DEATH MARK

MASON DIXON TROPICAL ADVENTURE THRILLERS - BOOK 2

NICK THACKER

Death Mark: Mason Dixon Thrillers, Book #2

Published by Turtleshell Press

PREFACE

(Or: I wrote a book.)

Hey. Mason Dixon here. Thanks for grabbing this story about me, I know the guy who wrote me will appreciate it.

But I want to talk about me for a second.

I the pages to follow, you're going to have a lot of fun hearing about some of my adventures and escapades. You'll *also* hear about my drinks — some of which I've invented, and some of which you've heard of and I've just perfected.

I don't just use drinks to take out my marks, either. I *drink* them.

And, recently, I started writing about those drinks.

I just published my first book, called *Classy Drinks for Classy People*, and I wrote it for *you*, classy reader.

It's a recipe book, a how-to guide, and a humorous history book all rolled into one. I think you're going to get a kick out of it. So what do you way?

Want to learn to mix drinks the Mason Dixon way?

Go here to find out more: http://www.nickthacker.com/CDCP

…and then come back here to continue reading about me!

CHAPTER ONE

I HAVE THIS IDEA THAT maybe morality is like death: we can buck and fight against it as long as we want, but eventually it's going to get us. And we're all given a specific amount of morality; a certain flavor of it we can't change or cash in, or alter in any way.

We can mask it, like our faces, but it won't do any good. At the end of the line, wherever that line is, we're as moral as we're ever going to be. We're as good or bad as we're ever going to be, or as 'us' as we ever were.

Okay, enough with the philosophical bullshit. What I'm saying here is that *I have no idea how the world works.*

I don't really care, either, because I know, generally, how *people* work. I get how they tick, what they want, how they intend to get it. I'm good at that part of it. I'm not so good at the part of it where I have to decide what to *do* about it.

You see, I'm good at my gig — I tend bar at a little place I own, and I like it. I love it, actually. The oldies take care of me, and I get to silently judge the younger idiots that come in and ask for things that no bar menu should even *suggest* to offer.

Like light beer.

And I don't mean 'beer that is light,' like a proper Belgian or some of the summer Germans or the pilsners and IPAs that are vying for hipsters' attention out west.

I mean beers that were designed to be tasteless, so men, women, grandparents, and children alike could hate them all the same, pretend they like them, and drink them by the bucketful just for the sheer hell of saying they could drink a bucketful of them.

Those beers are the types I don't want anywhere my bar. I've got a few taps, and I keep those taps full of whatever I can get for a reasonable price that comes out of Charleston, or when I'm feeling fancy or festive I might spring for a shipment of kegs of something a little more exotic. But I don't have your typical Applebee's-on-a-Sunday-night fare of brew selections.

So when these youngsters — anyone younger than me, I should say — come in and try to order something like that, I just shrug and serve them whatever I've got on tap in that's in a real beer format.

Want a Coors? I'll give you whatever I've got from Revelry. Have a hankering for a Bud Light? I'll toss you the latest from Tradesman.

The guy that walked in five minutes ago was one of these guys — I could tell by his swagger. There's always a swagger. They come in like they're the coolest cat in town and that I should be *honored* to serve him a 'cold one,' which is 'this guy'-speak for 'crappy beer.'

Sure enough, he sidled up and tucked his legs under the bar top and gave me a nod. No smile, no greeting, no nothing. Just that nod.

I nodded back.

"What can I get you?" I asked.

"Eh, just a cold one," he said.

Of course. Bartender one, this guy zero.

I poured him a legacy IPA from Revelry, waited for the head to peak up above the top of the pint glass, and slid it over to him on a brand-new coaster.

Joey made those coasters — they have a cute little logo of a bearded, mustached man holding a bottle of whiskey in one hand and a pint glass of beer in his other hand. It's green, mostly, but the guy's lumberjack shirt is checkered red and black, and his mustache and beard are a dark brown.

It's sort of a weird logo, but I wasn't on the design committee that made them. The oldies and regulars seem to like the coasters, at least, but I wasn't too thrilled that it was just another expense and not something we could make money from. You can't sell coasters, after all.

Joey, anyway, had printed up a few million or so of these stupid things and placed them in all sorts of strategic locations around the tiny estate of mine. I even saw a handful of them in the bathroom, on top of one of the toilets. I mean really, I guess it's a helpful thing, but I'd just as soon finish my drink *before* I expose it to the nasty shit floating around in the men's room.

"What's this?" the guy asked.

"Cold one," I said, without missing a beat.

"Tastes like shit," he said.

I pulled it back and dumped it out in the sink. "That one's on me, then," I said. "What are you looking for, *specifically*?"

He shrugged. "I don't know, Miller, Coors, Bud, any of those ring a bell?"

I frowned. "Yeah, I've heard of them. Don't have them here."

He looked like he was about to pop a gasket, but to his credit he held it together long enough to ask the famous question. "What is this, some sort of gay bar?"

I honestly don't know what it is with these guys. Look, if your drink really is a Coors Light, fair enough. I won't get in your way. But if you claim to *not really care* about what type of beer you're drinking, but then you bitch about it when I pour you a craft beer from a small local business that needs your support, I have no patience for you.

And if you top it off by adding some sort of 'color' to your opinion, you're about as good as the coaster that's been stuck to the floor near the drain in the bathroom to me.

"Nope," I said. "Just a bar. But we don't have that sort of stuff here because it's actually cheaper to work with the local places. I get a better deal, and they make more money. Win-win."

"Yeah? Well not for me."

"Well I'm not sure there's anything in this world that will make you a winner at anything, pal."

He looked at me then with those eyes that would have told me I was in trouble, if I thought this was even remotely the sort of guy who could make me feel like there was trouble coming.

Then, as if on cue, he got up and stormed out. The little bell above the door clinked violently as the door slammed shut, but only two or three regulars in the corner took notice.

"Who was that?" Joey asked. He'd snuck up on me, delivering dinner and placing it in front of me at the bar. Fish and chips.

"Just a guy looking for a cold one."

"Huh," Joey said. "Nothing here cold enough?"

"Nothing but the banter, I guess. Fish and chips?"

"Yeah," he said. "Thought we'd keep rolling with that English pub theme for a while longer."

Joey, since I'd made him manager, had done me quite a few favors. One of them was to 'theme' different seasons. We were currently running with an English pub theme, complete with a few English-style ales on tap. I was never a huge fan of English beer, but Joey had done a great job with the theming and menu design.

We're a small operation — just Joey and me — but we're sort of the talk of the town, if you consider that the town is about 800 people. Edisto Beach, in South Carolina. It's the town you run into when you're trying to run into the ocean.

Joey took the helm as planner of all things that needed planning, besides the liquor selection and the mixology. I'd started the place because I'd wanted to bring back the classiness to drink-making. The '-ology' part of mixology. So many younger bartenders were throwing together fruit juices and liqueurs, mixing them in with forty crushed berries and calling it a drink. Sure, it was liquid, and sure, it may count as a drink on a beach somewhere south of the border on spring break, but in my world it was trash.

I wanted the beauty restored to the mixology world. Just like the chefs that were breaking down barriers and expectations, I wanted drink-making to be as masterfully practiced an art form.

Joey got it, and he loved it. But we didn't need two of me — we needed me and Joey. Joey was master of the kitchen, the private chef of the patrons we served six nights a week. He was also in charge of decor, aesthetics, and generally everything else besides the liquor. He did a bang-up job, and I paid him better than anyone else in this town or Charleston.

"So it's working pretty well, then? The pub style?"

"Sure, yeah. Everyone seems to enjoy the beers, and the drinks you've mashed up are a huge hit."

I'd made about five custom drinks to match the English theme, using English gins and genevers, as well as a few specials, like the Cornish Pastis, to round out the palate. I had to admit, they were tasty. I liked creating the drinks, and I certainly liked *drinking* them.

I drank a lot, but never too much. Joey and I were the tasters, purchasers, mixologists, and bartenders, and I always harped on him that we needed to know our stuff. I wouldn't anything without my palate.

"So what's next, then?" I asked him.

"Like for themes?"

"Sure, yeah." I gave him that look he'd come to understand well. *Yeah, but not really. What's* really *next?*

He smiled. "I don't know, boss. You're kind of in charge of that, don't you think?"

He was referring, of course, to our *other* endeavor: moonshining.

CHAPTER TWO

I HAD ALWAYS WANTED TO get into moonshining, but never had the guts. Really. I'd always heard it was a 'good way to get yourself killed,' or 'great if you want to go to prison,' so I'd never really attempted it.

But the truth of the matter was that it's a misdemeanor in most places, and seen as one in all the places. Most cops — trust me, I've asked them — don't really care one way or another. It's when you *sell* the stuff they tend to get all bent out of shape.

I had the stuff all set up in the back area, near the tiny kitchen and against one of the walls. It wasn't much — a couple carboys, a couple large fermentation buckets, and lots of plastic tubing. Joey had figured out how to finagle the whole distillery apparatus onto the kitchen's water spigot using about a hundred adaptors, and a large electric burner served as the heating element.

I'm not interested in breaking the law, necessarily. I'm not really interested in *not* breaking the law, either, but the point isn't about the law. I wanted to start distilling my own stuff, and eventually try to get it sold in the bar, but in order to make sure I knew that I could do it, I had to practice. No point in paying the massive fees and working toward a license if I didn't even like the process.

Hence the tiny distilling operation taking place illegally in the back of my kitchen. Nothing fancy, but enough that Joey and I could get used to the process and try to produce something worth selling.

Joey was excited about our new little experiment, and I often found him in the back trying out a new mash or cooking up something strange. It took time — usually between three and six months — aging the distillate in the tiny oak barrels I'd bought for the purpose, so neither of us knew if our stuff was any good, but it was fun nonetheless.

"What do you have in mind?" Joey asked.

"I don't know, maybe something similar to Scotch?"

Scotch was tricky because, well, we weren't in Scotland. But the premise of Scotch was pretty simple: make whiskey from grain, but smoke the grain over peat before you distill it.

"Sounds hard," Joey said.

"It adds an extra step, but —"

I looked up from the bar just then, interrupting our small talk, and noticed the guy who'd just walked in. He was tall, not as tall as me but tall enough to be noticeable, but he carried himself the same way I did.

Confident.

I gave him a nod, but he kept on staring me down as he walked straight toward the bar. I wasn't entirely sure he'd slow down and stop, and I wasn't entirely sure the bar would be able to stop him if he wasn't.

Finally he stopped. He didn't sit down, and he didn't look down either.

Joey turned to look at me, then he shrugged. He knew the drill — guys like this came in every now and then.

Thinking they were worth someone's attention. Maybe they were, but they weren't worth *mine*.

I waited for him to make the first move. Confidence like that meant he was here for a reason, and that reason probably wasn't drinking.

He reached into his pocket. I moved my hand to the left, feeling the rounded edge of the shotgun's barrel poking out from where I'd mounted it just underneath the bar. I doubted I'd need it, but better to doubt and be ready than to be sure and be caught off guard.

His hand came out, weaponless. He smacked his palm on the bar top and then removed his hand. I looked down at the hard object he'd laid there.

A small, metallic circle. Embossed with some sort of design on the topside of it.

I looked back up at him. "What's that supposed to be?"

The man didn't respond at first. He was waiting, testing. Trying to figure out if I knew more than I let on.

"You don't know what this is?" the man asked.

"If it's money, it ain't going to work in here. Not sure I've ever seen that currency —"

"It's not money."

"Okay, well your *round metal circle* isn't going to get you any beer."

"I don't want beer."

I saw a few oldies shifting around in their chairs, but Joey was off helping a couple patrons near the door.

"Listen, pal, I'm not sure what you're trying to play, here, but I've got *paying* customers — using *real* money — to take care of."

The man nodded. "Go ahead. I'll wait."

I sighed. "Okay, here's how it's going to go down. If you're waiting for me to suddenly remember where I've seen that little thing, you're going to be waiting a long time. If you're waiting for me to have some time to chat, maybe play 'Antique Road Show' with you, bar closes at 2. That's in…" I stopped to check my watch, "about five hours."

She shook his head. "I want to know what you think of this."

"I don't think *anything* about it. It's a coin, probably from some other country. Why should it mean something to me?"

I shuffled away, grabbing the two beers I'd just poured and an Old Fashioned 'My Way' I'd mixed and placed them onto a serving tray. I swung around the end of the bar and walked them to the customers who'd ordered them.

I took another couple's order and began walking back to the bar.

"Look like your other little coin?"

I stopped in the middle of the bar, examining the man. I was positive I'd never seen him before, yet he looked familiar. Maybe in that 'looks-like-a-lot-of-other-people' sort of way.

"I know you?" I asked.

He shook his head. "No, but you're going to."

"Why's that?"

"This coin was found in a dead man's pocket three days ago.

CHAPTER THREE

I HAD POURED MYSELF A glass of bourbon — Michter's — and sat down at the bar stool next to the guy. He didn't want anything but a glass of water, and that was how I knew: he was a government guy. Paid detective sort.

"You FBI?" I asked.

He shook his head.

"DEA."

"I see. Well, DEA, I'm sorry I can't help with your investigation."

"Why's that?"

"Well, because I don't know what that little thing is."

"You don't?"

Joey's eyes met mine — he was still behind the bar, pouring for a few customers who'd just walked in. They were apparently here on vacation, from what I overheard. Nice folks, older than me with a son who was about half my age. They ordered some mixed drinks, and the son ordered a beer.

"I don't. Like I said."

"Got it." DEA-man pulled out a little notebook and started writing in it.

"You actually *use* those things? What are you, some 1950's detective?"

"No," he said. "DEA."

"Right. So, DEA, how many questions of yours am I going to have to answer before you let me and my patrons be?"

He swiveled around and looked at me after he'd finished scratching in the words 'doesn't know — coin.' "Well, I want to know what you know about this coin, or —"

"I don't anything about that —"

"*Or* any *other* coin you might have seen."

"I've seen lots of coins. This is a bar, you know that, right?"

He sighed. "Look, man. I've got a family. I've got friends, believe it or not. And a life. I don't want to be here any more than you do, but I was told by a… coworker you were the guy to talk to about this thing."

I frowned. "What coworker?"

"I can't say."

"Of course you can't," I answered. "What *can* you tell me?"

"This was found on some dead guy, three days ago."

"Three days ago the dead guy *became* dead, or three days ago you found it on a guy who was *already* dead."

"Does it matter?"

"Not sure," I said. "Does it?"

"He was on his way to a strip club in Charleston."

"Okay, so he was hoping to score with the ladies."

"It was a *gay* strip club. For men."

"So he was hoping to score with the *guys*." I was growing impatient, and I knew he was, too. "Look, pal — you got a name, or should I just keep calling you pal?"

"Jeff."

"Right, Jeff. Look, *Jeff,* I've got a business to run, and I, too, have a life. Tell me who your friend is, or tell me why they think *I* should know what this stupid little coin is in my bar."

"They think it's a copy."

"A copy… of what?"

"A copy of your coin."

I turned and frowned at the man. *Who the hell is this guy? Jeff. Jeff who? Why is he here?*

"I don't have any coins like that."

He sighed, again. It was like a sighing match, and I wasn't sure who was winning.

"I was told you had a little… operation. Something like this, months back."

"Tell me who told you that."

"Can't do that," he said. "But they told me your operation was successful. Then you got out, went clean."

"Okay, so if I'm out of this 'operation,' why would I know about this *other* coin?"

"Maybe they're paying homage to you, you know? Like honoring your legacy by minting another coin, something to track —"

I held up a hand. "Hold on a second, there. *Jeff.* I'm not doing this *thing* you say I used to do, so that means I don't know about anyone *else* doing this thing. Maybe you tell me I'm a suspect and I might be more apt to go along with this story."

Jeff raised an eyebrow, and I found another bourbon in front of me. I nodded at Joey, who'd snuck it in, then looked again at Jeff.

"Okay," Jeff said. "You're a suspect."

I laughed. "Well shit, that was easy. Fine — I'm a suspect. For what? Killing this guy?"

"Yeah, for that."

"Okay, fine. Who's the guy?"

He looked at me, no doubt getting ready to track my reaction and make another tiny note about it in his tiny book with his tiny pencil.

"You Mason Dixon?"

"One and only."

"Okay, Dixon. The man we found dead was identified as your father."

CHAPTER FOUR

MY FATHER — DEAD?

I RAN through the sentence in my mind once again. *The man we found was identified as your father.*

"H — how was he identified?" I asked.

"Found an ID in his wallet. Also had some neighbors and acquaintances confirm."

"Yeah," I said. "Probably too hard to drive *all the way down here* and just ask me yourself."

"Like I said," Jeff continued. "You're a suspect. So we needed to watch you, see if you made another move."

"And?"

"So far, the alibi's strong."

"Got it," I said. "Anyway, you've got a wallet — just one you *found* on your dead guy — and a few neighbors who *say* it's him. Sounds like a *strong* case you're building there, Jeff."

It was Jeff's turn to glare. "There's still a dead guy, and it's still a homicide. With a coin in his pocket that links your past to this guy, who we're saying is your father."

I chewed the inside of my lip for a bit before responding.

"Yeah," I said. "It does sound a lot like I should be your first suspect."

"So you'll come up to the office with me? Answer some questions?"

"I'm already answering your questions."

Jeff looked around. Saw Joey, then turned back to me and lowered his voice. "I mean *questions*. I want to ask about what *exactly* you did back in the day, uh —" he flipped through pages of his tiny notebook and then continued. "Back in the day, about seven months ago."

Seven months ago.

I knew exactly what he was talking about, and I knew exactly who'd told him about me. I shook my head, smiling.

This is too much.

Seven months ago was *Hannah.*

Seven months ago I saw my father for the last time, walking out from the life we'd built together, for the last time.

Or so I thought.

And I knew the guy who'd told Jeff about me.

"You the only one who knows?"

"About the dead — your father — or about your past?"

"My past."

Jeff nodded. "Yeah, pretty sure. I haven't told anyone, if that's what you're asking."

"Okay, fine. Good. Keep it that way. Here's how it's going to work. Unless you're arresting me, I need to finish up around here, check in with my bar man. I can head up tomorrow, first thing."

He seemed pleased with this, then he wrote down the address and tore it off one of the pages. He slid it over to me and cleared his throat. "First thing — so, 7am?"

I laughed. "Are you *nuts*? I run a *bar*, man. I don't even hit the sack until 4 am most nights — I'll be there *first thing*, my time. 10. 10:30 if it's a busy night."

His nostrils flared a bit, but he knew there wasn't much else he could do. *Unless he wants to arrest me.*

"Fine."

"Fine," I said. "See you tomorrow, Jeff."

CHAPTER FIVE

I WAS LATE, BUT I sort of already knew I'd be late. I knew I would be late the moment I told Jeff I'd be there around 10am.

The car ride was uneventful, and I got to Jeff's office a little after 10:00 in the morning. Actually, a little after 10:*20* in the morning. There wasn't an obvious place to park, as it was downtown Charleston, so I rolled around the block for a few minutes until something opened up. A businessman on his way to an early lunch, I suppose.

I parked, walked into the building at the address Jeff had given me, and was immediately struck by the plainness of it. Dark gray, marble walls slid straight up, forming the exterior facade of the place, and a single, narrow hallway provided access to a set of stairs that had been recessed into the middle of the building.

This isn't a police station, I realized. *Or a private detective firm.*

Police stations looked like, well, police stations — they had no reason to mask their true identity. PI firms, on the other hand, *loved* the subtlety and aesthetic of well-designed, yet well-camouflaged buildings. From the street a simple bookstore, perhaps, or a women's apparel store, but once inside a great oak or mahogany desk would welcome you in. Possibly even a secretary or admin assistant if the firm was large enough.

The point was that a PI firm or private detective's office had to at once alert its possible clientele to the fact that they were in the game, that they understood the nuances and necessities of espionage, yet they had to do it in a way that still wasn't shady or sketchy. Like a gambling ring for the rich and high rollers, it had to scream 'we're worth your money but we're still a secret' from the first impression.

My first impression of this building was: rented space.

Whoever I was going to meet in here was a vagabond, a nomad. They weren't here for business, they were here to meet me. To plan something, then to move on. They needed a room or three, and they didn't much care for where it was or what it looked like.

I walked up the concrete stairs and thought I could smell a faint whiff of urine. This building wasn't in a bad area of downtown Charleston, but I knew that there weren't any downtown spots in any cities that were safe from the 'street folks.' With such an unassuming and simple appearance, I wouldn't have been surprised if this was a common overnight setup for the homeless.

There was a single door at the top of the stairs, and I briefly considered knocking. I changed my mind and turned the handle, but soon as I did I could feel it moving on its own. Someone on the other side of the door was already opening it.

I took a step back and felt around my back for the 9mm I'd tucked into my belt. I was sure I wouldn't need it — no one schedules a meeting for the next morning just to kill you — but I wasn't one for being unprepared.

The door swung open and Jeff's bloated face pushed out from behind it.

"You're late," he said.

"I'm here," I answered.

He snorted, or coughed, I wasn't sure. He cocked his head and motioned me inside, so I followed him. He offered no introduction, no handshake, no formalities of any kind.

He also didn't offer me coffee, which sort of made me angry. He *knew* this was considered an early morning for me, and besides, wasn't he supposed to be still pretending he was a detective? What detective's office — or office of *any* sort — doesn't offer its visitors a cup of coffee in the morning?

I looked around, but it wasn't easy. Hardly anything was lit, and what was wasn't lit well. A couch in the corner, with a blanket and pillow on it, and a card table on the opposite side of the room. A mini fridge and a small television that had been made last century sat in the corner.

"What is this place?" I asked.

Jeff grunted again and kept walking down the hallway. There were three doors — one at the end of the hall, and one on each side of the hallway. He headed for the one at the end, then knocked twice when he'd reached it.

"Yeah," a voice said from the other side.

He opened the door and bright, yellow light came pouring out, suddenly illuminating the main room. The carpet, I could now see, was dirty, worn, and threadbare in spots. Stains and marks on the wall told me that this room had been used, abused, and subsequently evacuated quickly. The current tenants, of which Jeff was probably one, apparently had no desire to clean it up for guests.

Jeff held the door open and I walked in. I waited for him

to step inside, but instead he let it close and then I heard the lock engaging.

Great, I thought. *Locked in a dingy apartment.*

I didn't worry much about my location, however. It was the two men already sitting in the room that held my attention.

CHAPTER SIX

I SAT ON THE OTHER side of the power table. It was, of course, a normal table. But the *location* of this particular table made it into what I called a 'power table.' Situated inside a cell of a room, inside a crypt of a building, inside a maze of a city, I was at the mercy of whomever was opposite me at the table.

And, at the moment, the person opposite me did nothing to lessen the impression of the 'power table.'

"Where are you headed, Dixon?" the man asked.

I cocked an eyebrow.

He waited. *Power.*

I sighed. "God. You guys and your tables, and your ties, and your shitty black coffee."

Still, he waited.

"Fine," I said. "You know where I'm headed? Nowhere. I'm sitting right here, doing absolutely nothing but answering your questions?"

"Are you?"

"Am I *what*?"

"Are you answering our questions?"

The second man leaned forward. I assumed, by his expression and his clenched fists, balled up and smashed up against his jowls, that he was trying his best to play 'bad cop.' "Listen, Dixon," he said, with a voice that destroyed any chance he'd ever have at playing 'bad cop,' "if you don't like the coffee you don't have to drink it."

The room inside the station was barren, just plain drywall walls the color of steel and a steel table the color of drywall. The chairs were purposefully uncomfortable, and I had noticed within ten seconds of sitting in one that they had been designed just a few inches too low. I had to sidle up to the damn thing so far my chest hurt just to get my elbows high enough to lay them on top of it.

Their chairs, I noticed now, were *not* placed too low.

Power chairs.

"The coffee's fine. Fabulous, actually," I said. "I like it like I like my women. Bland, with that perfect amount of *je ne sais quoi* that makes you wonder where the hell you found it."

The 'good cop,' the guy doing most of the interrogating, looked at his buddy. No glance was exchanged.

"But I'll play along, since I know I've done nothing that warrants my being here. Maybe you'll believe me, and feel horrible for it, and throw yourselves off a bridge for putting me through it."

Good cop narrowed his eyes at me. Fat, pudgy things that could hardly be seen poking out through the rest of his face skin. I took a second and marveled — I wasn't actually sure which of the guys was fatter. I pursed my lips, really trying to focus and get into it, when the good cop snapped a finger.

"Okay, Dixon," he grunted. "So tell us."

"Well — let's see," I said. "You've told *me* absolutely nothing, because — I'm guessing here — that's what *you've* seen on TV. The 'good cop,' 'bad cop' routine, done up real nice in a place that actually *looks* like a station. You've got the table, the chairs, the fat guy just wanting to get home to his flat wife — still not sure which of you *that* one is — and all the little details in place for a real intimidation session."

I saw bad cop, the guy on the left, fidget. *He's considering it,* I thought. *He thinks I'm right.*

Or he's just fat.

I was no expert, but I've observed plenty specimens of the human race in my day, and the ones who were on the range of overweight to obese typically had a hard time getting comfortable. I don't know why — I'd always been skinny, even 'skeletal,' as my old man once *lovingly* said — but I tended to believe it.

So this guy was either acting fat or acting like he was considering my train of thought. So, never one to need much egging on at all to continue giving my opinion, I continued giving my opinion.

"Last night I was in my bar. Night before, I was in my apartment. Night before that, I was in my bar. Before that... look, you get the point, right? I work six days a week, and on the seventh day I work some more. Shopping for the bar, pricing and planning out for the kitchen stuff, Amazon for the cleaning and maintenance supplies. Joey helps with it, that's what I pay him for, but it's my bar.

"So you brought me here because you think I know something about this dead guy you found you think is 'my old man,' but I can assure you, I do not."

"Well we're after assurances, Dixon," the bad cop fat guy said. "What assurances do you have?"

"Besides a rock-solid alibi?"

"You got anyone to corroborate that?

I did — Joey. "No," I said, without hesitation. "My bad. I didn't think to put someone in place for the arbitrary and still unknown-to-me window of time to which you're referring."

"So… what assurances, then?" the good cop fat guy asked.

"Well, for one, you're bullshitting me. You have been from the moment you sent in your shitty excuse for a hired PI, and you kept it up — admittedly, good work — when I got here. This —" I waved my hand around and elaborately called everyone's attention to the perfect replica of a stereotypical interrogation chamber these goons had constructed, "this is grand, really. But it's nonsense. What the *hell* am I *really* here for, boys?"

Again, another expressionless glance.

"Explain."

"No."

"*Explain,* Dixon."

"*No,* asshole."

Bad cop sighed. I had been wrong. He was the good cop, I guess. He broke first. "Fine, Dixon. You're right. We're not a PI firm. Nothing like it."

"Got that. Thanks."

The other guy jumped in. "But I assure you, we're on the same side."

"Now *you're* giving assurances."

"We are. Just trust us."

"You've given me plenty of reason to trust you so far. Thank you." I wasn't sure if my no-bull voice gave them the assurance that my statement was loaded with bull or not, but I went on anyway. "So I trust you. You're the *pinnacle* of trustworthy. Stand-up guys, both of you."

Bad cop shook his head. Just briefly, just slightly. But it was there, and I caught it. I almost frowned, but I refrained. I didn't want to give anything away like he had, but I mostly just wasn't sure what that head shake meant.

"Anyway, I know this isn't a police station. And there's no PI firm on this side of the *country*, much less Charleston, big enough to justify a place like this. So who are you?"

It was an appeal to ethos: they tell me who they are, I might be willing to work with them to figure out their dead guy situation.

"Why are you ignoring the fact that your father is dead?"

"I'm not. It's just that it's not a fact."

"It's not?"

"I haven't seen the body with my own eyes. So no, it's not a fact."

"We have verified reports —"

"From who?" I asked. "My old man knew about four people, and two of them are long dead. The third is me, and the fourth…"

Shit. They'd caught me. I knew it, right then.

"The fourth is *who*, Mr. Dixon?"

I sighed again. *Fine.* Resigned to my fate, I looked both of them in the eye and then continued. "The fourth is my brother."

CHAPTER SEVEN

"YOUR BROTHER?"

THE QUESTION WAS genuine, which gave me hope. *He's not involved,* I realized.

"Yeah."

"You want to tell us about him?"

"Nope."

"Fine. Continue. So no one knows your old man?"

"Not really, no. Not enough to give me a feeling that they could satisfactorily determine whether or not your dead guy is actually him."

"Right," good cop fat guy said. "So you don't believe us."

"Guys," I said, "cut the bullshit. You ever *been* in a room like this? A *real* room? Meant for interrogation of a suspect, or even a witness?"

Bad cop sniffed.

"It's *nothing* like this. For one, the chairs are comfortable. They're spending a lot of time in here, so why not get a decent chair? And the chairs are all the *same,* none of these unmatching kids-table-at-Thanksgiving pieces of crap you shoved me in."

Bad cop sniffed again.

"And don't even get me started on the walls. You realize that *every* room in *every* station in literally *every* city — all around the world — has finished walls? Just throw some spackle and paint up there, it costs about thirty bucks. And the table? Is there some sort of special 'fake bad guy IKEA' you know about?"

The bad cop, at this, actually laughed. A quick chuckle, just a snort, really, but he stopped almost as quickly as it had begun.

"So don't try and convince me you're anything *but* just some guys who found another guy, and you want to figure out why he's dead. And who he is."

The pause, on both sides of the table, told me everything I needed to know.

I'm right. And they need me for something. And my old man may not be dead.

"Fine, Dixon. You're right."

"I am?"

Good cop nodded. "But that's all you're going to get for now. We still want to know why this guy's dead and why your little token was found in his pocket."

I looked up at the ceiling, throwing my head all the way back and leaning back into the sharp metal of the chair. *So that's what this is about.*

"I figured," I said. "I figured it was about the token."

"The *mark*, you mean?"

"Right, yeah. Whatever you want to call —"

"Whatever *you* want to call it. It's yours, right?"

I was shaking my head before he'd even finished the sentence. "No, it's not, guys. Sorry to disappoint. It's not mine at all."

"But you admit you know what it is?"

"I don't admit that at all."

"You admit you used something similar to this *mark* in your line of work?"

"Bartending?" I asked. "Yeah, we had coins come into the bar all the time. *Money*. People spent it, and I took it."

"We're talking about a *mark*, Mason."

I shook my head. "What makes you think I know a damn thing about this stuff?"

I sensed we were close to the big reveal, the connection, the reason why I was in here in the first place, why the whole story had been concocted and sold to me, albeit in a highly unbelievable and lazy sort of way.

I was right.

"We believe this mark was meant to pull you in. To get you back in the game."

CHAPTER EIGHT

"YOU THINK… YOU THINK THIS mark was meant for *me*?" I asked. My shocked expression apparently had an effect on the guy on the left.

He shook his head. "No, not like that. It's not about you — they wanted your *father* dead, and now he is. But they're taunting you. Trying to lure you in."

I nodded, pretending like I understood. I had no idea what they were talking about. I looked around the tiny room once again, examining it. It wasn't a police station's interrogation room, and if it was, in fact, a room inside a large private investigation firm, my opinion was that they needed to hire a designer.

"So what are they trying to lure me into?" I asked. "By killing my dad? Seems a bit… over the top."

"We agree, Mason," bad cop said. "That's why you're here. We think it's a bit much, and that your father's death was an unfortunate side effect. Collateral damage."

"No," I snapped, "it wouldn't *collateral damage* unless it didn't mean anything. A bomb blowing up and taking out a cafe and a woman and her child dying, *that's* collateral damage. Hell, there was a movie about it."

Good cop nodded. "Right, yes, we know. Sorry — a poor choice of words."

I raised an eyebrow.

"What we mean, I guess, is that your father was *targeted*, but only to get to you. He was killed because they wanted *you* back in the game."

"I'm just a bartender now, boys."

"Right. And I'm just a PI."

I looked at him, good and hard, stared him down like I knew only I could. This was the point in the investigation that the truth — the *real* truth — started tumbling out. On both sides, which meant I needed to start coming clean and at least admitting to these grunts that I was, in fact, exactly who they thought I was. Way I figured, it didn't cost me anything, since they already assumed I wasn't *just a bartender*. They'd proven that much, so the least I could do was come clean about it and see if they'd return the favor.

"I'm a bartender," I said again. "But I'm certainly *not* a detective."

"As your previous exploits have proven," good cop said.

Bad cop flashed him a glance, but it was already too late.

"You've been spying on me, then?" I asked.

"It's our job. If it's happening in the city, we're supposed to know about it."

"Okay, that *definitely* sounds like something a PI would say."

"You joking?"

"Yeah." I looked at bad cop. *If anyone's going to come clean, it's him.* "Who you working for?" I asked.

He shrugged. "Some guy. Don't worry about it yet."

"Fine, but you have to give me something."

"Fine."

Good cop started talking almost immediately. "The guy that offed your old man, he's the one we're after. Name's Rockford Elizondo. We want him taken out, and we need it done quick. By Sunday."

"Rockford Elizondo?"

"Yeah. Mexican father, but his mother is East-coast born-and-bred. Attended a fancy Ivy League school or something like that."

"Name checks out," I said, shrugging. "So you thought you should ask me. Because I'm a bartender."

"Something like that, yeah," the guy said.

Bad cop shook his head. "No, we figured you'd want a chance at this guy that offed your father."

I frowned, pausing to feign interest in the question. "No," I said. "I'm good. Thanks though."

I stood up to leave, and the two men at the table with me stood as well.

I laughed. "That how this is going to play out? Two grunts beating me with a stick until I agree?"

The man now standing directly in front of me, bad cop, glared. "We didn't bring any sticks."

"Shame," I said. "You're going to need more than a couple sets of fists to fight me off. I may be old, but I ain't dumb. You think I came in here thinking I'd be walking out without a fight?"

Good cop jumped in. "We don't need sticks *or* fists. Man, where you been? Business happens *different* these days. You should know that, *barman*."

He enunciated his last word by smacking a folder down on the table in front of him. The hollow steel rang, the slap reverberating only to the walls, the sharp noise dying quickly.

Still, it was effective. I hadn't even noticed he'd been holding a folder in his hand, and the abrupt sound of it hitting the table made me jump.

"What's this?" I asked. "Money? You trying to buy me?"

Good cop shook his head.

"Good, 'cause my old man tried it for years. And I doubt you two would have enough to afford me."

"Open it," bad cop said.

I did. The folder was a typical office issue, light beige and thin, barely cardstock. It had nothing on the front of it, not even a brand marking or logo. I reached for it, feeling the smooth outside of the cover before I flipped it open.

Page one was a picture. Grainy, pixelated, and taken at night with what had to have been the worst camera ever designed. I could barely see what it was supposed to depict, but when I did, I pulled my hand back.

My bar.

It was, without a doubt, my little space downtown. Editso Beach, South Carolina. On the 'strip,' which was certainly a generous term.

But it was mine.

"What's this all about?" I asked.

"This your place?"

I nodded.

"Well, it's going to be *our* place if you don't help us out."

I made a smacking sound with my lips. "Right. Well, bad news, boys. The place ain't for sale, and I ain't rich — I'm still paying the place off."

Good cop nodded, then flipped over the first page picture and let me read the second page.

I read what I could, but there was a lot of legal mumbo-jumbo. I had never been a fan of lawyers, mostly because I couldn't stand the way they wrote. Just walk up to me and tell me what the hell you're talking about, in plain English, you know?

So I wasn't *entirely* sure what this page was trying to tell me, but I got the gist from the top few lines that *MASON*

DIXON, hereafter referred to as SELLER, was going to be selling his bar and all remaining debt on the property to some bank in Charleston.

I looked up at my new friends. "This supposed to be real?"

Bad cop shrugged. "If you want it to be."

"I don't, I'm pretty sure." I paused. "Yeah, now that I've thought about it, I really would prefer to keep my bar."

"That's what we figured, too." He reached down and grabbed the paper out of the open folder. "But the thing is, my boss *really* wants to get this little job done, and he tells us you're the guy for it."

My turn to shrug.

"So we had this little contract written up. It's not really worth anything, as you know, since there are lawyers and signatures and stuff needed, but — and this might make a difference — *our* lawyer is pretty good friends with the guy who'd be signing this contract."

"Who, me?" I racked my brain, trying to figure out if I knew any lawyers. I had made it a point in my almost-49-years of life to distance myself from the legal profession, so I figured I was safe now.

"No, Dixon," good cop said. "The guy at your *bank* who'd be signing this."

"But you'd —"

"Still need your signature? Yeah, we know. But we're pretty good at getting what we want."

I let out a long sigh. "Right, okay. I got it. You're like the mafia or something, and you're going to break my legs if I don't do what you want. And then, if I *still* don't do what you want, you're going to take my bar away from me."

Both men across the table from me nodded in unison.

"Got it."

My mind raced. I tried to figure out if they'd forgotten

something. If there was anything I had on *them*. Or if there was still a back door, some way to maneuver out of this mess I'd somehow gotten myself into.

"So you'll do it?"

I frowned. "Do what? Kill Elizondo? The guy who murdered my old man?"

Another nod.

"That's the thing, boys," I said. "I don't really… *like* my old man. I'm not saying I like him better dead, but I'm not sure I want to take on a project like this when it seems like you're not exactly *trustworthy* individuals."

The bigger man, bad cop, sniffed. "Dixon, we already explained —"

"You explained *nothing*. You just threatened me with taking away my bar. You know it's not that hard to *go find another bar*, right?"

"We know. But there is that whole part about breaking your legs, remember?"

I nodded. "Yeah, sure. Right."

I took a deep breath. Whatever they were threatening me with was serious, judging by the looks on their faces and the folder in front of me. This wasn't just some half-assed attempt to scare me — they'd thought this through, and prepared for it. They'd hired a guy to pose as a detective, and they'd even gone to the trouble to print out a whole folder of documents and bank-ish type statements.

No one printed anything these days.

These guys meant business.

"Look," I said. "I want my lawyer to look at these documents. That cool with you?"

"No."

"Right. Figured. Okay, well, in that case, *I'd* like to look at them. Is that okay?"

"No."

"Well then. Hmm. Seems like you've wasted a lot of time and dead trees printing it all out, then. You've also made quite an offer, gentlemen, but I'm afraid I'm going to have to —"

"We'll pay you."

I cocked my head sideways. I didn't necessarily *like* this opportunity, but they had suddenly started speaking my language. "Yeah? What are we talking?"

"We'll cover your expenses, as long as they're reasonable. And we get to decide if they're reasonable."

Bad cop jumped in. "And then there's a 'finder's fee.'"

"For finding the guy?" I asked.

"For finding the guy, and *taking him out*. Ten percent."

"Ten percent of *what*?"

"Ten percent of what he stole from us," good cop answered.

I nodded. "That's fair. What, uh, did he steal from you?"

"Thirty-two million."

I choked, out loud. "*Dollars?*"

"No, Dixon, *pickles*. Yes, dollars. Thirty-two million of them."

"That's — that's three-hundred twenty thousand. As a finder's fee."

"Glad to see you can do math. You in?"

I still wasn't convinced this was legitimate, but I also knew that just about *all* of what I did outside of tending bar was *not* legitimate. I had never been one to abide by the law, but I also knew I needed to get confirmation on the mark. I needed to know the mark was *worth* being marked.

Call me softhearted, but I don't kill innocent people.

Good cop reached down, then pushed the documents toward me. "Listen, Dixon," he said. "These documents are real. You can look at them all you want, but we're not leaving this room until we've got a verbal confirmation from you.

You help us get this guy, we leave you — and your bar — alone."

That seemed reasonable, but I *hated* when people tried to tell me what to do. It was just… disrespectful.

"Can you ask nicely?"

"Come again?"

"No. I don't think you misheard me. There are two of you, after all. Put your heads together and figure it out."

"You — you want us to ask *nicely*."

"Is that so much to ask? My old man just died, so maybe it's the least you can do?"

The two grunts looked at each other — apparently my attitude was completely new to them — then they turned back to me. Bad cop nodded.

"Yeah. Okay, fine. Will you *please* help us find Elizondo? By Sunday?"

"And take him out?" good cop added.

I waited, basking in the moment. A small victory. I'd learned a long time ago to really stop and appreciate those little victories — they were, when you think about it, everything.

I crossed my arms.

"Fine."

CHAPTER NINE

"THEY WANT US TO *WHAT*?" Joey asked.

Joey was my right-hand man, the manager of my bar, the head chef, and the man I trusted with, well, just about everything. He knew my secrets and he'd so far proven himself worthy of keeping them to himself.

"They don't want *us* to do anything," I answered. "They want *me* to find some guy."

"Some guy who killed your old man!" Joey said.

"Calm down. Yeah, something like that. Some guy — Rockford Elizondo — who murdered my old man."

"Did you see him?"

I shook my head and poured myself a drink. No sense reaching for the cheaper stuff — I grabbed at a bottle of Jefferson's Ocean, No. 11. A bourbon that tasted like it was made for king, at a peasant's price.

A peasant who made shit ton of money a year.

Ocean was a bourbon that I'd coveted for a long time. It had taken me some time to get into it, what with its polished logo, simple and corporate, the name itself, and the kitschy novelty it promised on its little stretchy-band label: aged at sea, by letting the bourbon barrels sit on deck and slosh around in the sunlight and moonlight for a year. The bourbon would, therefore, take in more of the wood's delicious flavors of vanilla and oak, at a much faster rate.

Ostensibly.

I'd put off tasting it for years, as I never was one to fall for the scams of marketers and advertisers. Or at least I didn't want to *think* I'd fallen for them.

But Joey had a bottle of it in hand when he'd returned from Charleston a few months ago, and had offered me a sample. The bottle, a standard 750mL, wasn't cheap, so I immediately wasn't impressed. But the first sniff, then the first taste, then the second sniff, began to change my mind. Deep, rich vanilla, just enough caramel, and the right amount of oak to make the drink smooth, but not cloying. Bite that matched its alcohol content, and overall the feeling that I was drinking something that deserved the reputation it had.

Jefferson's Ocean, in my opinion, was a fantastic purchase, and we began to stock it behind the bar. It tended to fit in well with the English pub theme we were currently running with, even though it wasn't technically English anything, and most English hard liquor that was aged at sea was rum.

So I splashed a few fingers into a rocks glass and dumped in a huge sphere of ice, then swirled it after giving it a respectful sniff. When I felt it was cooled enough, I brought it to my lips and thought about our next move.

"No, but I'm going to find the guy," I said.

"Don't," Joey said, matching my movements with his own glass of bourbon — Bulleit, another popular mix-worthy bourbon we kept stocked.

"Why?"

"Because they're obviously playing you."

"How so?"

"Did you see the body? Your dad's, I mean."

"Well, no. But… but that doesn't mean anything."

He stared me down. Or up, as I was a bit taller than him. "Really?"

"No," I said. "It shouldn't. They want something from me, and that's to take out their mark. Another guy, one they are claiming killed my old man."

"But what if he didn't?"

"What *if* he didn't? It doesn't change anything. They're claiming they have something on me, enough to take the bar."

Joey smiled. "But did they threaten to break your legs?"

I laughed. "You know, it did come up."

He took another sip, and I followed. The whiskey was good, and it got better the cooler and more diluted it became. "So they want you take out their guy."

I nodded.

"Any idea who it is? This 'Rockford Elizondo' gentleman?"

I nodded again.

"Really?"

"Yep. They told me who he is, where he is, and when it needs to be done by."

Joey's eyes widened. "Christ, Mason, they're not *asking* you to take him out, they're *telling* you. This is a planned hit, and you're the unlucky SOB who has to do it."

I sighed, then downed the rest of the bourbon. "Yeah," I said. "I know. That's why I'm doing it myself this time. Without you."

Joey laughed again, then refilled my drink. "Bullshit."

I glared at him.

"Seriously, Dixon. No way I'm out on this one. You haven't been in the game since… well —"

"Don't say it."

"Fine. But you've been out since then, and you know you're getting soft. I'm —"

"Like hell I am."

"You were better at this, your mark would already be dead."

I wasn't sure what to say to that, since I couldn't tell if he was right or just trying to piss me off. I decided to drink another shot of bourbon, but I cut him off when he tried to top me off once more. It was, after all, a work day. The bar would be opening in a few hours.

"There's no way I could have known —"

"Maybe," Joey said. "Maybe not. Point is, your old man's dead and they want you to find his killer. They're probably into something big, and they can't be bothered with, or they don't have the manpower, to off him themselves. They've got enough brains to know they need plausible deniability, *and* they have the added benefit of knowing the old dead guy's son is an assassin."

"Don't call me that. I hate that word."

"Whatever. You're a… dealer of vigilante justice."

"You make me sound old."

"No, *you* make you sound old."

I glared at him again, simultaneously doing a walkthrough of the bar area and prepping the few liqueurs we kept on hand. It was a quick job, as I made sure the bar was in perfect shape every night after close. Joey had picked up the habit as well, so when he was closing without me I knew I'd come in the next morning to a beautiful, fully stocked bar.

"I'm helping you."

"You have to run the bar, Joey."

"No we don't. It's the middle of the week. There's no one

but a few oldies who'll care that we're closed, and we can buy them off pretty quickly."

He was talking about the little BOGO cards Joey had printed up — discounts or buy-one-get-one free coupons that offered a free meal, a discounted drink, or something else valuable to our regular customers.

Besides those cards, our regulars thought I was quite the fisherman. Joey had a sign he'd hang on the door whenever we were out and the bar had to be closed temporarily that claimed we were going fishing.

The ruse worked, I'd always assumed, because Joey cooked the best damned catfish this side of the Mississippi — and any place on the *other* side of the big river didn't have catfish worth talking about.

He was *mean* with a spatula, and he knew it. He'd turned my little bar into a full-fledged restaurant, complete with fancy-looking menus and often-shifting delicacies, like imported lobster and English beers. He was a true asset to my business, but he was also a true asset to my *extracurricular* business.

I sighed. He was right, and he knew it. He would help me, no matter what I tried to do to keep him away. I'd learned the hard way to keep him close and let him be part of the team, and as much as I railed against the idea, he would be an asset to me there, as well.

"Fine. But I'm not going to let you —"

"I'll help you however I can. No constraints this time."

"You'll help me however I *tell* you —"

"I'll quit. You can cook the catfish yourself."

He was smiling, and even though I knew the threat was empty, I balked. "Yeah, okay. Fine. I need help. Just... just don't get... don't get killed."

"Sounds like good advice," he said. "Want to head out on the water and make a plan?"

CHAPTER TEN

JOEY AND I SPENT THE rest of the night like we always did — cooking up fish and serving up drinks. He manned the griddle and took care of the house, while I made sure our patrons at the bar weren't going thirsty.

I thought a lot about the offer. Not much of an offer, really. They were twisting my arm, forcing me into it. They knew I could do the job, and they knew I'd have no choice when I found out about my old man.

And then there was the money.

It was *a lot* of money. I didn't typically see that kind of money come through my bar in an entire year, and I definitely could use it. I'd made some headway on buying the place outright, but there was still a ways to go, and there were still things I wanted to do with the place — all of which cost money.

Or rather, there were things *Joey* wanted to do with the place.

He'd already fixed the lights — something that had always bugged him. They were either always too bright or too dim, or something. He was a Goldilocks about the aesthetic stuff, and I didn't care one way or another, I just wanted it to be cheap.

So he'd found some inexpensive LED lighting fixtures online that were dimmable, wired them up, and even recessed them into the fixture sockets that had been there before. Then, as if to rub in how much younger he was than I, he even got a little app for his smartphone to control them.

When the bar opened, the lights turned on. When it got dark out and the oldies' and guests' palates shifted from fish and chips to bourbon, the lights dimmed just a bit.

I had to admit it he'd done a bang-up job, but I refused to let him know. He always smiled at me, big and dumb, whenever the lights changed according to the 'mood' of the room, which always seemed to be a 'mood' I wasn't tuned into. He'd wait for me to see him, with that big dumbass grin on his face, then he'd break out into laughter.

"See, much better, ain't, boss?" he'd ask.

"I don't see any difference."

I always tried to make my response seem crustier every time, but I knew he saw right through it. I like the lighting, and liked that he was making improvements, large and small.

I *really* liked that he cared about it all. It was like having another me walking around, with a different skill set and different personality, but cared about it all just as much as I did.

I always gave him a hard time, but I tried to make him know he was a valuable asset — and good friend — to me. One of the ways I did that was by giving him access to the *Wassamassaw*, the 131-foot yacht that Hannah Rayburn had given to me.

We were on it now, heading out into the bay, just past the last buoys and before the breaks started. During the hotter months there were windsurfers and paddle boarders out on the surf, and you could see the cruise ships heading to and from the Bahamas out on the horizon.

Now that it was cooler the wind picked up a bit and only the die-hards were out in the water. The majority of the traffic now was sailboats and catamarans, each vying for control of their own narrow little slice of the vast expanse.

I loved being on the boat. She had been completely refinished, from the carpet to the furniture, thanks to a generous clause in the Federal Bureau of Investigation's operating agreement.

Or, at least, thanks to a friend of mine who *worked* there.

I still didn't know if it was common practice at the FBI to let their case victims keep huge boats after a traumatizing incident, but I didn't ask questions, and I didn't care to know the truth.

The boat was mine, and that was that. I had the papers for it, the registration and license, and a dock for it two blocks away from my bar.

If anyone loved the boat more than I did, it was Joey. He and his new girlfriend from the city would come out and sleep on it, even while it was docked. I'd let him take it out a few times as well, but there was hardly a time I wasn't also available for a quick jaunt up and down the bay.

"Hey boss, you have dinner plans?" Joey's voice called up into the bridge. He and his girlfriend, Shalice, with an 'S,' were cozied up on the couch in the adjacent room, the long, large dining and entertainment lounge. Joey had already made his way through half a bottle of one of the more expensive bourbons I kept stocked, Shalice a bottle of red.

"Me? You're the chef."

Joey laughed. "Well, yeah, but I'm probably a little too buzzed to cook. There's fish in the fridge — you can just grill it."

"Oh?" I said. "That right? I have your permission to cook you dinner?"

I had already planned on grilling fish, and I'd already told Joey and Shalice that, but it was funnier to give him crap for it.

"Unless you want to risk me falling overboard."

I stared him down from my chair in the cabin. "I might take my chances."

Shalice laughed. "I would."

Joey returned — slowly, so he wouldn't fall — to his chair, pouring himself another generous splash of whiskey, then sipping it as he closed his eyes. I stood in the doorway, watching. *To be young again.*

"What?" Shalice asked, her bright smile lighting up her face. "You wishing you weren't so old and worn out?"

I shot her a glance, trying to feign anger. It was impossible — she was absolutely gorgeous, yet still had the youthful cuteness of a college schoolgirl. She was African-American, with long, skinny legs and wiry arms, but in a lithe and fit way. I couldn't remember how she and Joey had met, but they'd been inseparable for the past few months.

"Not any more than you're wishing you weren't named after a cup."

She frowned.

"*Shalice — Chalice.* It means *cup.*"

"It's *Shalice,* with an 'S,'" she said. "And it's pronounced 'Sha-leece."

"Not my fault your parents can't pronounce *cup.* What kind of dancer did you say you were, by the way?"

She scowled. "I told you about fifty times, Mason. I teach *ballet.* To *children.*"

"Yeah?" I asked. "That what they're calling it these days?"

I knew she had a sense of humor, so I wasn't too worried

about her feelings, but I still didn't want to come across like a jerk, so I let up.

"Dinner's ready in half an hour," I said. Shalice nodded, and Joey rolled his head side to side and then back and forth. I took that as a confirmation that he'd heard me, then retreated to the small kitchen to start dinner.

CHAPTER ELEVEN

DINNER WAS GOOD, BUT NOTHING special. I secretly wished Joey would have sobered up enough to cook it, as he was a master cook, even when it was as simple as fish on the grill.

We shared a bottle of wine I'd dug out of a cabinet, then the three of us parked it up on top in the deck chairs, waiting for the sunset. Sunsets on the *Wassamassaw* were a new favorite of mine, and I'd spent many evenings up here alone or with Joey, or with Joey and Shalice.

Since Hannah, I hadn't dated or seen anyone, even though I often felt like it would be quite nice to hang out with a lady closer to my age once in a while. Joey and Shalice were nice, but they were, well, together. Even though it was my boat, when they were here there were times I felt like a third wheel.

They bunked up in one of the guest rooms, which were plenty big enough for two people and luggage. Joey had a few clothing items in the closet and some hygiene accessories in the bathroom, ready to go in case we decided to make a jaunt somewhere. As my only friend, he was a good one: ready for anything, whenever I said the word.

His background in the Navy didn't hurt, either. A scrapper, learning the ropes from having to figure them out on his own. No family that he talked about, and I didn't ask. Shalice perhaps knew more about the guy than I did, but I knew one thing: I could trust him, and I could count on him to pull through.

It was no different now — I was going to find this guy who'd killed my old man, and I knew Joey would help. I couldn't keep him from doing it anyway, even if I'd wanted to.

I knew that was the topic as soon as Joey turned to look at me from his chair on the top deck.

"Finally sober up enough to chat?" I asked.

He smiled. "Yeah, and I was waiting for Shalice to head down to the room."

Shalice had gone down to shower, or put makeup on, or something women did after dinner. It gave Joey and me a minute or two to talk about the situation, and even though she'd eventually know what we were up to, it would save her from getting too wound up about it before we'd even started.

"Well, what are you thinking?"

He shrugged. "Still going through with it?"

"Damn right I am. The guy killed my old man, and I —"

"It's not about that," Joey said.

I frowned. "What do you mean?"

"I know you, Dixon. It ain't about your old man." He paused, sniffed, then took a pull from a long cigar he'd been cradling. "I mean it *is*, but it's not *really*."

I looked him up and down. He did know me, better than anyone with the possible exception of Hannah, but that didn't mean he could read minds. "What do you think it's about, then?"

"They want you to take this guy out. Sure, he offed your dad, but they know that you're still their best option for getting their mark."

"Yeah, and?"

"*And*," he continued, "it means they're paying you."

I chuckled.

"When were you going to tell me, and what's my cut?"

This time I actually laughed out loud. "Your *cut?* You think just because you're a mediocre sidekick you get more than your current share?"

"My 'current share' is a manager's salary and some perks."

I laughed again, looking out at the sunset over the Atlantic and taking a puff from my own cigar. I wasn't much of a cigar smoker, but I could appreciate them. Joey had picked these up from Charleston, and I had to admit the kid had decent taste. Mild, sweet, and very aromatic, it was right up my alley.

"Your manager's salary is a *very* generous salary, kid. And those *perks* you're referring to — wining and dining in the fanciest yacht from here to Boston Harbor? You think they're just little perks? This baby costs money to run."

Joey smiled. "I'm messing with you. But seriously, you wouldn't be as gung-ho about this if it was *just* your father's death motivating you. You might look around, poke into some of the undercurrents in Charleston, maybe even call in some professional help. But you wouldn't take it on just by yourself. And you certainly wouldn't be *that* interested in getting it done quickly."

I looked at the stairs, then listened to hear if Shalice was returning yet or not. All I could hear was the splash of waves falling gently on the hull of my boat, and the distant wash of the same waves crashing against the beach. We were only out about a quarter mile, enough to get some decent fishing in but not too far we couldn't get back to the bar in a hurry if we had to.

"Fine," I said, turning back to Joey. "You caught me."

He smiled again. "I knew it. So what's the payout?"

"Ten percent. Typical."

"Okay, so this guy *stole* money from them — they want it back, and ten percent of that makes sense. But ten percent of *what*?"

I waited for him to take a sip from his scotch. It was expensive, and I had bought it, so planning for him to spit it out wasn't probably the smartest decision I'd made that night, but it would be funny.

"Three-point-two," I said.

His eyes widened a bit, then shrank. He was thinking about it. "Three-point-two..."

"*Million.*"

As if reading my mind, he looked me in the eye, carefully swallowed every damn drop of the whisky, then took a deep, long, puff from his cigar.

"Come on, Joey. That's a *lot* of money."

He laughed. "Sure it is. Your payout then is three-hundred twenty thousand?"

"Yep."

"Damn. That *is* a lot of money. I figure we can still split it fifty-fifty, get you some nice wallpaper for the bar, and —"

"Like hell we will."

"What? You don't like wallpaper?"

"Fifty-fifty."

He laughed.

"More like eighty-twenty, if you're good."

"You mean like if I save your ass like last time?"

I blew out a puff of smoke. "Yeah, like last time."

He immediately reached a hand over. "Deal, boss. Only this time you let me in the action."

"Joey," I said. "Let's hope there won't *be* any action."

As soon as the words escaped my lips, the sound of a large boat motor ripped through the serenity of the orange-cast sunset.

CHAPTER TWELVE

THE BOAT WAS SMALLER THAN mine, but certainly faster because of it. Even with only one of their twin engines they could burn me in a race, and I knew it.

"We're not going to outrun them," I said.

"Why would we?"

"Because they're not our friends."

"How can you —"

Joey cut himself off as soon as he saw it.

At the bow of the boat, standing on the rounded covered section on top, stood a man, his legs firmly at shoulder's length apart, one hand holding the deck rail of the speeding motorboat.

In his *other* hand he held an assault rifle.

"Shit."

"Shit's right," I muttered.

"What's the —"

"You and Shalice get belowdecks, stay out of sight, and wait for —"

"What's going on?" Shalice's voice cut through the night

air, rising above the increasing roar of the approaching watercraft.

"Shit again," I said. "You two need to stay down. No sense letting them know there are three of us here. They're here to talk to me."

"No, but it doesn't matter. My boat, my rules."

"We can't get belowdecks without being spotted."

He was right. "True. Okay, just stay up here. It'll give you a perch to listen from, and if you're careful about it maybe even a good line of sight onto their —"

My world suddenly lit up with the brightness of a million suns.

"*Dammit*," I shouted. They had opened fire with a massive light, one of the coast-guard-quality million-candle-power bulbs that could be focused on a target from over a hundred feet away.

And they weren't even *close* to a hundred feet away.

The light burned my eyes, blinding me.

"What the hell," I heard Joey say from next to me.

'Don't move,' a voice said, booming out from a speaker system from somewhere on the smaller craft. *'We see you — all three of you. Do not attempt to escape. We need to talk.'*

"Yeah," Shalice said. "Sounds like that's all they want to do."

"Never know," I said. "They might just need to chat with me about something."

I saw Joey's face, met his eyes. *Don't tell her*, I silently pleaded. He nodded.

I turned back to Shalice. "Stay up here, just like they said. Don't let Joey do anything stupid."

She nodded. "Want me to call the cops? Or Coast Guard?"

"Can't get cell service out here," I answered as I stepped

onto the first stair. "And there isn't a radio on the top deck to get the Coast Guard. Just hang tight, stay cool."

I walked down the stairs onto the main deck, wondering the whole time if I had time to get to my cabin and grab one of the pieces I kept on board at all times. I had a few to choose from, everything from a couple smaller .380s to my trusty .45-caliber Glock.

I knew, however, that the answer was no. They were already preparing to board, and I had a feeling the guy standing like a pirate at the front of their boat was more than ready to pop off a few rounds. I walked over to the port side, stood at the rail, and held my hands up.

"Keep 'em up, Dixon," the guy with the gun said. "Don't worry about helping us board — we'll take care of that on our own."

He was right, as almost immediately after he'd said it I saw two more gentlemen throw ropes over to the *Wassamassaw* from the smaller boat. The boat was unnamed, unmarked, and painted black. *Great.* They were in the business of staying out of sight.

I wondered if they were pirates, but thought it seemed a little unlikely that they'd be targeting yachts and smaller vessels that weren't in a shipping lane, and American boats at that. Pirates these days were far smarter than the general public wanted to believe, targeting ships that had strayed off the beaten path for whatever reason, and specifically focusing on large pulls — ships carrying valuable cargo that could fetch a hefty sum on the black market.

The pirating industry, I'd been told, was alive and well, but it was rare to see or hear anything about them in the States — it was too far from the markets for the bastards to risk it.

So these men weren't here to loot my boat. They weren't here to hold me hostage, demanding an ungodly sum of money to warrant my release. They were here for something else entirely.

Something that was probably related to this latest operation I'd found myself in.

"Hello, Mason," a voice said.

I turned, my hands still above my head, and looked at the man who'd boarded. He was short, squat even, but seemed like he could handle himself well. A bowling ball made of pure muscle.

"What do you want?" I asked.

"I need to know that you're not going to make a move on Rockford Elizondo."

"I'm not."

"Good," the man said. "I guess we're done here."

I frowned. "Really?"

The man smiled. "No asshole, we're only getting started. You know how these things work. You've been in the business a long time, Dixon. You *and* your old man."

"What do you know about my old man?"

"That doesn't matter now," the man said. "I'm employed by the guy *you're* supposed to be trying to kill. He's *very* interested in *not* getting killed."

"So you kill me, he's safe? That it?"

The man shook his head. "No, Dixon. It's not that simple. Again, you know how this stuff works."

I shook my head. "No, I guess it's been too long. Why don't we have a drink, talk about it like gentlemen?"

He smiled. "Thank you, Dixon. I thought you'd never ask."

He motioned with his pistol for me to start walking.

"I'll follow you. Hope you have something worth drinking in there."

CHAPTER THIRTEEN

NATURALLY HE WENT FOR THE Johnnie Walker Blue — the overrated scotch that I keep on display in the lighted liquor cabinet. It really was meant for display. I'm not a scotch guy, really, and I'm certainly not a showy fellow, so having anything that costs more than a Benjamin in my liquor cabinet means it's either got to be *really* good or was a *really nice* gift.

My JW Blue, as it turned out, fell into the latter category. A gift from someone I can't even remember when my late wife passed away. That was the funny thing about gifts — the ones you remember aren't the most expensive, but the most meaningful. I'd have remembered the hell out of someone who'd gotten me *her* favorite drink rather than their own.

If they'd have known me any better they'd have opted for a bourbon, or a rye, or even just a plain 'ol American whiskey. But scotch has *zing* to it, a certain *je ne sais pas.* It says 'I bought you a gift that's expensive because I want you to remember that I bought you an expensive gift,' rather than 'I bought you this because I know you well.'

Whatever.

Regardless of the history of the items in my liquor cabinets — the good-sized one here, the minuscule one back at my apartment, and the massive, impressive one at my bar — I don't want schmucks drinking my stuff.

Especially if they're not paying for it.

"That's a $150 bottle of scotch, my friend," I said to the newcomer on my boat.

The squat man looked at it as he poured two glasses, then lifted the glass up and looked at through the light.

"It is fascinating, isn't it?" he asked. "How they can charge so much for swill like this?"

"It's just blended," I said, "but it's a well-known distillery. They can get away with it."

He scoffed, then set the bottle back on the shelf in the cabinet. At an angle, so the label faced the wrong direction. I made a mental note to fix that later before it started driving me nuts.

"I can fetch about $30 a pour at my bar for that."

"For *this*?"

"It's not a common request, believe it or not. And by pricing it high, I turn their attention on the lower-priced — and better — options."

He nodded in approval.

"What do you want?" I asked.

He sniffed, then smacked the scotch in his mouth after sniffing and sipping a finger of it. At least he seemed to know his whisky. I wondered if he was a drinker at all or if it was all for show.

"I normally don't drink on the job, Dixon," he said as he took another smaller sip. "But considering the company, I figured I could stand to indulge a bit."

"Keep drinking. Have all you want," I said.

He laughed. "It would make it easier to get rid of me that way, wouldn't it?"

"How else can I get rid of you?" I shot back. "I'm normally pretty good at boozing up the clientele, but something tells me you're not going to fall for any tricks."

"Good," he said. "We're on the same page."

"What do you want?" I asked again.

"I want you to back off Elizondo," the man said.

"I *am* off" I said. "I've done nothing so far. Don't really have plans to."

"Correct," he answered. "And I thought we could talk about the logistics of it down here, to keep it that way. Like gentlemen."

I thought about, then took a sip. "Well, listen, er —"

"Franzen," the man said. "Jacob Franzen."

"Okay, Mr. Franzen," I said. "You're here because you want me to *not* kill some guy, but there are guys who *really* want me to kill that same guy, and they're willing to pay me —"

"Three-hundred thousand," he said immediately, cutting me off. "Yes, I heard about that."

"It's a lot of money. You offering me that much to *not* kill him?"

He shook his head and smiled. "No, I'm afraid not. My boss doesn't have the resources to begin to pay off all the other men who want him dead."

"Right," I said. "So you can understand my conundrum, I'm sure. On one hand, I stand to make a lot of money. On the other hand…"

Franzen leaned forward a bit in the couch across from me. His legs parted a bit to allow for his roundish gut to fall between them. "On the other hand," he said, "you stand to *not die.*"

I leaned my head back. *Why does this shit always happen to me?* Everything about Franzen told me he was telling the truth. Everything told me he was a player, and possibly a major one, or at least a man playing for a major player. His boss, the man I had been instructed to kill, was now threatening me *not* to kill him.

Crazy world we live in.

"You're going to kill me."

"If you don't comply, yes."

"But... everyone dies."

He laughed. "Sure, Dixon, everyone dies. But my boss was very clear about the *timeframe*."

"Yeah," I said. "Sunday. I keep hearing that. What's Sunday, and why's it so damn important to this Rockford Elizondo guy?"

He shook his head. "Listen, Dixon. The only thing you have to worry about is making sure Elizondo stays alive until Monday morning. That's it."

"Great. So I'll make sure to cross out 'kill Rockford' from my planner."

Franzen laughed again. "That's just it," he said. "You see, Elizondo, after hearing a little about you, figured it would make *more* sense to have you on our side with this whole fiasco."

I squinted with one eye. "What — what are you talking about, Franzen?"

"I'm talking about making sure my boss doesn't die."

"Yeah," I said. "I got that. We already talked about *that*."

"No," he responded. "We talked about *you* not killing him. *Now* we're talking about making sure he doesn't die. Before Saturday."

"Wait — you're telling me you want me to *protect* him?"

He nodded. "My boss is convinced you're the right guy for the job."

"But the other guys are threatening to take my bar away if I *don't* kill him —"

"And *we're* threatening to kill you. If Elizondo dies."

Shit. Something about a rock and a hard place fits here, I thought. *But I'd honestly rather* be *between a rock and a hard place.*

I couldn't think of anything else to say. "Shit."

He nodded. "That's about the extent of it, yes. It's a shit deal, but it's the deal."

Franzen downed the rest of the glass and set it on the edge of the bar. No coaster. I'd have to clean up the wet ring of condensation after he left.

"I don't like that deal," I said.

"That's cute, Dixon. Sorry it doesn't fit your agenda. Hate to break it to you, bud, but *that's the deal.* Keep my boss alive, and we keep you alive."

I shook my head. "No," I said, clenching my fists. "I — I won't do —"

The punch hit me much quicker than I'd expected. It also hurt a *lot* more than I'd expected. The guy *was* pure muscle, I guess, and he was certainly in shape enough to move quickly.

I licked my lip and felt the beginnings of a massive welt forming. I was on the floor somehow. The punch and the whisky combined, perhaps. Or he was just that damn strong and knew how to use his hips to throw a hell of a punch. I crawled forward a bit on the carpet, trying to get to the other chair next to me to pull my self up.

"You son of a —"

The next hit was from a foot, and it landed in the soft part of my stomach.

I felt and heard the air leaving my insides as I crumpled down onto the carpet. *Shit,* I thought again. *Shit. This is not going well.*

"Dixon," the man said, not even breathing heavily. "I didn't want to have to tell you more than once. But this is something you'll learn from me."

He walked over to me, stepped over my prone body, and

reached down for the glass of scotch on the end table next to my chair. He downed the rest of it, then set it by his glass on the edge of the bar.

"I don't like to repeat myself. I *really* don't like to repeat myself when I know for a *fact* that the person understands me just fine. So when I *do* repeat myself, it costs."

I looked up at him, still catching my breath.

"It costs *a lot*, Dixon."

He swung his foot back and sailed it — perfectly aimed — right into the exact same spot he'd landed it before. The *oof* that escaped my lips was nothing compared to the feeling of everything inside of me trying to get out at once. I wanted to vomit, scream, and crawl away all at the same time.

Instead, I just lay there, pitiful, staring up at the bowling ball of a man who'd single-handedly laid me out and decimated me.

"It's going to cost you, Dixon, but consider yourself lucky. We're only going to take some collateral this time. Next time, it's their life."

I didn't have time to contemplate — or understand — what he was talking about before the swinging foot wound up and came back down.

This time it landed just under my eye, sending me rolling backwards and into the chair behind me. I made it through about a half roll before everything went black.

CHAPTER FOURTEEN

I GROANED. TRIED TO MOVE. Groaned again.

Dammit, I'm getting old.

My neck hurt, which was relatively normal, but as soon as I tried to turn it to the side a sharp flash of pain shot down my spine. I yelled, cursed.

My hands worked, so I used those to try and massage the kinks from my neck. The pain, apparently, was far deeper than a simple muscle-based massage could mend. I wondered if my neck was broken, but after writhing around on the carpet and shifting to a sitting position, I realized I was fine.

Just in severe pain.

I stood, keeping my balance by holding onto the chair. I looked around at the living room. Two empty glasses of scotch sat on the edge of the bar in the corner, the liquor cabinet closed but the bottle still spun out at the wrong angle, the label hidden from view.

Then I remembered what had happened.

I wanted to hustle, to move quickly, but I couldn't. I could barely move at all, so it was enough to shuffle toward the door and the stairs, then pull myself up slowly. Carefully, steadily, I made it to the top deck, the smaller area above the main deck that held the three deck chairs and a table with an awning cover over all of it.

Joey was still there.

Alone.

"J — Joey," I said. "You alright?"

He didn't respond.

Shit.

I walked over, still shuffling slowly so as not to upset my aches and pains any more than needed.

"Joey," I said again, louder this time. "Wake up."

He was facedown on the deck, the hard floor smashed against the side of his face. I tried to get closer and bend down, but my back wouldn't let me. Instead I just stood there, standing over him, useless and unable to help.

Finally he stirred.

"Joey, where's Shalice?"

His girlfriend's name seemed to wake him even further, and his eyes shot open. He groaned, loudly, then grabbed at the side of his head.

"They knocked me out," he whispered.

"Yeah," I said. "Me too."

"Someone else came aboard and came up here right after you and that other guy went down below. They — they forced me up against the railing and took Shalice."

I cursed. "Any idea where they went?"

He shook his head.

"How long ago?" I asked. I didn't know how long I'd been passed out, but I figured it had been longer than Joey.

"Not sure," he said. "I — I just remember them grabbing her. She screamed, and I tried to fight back."

"You were unarmed."

"Yeah, well screw that. I wasn't going to let them just…"

He didn't finish the sentence, and he didn't need to. I knew what he meant.

"You okay?" I asked.

"I think so. Shook up a bit, but I'm not injured. You, on the other hand —"

"I'll be fine," I answered. "Don't worry about me. Listen, Joey —"

"We're going to find them," he said quickly. "We're going to *kill* them, Mason. I'm going to personally rip that asshole's fu —"

"I know," I said. "I know. I'm with you. We'll get her back. They took her for collateral."

Joey stared at me like I was insane. "The hell's that supposed to mean?" he asked.

I walked closer to him, my hand on the rail. The wind felt nice, but nothing else did. All of it sucked. Ruined. A waste of a beautiful night.

And this is all my fault, I thought.

"First," I said, "this is my fault. My problem. You don't have to —"

"I'm doing whatever it takes to get her back, Dixon. Just try and —"

"I'm *not* going to try and stop you, Joey," I shot back. "I'm just going to say this because it's true, and I need to say it."

"Okay, go ahead then."

"This is my fault. Okay? Mine. My fault, my problem. Don't forget that. Whatever we're getting into, it's *my fault.*"

He nodded, then looked out over the water.

"Okay?"

"Yeah, Dixon," he said.

I could tell he wasn't done, and I could tell he wanted to scream. I wanted him to; hell, *I* wanted to. But he wasn't that sort of guy, and neither was I. He needed to vent, to get out some frustration, and the best way for both of us to do that was to start planning our attack. Figure out our next move, then start moving.

He also needed to figure out what he was feeling about Shalice.

She wasn't in immediate danger, but I hadn't yet told him *why* they'd taken her. I remembered the conversation, but it was likely Joey had no idea what they wanted with her.

"Joey," I said. "You good?"

He nodded. "I guess."

"We need to talk. Make a plan."

"Yeah," he said.

"And I need to tell you why they took her."

He whirled around and glared at me. "They took her because she was *here*, Mason. Because we're a mess, and she walked right into it."

I shook my head. "No, man. That's not it. *I'm* a mess, and you're part of that. And yes, she was in the wrong place at the *very* wrong time, but it's not her fault, or yours."

"I know that, Dixon. Get to the point."

"Okay, fine. The point is this: she was taken as collateral."

"She's a hostage, Dixon."

"No," I said, shaking my head again. "No, she's not. I mean, yes, in a way, but she's not in any immediate danger. They're not going to use her to negotiate with us."

"How do you figure that?" Joey asked.

"Because they've *already* negotiated. Down below, in the room."

He waited for my explanation.

"They want their boss kept alive. They needed assurance that he would be, so they came here. To me. Not to you, not to Shalice. Like I said, she was just in the wrong —"

"Doesn't *matter*, Dixon," he said. His eyes were wide, nearly bugging out of his head, and I could tell I was about to lose him. "They *took her.* You got that? It doesn't matter why, or for what reason — she's *gone.*"

"It does matter," I said, trying as hard as possible to keep my voice calm. "It matters because as long as their boss doesn't die, she stays alive."

"Yeah?" he asked. "And you have any idea who their boss is?"

I nodded. "I do," I said softly. "It's Rockford Elizondo."

CHAPTER FIFTEEN

WE'D MADE IT BACK TO the dock and parted ways in record time. Joey had nothing to say, and I had nothing to offer that would make our situation any better. So the entire ride was silent, punctuated only by the squawking seagulls following us in to shore and then the other yachters as they disembarked from whatever excursion they'd been enjoying.

Our separate cars were waiting, and Joey headed to his without saying goodbye. I knew he was going back to the bar, to clean up for tomorrow. He'd probably make his way through a small bottle of something heavy as well, but I couldn't fault him for that.

I went back to my own apartment, still shaken and still unsure of what my next move should be. Whatever it was, Joey was in on it. He would grieve for a day, maybe a little longer, then he'd be ready for action.

He'd be ready for revenge.

Joey wasn't a hothead, but he wasn't a completely cool, levelheaded guy either when the shit hit the fan. He was like me in that way — ready and willing to rush in and get things done, no matter the consequences.

But Joey was no good to me or Shalice dead, so I needed to figure out how to keep him from doing anything rash. I hated planning — it always seemed like a pointless task, as plans were guaranteed to change midstream, no matter how well thought-out.

Joey was typically all for a solid plan, but I knew that since he had more at stake now than ever before he'd be more of a loose cannon.

I was a loose cannon, and we only needed one cannon.

Whatever I could do to reign him in was a good idea.

But, also like me, Joey was stubborn. Between a background in the Navy and an adult life spent figuring things out for himself, Joey would be hard-nosed about any sort of 'backseat' plan for him I could come up with.

If I was playing offense, he'd refuse to play defense.

Which meant I needed to call in some heavy-hitters. If I could make Joey *think* we were going on the attack, yet have someone besides us running point, it left room for us to fall back and help with some behind-the-scenes stuff. Support, recon, whatever they might need.

I picked up my archaic cellphone and dialed the number. It was well after normal business hours, but the person I was calling didn't maintain normal business hours. Or, for that matter, conduct normal business.

It rang, twice, before the man on the other end answered. "Dixon?"

"Hey, Truman."

"Shit, man," he said. I could hear the smile in his voice. It had already been too long since I'd seen him last — recovering from a close encounter back with Hannah. He and his team at the FBI had spent a night on the *Wassamassaw* as a gift for helping me out, and I'd told Truman then that we needed to hang out more often.

But, as it turned out, neither of us was any good at

keeping in touch. It had been since he'd walked off the boat that next morning that we'd last spoken.

"Yeah," I said. "Sorry — I'm… I'm bad about this stuff."

"No worries," he said. "Good to hear your voice. What's up?"

Truman probably already knew that I wouldn't call to set up a time to 'hang out,' and I certainly wouldn't do it on a weeknight. He also probably knew that from the sound of my voice.

"There's… there's a situation," I said.

"You got to be kidding me," Truman said. "Again?"

"Truman, I need your help."

I heard him sigh, then he went silent.

"I'm after someone. He killed my old man, and someone wants me to retaliate. There's a finder's fee."

Another sigh, but this time Truman's voice picked back up afterward. "Look, Mason," he said. "Besides the *very obvious* and *blatant* illegalities here, this is your business. Right?"

He wasn't talking about my bar.

"Right, yeah. But —"

"But now you're in over your head."

"Something like that, yeah."

"Not surprised, Dixon. And may I remind you, considering what you're about to tell me, that I work for the *Federal Bureau of Investigation?* The *government,* Mason."

I wasn't sure if I was supposed to take that as a 'be careful what you're about to say' or a 'don't say it at all,' so I did what I thought best.

I said it.

"Truman, listen. Someone else is in the game, and they want assurance that I won't move on their boss."

"Christ, Dixon. They've got something on you, then?"

"*Both* sides have something on me."

"Yeah?" Truman asked. "What's that?"

"My bar on side."

"Great. That's just great —"

"And Joey's girlfriend on the other."

"*What?*" Truman's voice rose in pitch and volume through the tinny speaker.

"Yeah," I said. "I told you, I'm in —"

"It's not *you* who's in it, Dixon. Hell, this is your *life,* pal. It ain't the first scrape you've been in, and — against your better judgement — it probably won't be your last. It's not *you* who's in trouble, pal, it's this girl. And Joey."

It was my turn to sigh, and I made it a good long one. I wasn't one for feeling sorry for myself, but at the moment I couldn't help it. "I — I know."

"Mason, I can't help you."

"I know you can't, I just —"

"Just *what,* Dixon? You thought that by calling me and spilling it all over the phone you'd bind me to some agreement? Some 'rule' about negligence that would force my hand?"

I wasn't prepared to be berated, but I figured after he'd started that it was probably his first reaction. If the tables were turned, I guess I'd have done the same thing.

"That's the thing with you, Mason," Truman continued. "You don't think there are consequences for what you do."

I was started to get worked up, pissed even, and I certainly had better things to do.

"Stop, Truman. Just stop. I called because I wanted your advice —"

"You want *my* advice?" Truman said, still nearly yelling into his cellphone. "*My* advice is the same as it always is. The same as it always *has* been. *Get. Away.* Run away from this madness, and stop acting like a vigilante idiot."

"I'm not a vigilante idiot —"

"Save it, Dixon," he said. "You and I both know that what you do is, generally, a good thing. It's dangerous as hell and I have *no idea* how you haven't left a wave of innocent dead people behind you, but I guarantee you that it is not *skill.* It's luck, and you're a lucky son-of-a-bitch, but that luck has changed. It's changed, Mason, and you just had your last battle."

"Truman, I don't need this right —"

"No *shit* you don't need this right now, but you called anyway. What'd you think would happen? I'd drop everything and come running? That I didn't have *enough* on my plate already? I'm neck-deep in a counterfeit operation in Puerto Rico, and we can't even decide on *jurisdiction,* Dixon."

He stopped to breathe, but I knew he was far from done.

"*Besides* all that, what do you expect me to do? This is all an illegal operation, no matter how you crack it. I come in, guns blazing, take out the bad guys, you're going to jail. For a *long* time. There's no way to 'report that away,' Dixon. There's no fudging those numbers."

"I *know* that, Truman. I'm just trying to see what you would do."

"I would go to the police."

"There's no way in hell I'm doing that."

"I know. But you asked me what I would do. This isn't something you can fix on your own, Dixon. You got yourself into this mess, no matter how you choose to see things. The police can't help you either, but at least you remove some of the liability from your own head."

"I'm not going to the police."

Truman breathed in and out again, a short string of sighs, then got back on the phone. "I can't help you, Dixon. I wish I could, but I can't. I can't give you information because I don't have it, and even if I could, I wouldn't. I'd be sucked into this mess, and I *will not* be sucked in."

I nodded. "Yeah," I said. "I know. I'm not asking you to, either. For the record. I don't want your hands getting dirty, trust me. I just — I just wish..."

"I know, Dixon. It's like when you're a kid in school and you get in trouble, you want your best friend to be there with you, because getting in trouble alone sucks."

"Yeah," I said again. "That's pretty much it."

"Well I may be the closest thing to a best friend you have, Dixon, but I'm not getting in trouble with you on this one."

"I know. Don't worry about it."

"Listen, Dixon," Truman said. "I really wish there was something I can do, but it's not possible. You get out of this mess, and we'll get a beer. Until then, I'd suggest you pour yourself a stiff drink, get on that fancy boat of yours, and point it toward Africa and don't stop until you get there."

"You got it, Truman," I said. "Thanks."

He hung up without saying anything more, and I knew he was sincere. He wasn't available, and no matter how much I wanted to try to drag him in, I couldn't.

This is my mess, I thought. *And I have to clean it up.*

CHAPTER SIXTEEN

THE BAR WAS DIFFERENT THE next morning, even though I knew it was exactly the same. It was the same place I'd started, the same place I'd renovated, and the same place Joey and I had served countless beers and poured countless old fashioneds.

Yet it was different.

There was a haze almost, something in the air. Hanging there, like dead weight.

Joey was silent, still, and I wasn't trying to get him to talk. He was thinking, and I didn't need to ask him about what.

I was thinking too, and even though I knew there was no way I could figure it all out, *not* thinking wasn't going to make the clock stop. We had until Sunday to find this guy, Rockford Elizondo, and kill him.

Or *not* kill him.

Depending on which side I decided we were on.

My dad was dead, apparently killed by this man. People who wanted Elizondo dead were threatening me with my bar, holding it out over me to get me to off him. They were even offering to pay me a lot of money to do it.

On the other hand, Elizondo's men wanted to make sure I *didn't* move on him. To enforce that, they were threatening at least Shalice's life, and probably mine and Joey's as well.

They could try to kill me all they wanted, but there was nothing I could do to protect Shalice from here.

So I was in a bit of a conundrum. A rock and a hard place. Up shit creek without —

"Yo," Joey said.

I looked over. "What's up. You okay? You need any —"

"I'm fine, Mason," he said. "Just got off the phone with our distributor."

I cocked an eyebrow. "Which one?"

"The big one in Charleston."

We worked with about five main distributors, all of whom offered something we liked at the right price. As usual, no one offered everything at a reasonable price, so one of the many things Joey and I split duties on was ordering and restocking the liquors behind the bar from our approved vendors list.

The vendor we did the most business with in Charleston was Jonathan Frey, a somewhat naive yet likable chap who gave us a great deal on rum and other Caribbean imports — bitters, liqueurs, fruits, that sort of thing.

"What'd he say?" I asked. Joey was obviously trying to keep his mind off the obvious, at least until he was ready to move and make a plan, and he'd chosen to do so by throwing himself into his day job. I was fine with that, even though I knew we were running out of time.

"Normal delivery for the smaller stuff," he said. "Bitters and pineapples are coming up tomorrow, but the rum's a bit behind."

"Why's that?"

"Storms, I guess," Joey said. "Lots of big distributors coming up from the Caribbean this weekend, apparently. Trying to unload before the storm hits, so the harbor will be packed with them. He said it'll be Sunday before the ship arrives. "

"Before the…"

"Ship arrives," Joey said. "Yeah." Then he paused, looked at me. "Why?"

"Before the *ship* arrives?"

"Yes, Mason, that's what I said. What of it?"

I thought back to the encounter I'd had with the first guys who'd brought me in. Jeff and his two cohorts. They'd told me the man's name — Rockford Elizondo — but not much else that was useful. They'd told me that he was somewhere in Charleston, and what he did for a living.

Shipping.

He was in the shipping business.

"Joey, I think one of those is our ship."

Joey frowned. "What are you talking about?"

It was all starting to make sense now. I wasn't just pulled into this because my dad was killed by Elizondo, a rich shipper from Charleston. It wasn't even because I was the kind of guy who could take out Elizondo without people knowing about it.

They had targeted me because, without knowing it, I had become *deeply* embroiled in their plan.

Elizondo was a shipper, and I had a feeling I knew what he was shipping.

"Joey, pull up something about Elizondo."

"What? Why?"

"Just *do it*, Joey."

"He's — he's not exactly… I mean, I already have."

"You have?"

"Well sure, boss. I came in and did it last night, after…"

Typical of Joey. He was already moving, making a plan. I had underestimated him, assumed he'd needed to rest, to grieve. But he'd been hard at work already.

"You didn't find anything?"

"Nothing useful. A LinkedIn profile that hasn't been —"

"A what?"

Joey smiled. "LinkedIn. It's like Facebook for —"

"What's Facebook again? Is that the networking site? Like for businesspeople?"

"No," Joey said. "You're thinking of LinkedIn."

"Oh," I said, thoroughly confused. "So what's Facebook?"

"It's like — you know what? Never mind. Back to Elizondo."

"Right, okay sure." I was moving chairs around and sweeping beneath tables, so it was good just to have Joey talking, if only to drown out the monotony.

And, I had to admit, it was good to hear his voice again.

"So he's got an old profile, if it's even him, and then a page on the shipping company's website, but I have a feeling it's outdated."

"Why do you have that feeling?" I asked.

"Because there was a note at the top of the page that says *'last updated September 14, 1998.'*

"1998?" I asked, incredulously. "I didn't even know the Internet was around back then."

"I'm surprised you know it's around *now*," Joey responded.

I shot him a Clint Eastwood stare, then turned back to the broom.

"So there's nothing useful online," I said. "Yet the guys in Charleston — and the guys from the boat last night — seemed to assume I knew exactly who Elizondo was."

"But you don't."

"But I don't," I answered.

"You were on to something, though," Joey said. "What was that?"

"Well, I just remember them saying he was a shipper, from Charleston. I didn't think much of it, but — maybe this is a stretch — maybe he's got a big shipment coming in on Sunday."

"Which is why they'd want this all wrapped up by then."

"Right," I said.

"I don't think it's a long shot at all. You said it yourself they thought you'd know exactly who this guy is, or at least they implied it. If they were really that dead-set on getting him killed, they could have at least made sure you knew who he was."

"Yeah," I said. "Sorry, I guess I didn't think to ask."

"We can figure it out, though," Joey said. "If they were that sure, it shouldn't be hard to find him." He pulled out his phone again. "Actually, hang on a sec."

I watched him flip through the screen on his smartphone, then press on something. He held the phone up to his ear.

"Yeah, hey — it's Joey again," I heard him say.

I frowned.

"Yeah, no problem. Hey, can you — would you mind doing me a favor?"

My eyes widened. "Joey," I said. "Don't." I wasn't sure who he was talking to, or what he was about to disclose, but I couldn't risk getting anyone else involved.

Joey laughed, then continued, holding up an index finger at me. "Yeah, yeah, of course. We'll have to grab a drink sometime when I'm up there. Anyway, listen. I'm wondering if you can give me any information about your suppliers?"

Joey made a face, then his expression softened. "Oh! No, man, no way. You're still our guy. Has nothing to do with that, and you shouldn't worry about it. I know we can't buy direct anyway. We — I just want to know someone's name, if possible. Or, actually, if *you* know a name."

I watched Joey's face, silently wishing he'd both hang up the phone and also hoping he'd put it on speakerphone so I could hear.

"Rockford Elizondo. That ring a bell?"

Joey listened for a minute. "That's the one. You sure?" he nodded. "Dude, *thank* you. That's great. Yeah, why don't you come down? You said you're driving anyway?"

Another nod, then Joey thanked him again and hung up.

"What was that?" I asked.

"That was our supplier. Charleston."

"Frey?"

Joey nodded. "I was just talking to him earlier like I said, and he knows a bunch of the guys in the area who ship in weekly and monthly. Figured it wouldn't hurt to ask."

I could tell Joey was getting excited about whatever it was he'd just found out, so I didn't interrupt him.

"He's stopping by to grab a drink, since he was already on the highway."

I waited, but Joey had turned away, wiping down his side of the bar and preparing to move toward the tables on that side of the room.

I raised an eyebrow. "You going to tell me, or do I have to guess?"

He grinned. "He knows. He's in."

"Wait, what? What do you mean, *he's in?*"

Joey sighed. "I didn't tell him anything — obviously. You heard the call. He just —"

"Joey," I said, suddenly feeling myself grow very serious. "Joey, this isn't something we're bringing anyone *in* on."

"No, I know that, boss," he said. "I just… I may have told him before about the boat, and how we…"

I frowned.

"He and I are sort of friends. Whenever I'm up in Charleston we try to grab a beer. I've told him about your boat, and how we're always out on it and stuff. He's a good guy, asks a lot of questions and stuff. I like that."

"But you didn't *say* anything about the boat this time, Joey," I said. "Why in the hell would he assume that we're heading out on it again?"

"Well, it's... I might have told him once or twice that we've been unavailable when he's wanted to meet up, and he's — I guess — jumped to conclusions."

"He's *jumped to conclusions?"* I was starting to get pissed, and Joey's calm, careless demeanor wasn't helping. "Joey, what we do — what happens *outside* of this bar — is *classified.*"

"I know that, and I've told him nothing. But what was I supposed to say when he wanted to meet up, or drop off a delivery, and neither of us was here?"

"You're supposed to tell him we're *not here*, Joey. It's not that difficult."

"Right, but it's happened more than once. And he's inquisitive, and he doesn't really have a life. No kids, no wife. And it always felt like he wanted to hang out, maybe figure out why you and I were always going out on these little excursions."

I glared at him. "So you felt *sorry* for him?"

He shrugged. "I don't know what the big deal is. I didn't tell him anything, and he's a cool guy anyway."

"Joey — listen to yourself! We can't let him *help* us. Hell, how *could* he even help us?"

"I'm not saying he could," Joey answered. "I'm just saying he might know something, or get us information. He's connected, and it sounds like our guy is in Frey's world too, so it's a good relationship to have."

"I don't like relationships."

"Clearly."

I was grumpy, but I still didn't want someone digging around my business. Either one of my businesses.

As usual, though, I trusted Joey's gut almost as much as I trusted my own, so I figured that if Joey was vouching for this distributor, I could at least give him the benefit of the doubt. Joey, I knew, wouldn't have told him about any of our 'adventures' together, and —

"Joey," I said.

He turned, quickly. "What's up?"

"You told him we went on 'adventures' together?"

"No, I, uh… I mean I didn't really have any other way of explaining…"

"You realize how that sounds, don't you?"

He laughed. "Oh come on, old man. He doesn't think we're…"

"Together?"

He laughed again. "No, I guarantee you he doesn't think that. He knows I'm not gay."

"Why?"

"Because Shalice and I have gotten a beer with him. He's met her."

"But…"

"*But* I never told him *you* weren't." He shrugged.

"Right, I said. "Thanks for that."

"You got it, boss." He paused, silently considering something for a moment. "Hey, listen. I mentioned Shalice, and… and I know it's hard for me to think clearly. I'm sorry for bringing Frey into this, no matter how little he's actually going to know. I just… I guess I was being rash, trying to get as much on our side as possible."

I immediately forgot all about my anger toward Joey for pulling in Frey. I knew exactly how Joey felt, and I knew exactly what I would have done in his situation.

"Joey," I said. "I'm with you, man. I get it. You don't owe me an apology. *I'm* the one that got us into this mess, remember? And I'm the one who's going to get us out of it. If you and Frey want to help, that's fine by me."

He looked out the small window for a moment, then back at me. "You sure about that?"

"Dead sure, Joey."

"Sounds good, boss. Let's feel him out, see if we think he can be helpful at all, and if he's interested. He might just want a free ride on the boat. But if he's gunning for some action, and he understands the risks, he could be an asset."

I knew that an innocent civilian just 'gunning for some action' would *never* be anything more than a major liability in *any* situation, but I nodded along anyway. "Sounds good to me. When's he going to be here?"

CHAPTER SEVENTEEN

I'D MET JONATHAN FREY A couple of times, though there was nothing much about him that I'd deemed memorable, so I almost didn't recognize him when he walked in. After he'd looked both ways as soon as he entered the front door, as if he was about to cross a busy street, I knew it was him. The two things I *did* remember about him was that he looked far younger than he actually was and had a nervous tick or something about him.

He was on edge, jittery. Even as he strolled over to my empty bar he was looking around, but not in a 'taking it all in' sort of way, like a tourist, but like a 'something's going to jump out at me' sort of way.

"H — hey," he said.

I glared at Joey. *This is the guy you thought might be able to help us?* I thought. *He can't even get a single word out without losing his mind.*

I wondered if he was a sociopath. Sometimes these types seemed almost normal, almost balanced, and then lost their shit. Maybe he was one of those.

"Hey, Frey," Joey said, a huge smile on his face. "How you been?"

"Yeah, hey Joey," he said, his voice almost a whisper. "I — I'm good."

This guy a junkie or something? I thought. I reached a hand out. "Good to see you again, chap."

Chap?

Apparently I had a nervous tick of my own: calling weird people weird things I'd never call anyone else.

"Oh, yeah, hey there Mason," he said. He sounded Canadian, really digging into those 'A' sounds. "How are you?"

"I'm good, thanks for asking. Can I pour you a drink?"

He frowned, as if I'd just asked him if I could sleep with his sister. Finally, after *far* too many seconds, his face melted back to normal and he looked me in the eye. "Oh, uh, thanks. Yeah, maybe a beer?"

I sighed. "Any particular *kind* of beer?"

"Just, uh, something lighter?"

"Lighter than *what*?"

I guess he had inferred my growing impatience, so he suddenly snapped to attention and then swung into a barstool. "Sorry. You know what? I'll have a bourbon."

I cocked my head sideways. *Okay, this is a change of pace.* The guy in front of me had just won a couple points in my book.

I nodded, turned around, and grabbed an interesting choice: a 291-distilled raw spirit, from Colorado Springs, that I had aged myself in a small barrel. I poured three glasses over our standard large cubes and pushed Frey's toward him.

He took a long, slow sip. He examined the color, then sniffed it.

Whatever preconceived notions I'd had about the man

quickly vanished. Still, I wondered what had brought upon the strange nervousness he seemed to be suffering from.

"Sorry," he said. Joey and I looked at him, simultaneously. "I… I know I sound nervous. It's just that…"

I looked over at Joey. *What did you tell this guy?* I thought. He shrugged in response.

"Speak your mind, Frey," I said. "We don't bite."

He took a long, deep breath. "It's just that I… I couldn't help but jump to some conclusions."

For the thousandth time that day I glare at Joey. I stared bullets through him. Again, as if it was no big deal, he simply shrugged.

"What sort of conclusions are we talking about, Mr. Frey?"

Jonathan Frey took another sip of whiskey, swallowed, then seemed to visibly steel himself. For a moment I lost sight of the small, timid man in front of me and instead saw an experienced, been-around-the-block-a-few-times savvy guy. He looked from me to Joey, then back to me.

"You kill people for a living?"

I laughed out loud. "Wh — what the hell? Where'd that come from?"

"Look," he said. "I really don't care one way or another. I just want to know."

For the firs time since I'd met him, I didn't know what to say. Of all the things I'd expected upon meeting with Jonathan Frey, one of our most loyal distributors, being completely taken aback was not one of them.

"Uh… no," I said.

"Come on," he said again, his voice growing more and more confident. "You can tell me. I've heard things, up in the city."

"Like what?"

"Like, you know, rumors."

"Rumors."

"Like there's a place down south you can send people, to uh, get *gone*."

"Get *gone*?" It was Joey's turn to laugh. "What is that, some sort of turn-of-the-century phrase?"

He shrugged, then helped himself to another glass of the 291. "How should I know?" He poured the drink, then looked up at us again with an odd crooked smile. "I'm just a distributor."

"Then why the hell are you digging around in my business?"

"Hey, brother," he said. "Joey called *me,* remember? You want to know more about this Rockford Elizondo situation?"

I nodded, then put my hand over his drink before he could take a sip. "What do you mean, *situation?*"

"I mean it's a *situation.* Every distributor on the East Coast knows about it. Shipping tycoon, works for one of the major importers. But he's in with some bad dudes."

I removed my hand and let him take a quick drink. "And you think *we're* those bad dudes?"

His eyes widened a bit as he swallowed his sip, then he smiled and shook his head. "N — no, not that. Sorry, no offense. You guys just don't have, uh, *oomph.*"

"And what's *that* supposed to mean?" Joey asked. "I got oomph."

"Yeah," I added. "Joey's the *oomphiest* guy around."

"Hey," he said. "No offense. You guys are great. Chill, unlike a lot of my clients. No purchasing crap to deal with, and Joey's always open to a recommendation."

He sat back a bit, no doubt feeling more in his element. "And I do know my way around the industry, so I like giving helpful recommendations."

He paused for a moment, then remembered his train of

thought. "It's just that you guys seem to be a, uh, bit smaller of an operation. Just two people, right? Nothing fancy. I like that, actually. Keeps things simple."

I leaned in, letting the little gut I had get squashed by the edge of my bar, and pushed my face right up into Frey's circle of comfort. It was no-man's land for a bartender — you never got up into someone's face like that, and you never let anyone else get up into *yours*, unless you meant business.

"Frey," I said, my voice a whisper. We were the only three people in the bar, and probably the only three people alive in a half-mile radius, as my place wasn't exactly in the middle of the hustle-and-bustle of a tourist town. But the whisper added to the effect. "Listen, man. I like you — always have. Joey's got a bit more of a hankering for you for some reason, and I respect that. But — and we're just going to leave it here — we need some information. Because of… because of *our* situation."

"Is your situation that you need to kill Elizondo?"

I pushed up from leaning over the bar and crossed my arms. "Alright, champ. Who told you that, and why in the world do you think we're out for blood?"

He smiled again, still maintaining that look of a deer in the headlights: unsure of his next move, but still confident that he was where he needed to be. "Look," he said. "I don't. Honestly. It's a guess. I don't know how these things work, but think about how it looks to the rest of us. The guys up in the city are saying things like, 'there's a guy for that,' and 'they'll take of that,' and then they talk about someone down south who… does stuff for them, I guess."

"Who?"

"I don't know. Guys who know people like Elizondo, and guys I prefer *not* to know. They're everywhere up there — they practically run the importing business, especially for the spirits industry."

"So you know, or *don't* know, some of these guys," Joey said. "And they're talking about someone down south of Charleston who can 'get things done?'"

He nodded.

"Things like what?"

"Well put the pieces together, man. You remember that car bombing a year ago?"

I knew exactly what he was talking about. *Yeah,* I thought. *The one up on the highway.*

I sniffed. "I thought it was a car fire. Just an accident."

"Well whatever it was, the police never did a thorough investigation. Just enough to figure out who the guy was. The talk around the city is that it was some rich schmuck, a guy who lived up in Jersey somewhere and came down to Charleston to, uh, get his fill of some less-than-reputable entertainment."

Frey was being unnecessarily kind. The 'schmuck' he was referring to was worse than dirt. A true son-of-a-bitch, the kind with money *and* a sick desire to spend it in despicable ways.

And his preferred 'flavor' of entertainment was underage children, specifically boys.

He'd sidled up to the bar one night, flashed the mark — a small coin — at me, and told me he'd 'come for what he deserved.' Then he'd ordered a shot.

An Irish Car Bomb.

I smiled. It usually wasn't that easy.

Typically the marks were a *little* more subtle. They either didn't have as much money as this schmuck had or they just cared more about the trail they were trying not to leave. Either way I took care of them, got them all *exactly* what they deserved.

Joey had started helping me out years ago. He was a capable soldier, a fine strategic thinker, and — best of all —

he had character. He felt the same thing I felt when these assholes would come knocking.

They deserved to die, and I was the man to help them with it.

It wasn't personal, and it wasn't a pleasure. It was just a chore, like cleaning the bar after a hard day's work or taking out the trash. I was good at it, and I liked the feeling of taking care of something that was usually a bit higher-level than local police but still under the radar of the Feds.

Still, I always thought we were subtle. Sure, there were the few times the smoking hull of a vehicle would be a bit difficult to hide away, but the vast majority of the time Joey or I could easily dispose of the bodies in a way that was discreet, simple, and cost-effective, and it had the added benefit of fitting the 'circle of life.'

I called it 'fish-baiting.' To fish bait a dead mark, we'd just bleach the body to remove anything that could be somehow chemically traced back to us and then cart it out to the water on a tiny fishing boat, then dump it out by the breakers using a couple cinder blocks and a lot of heavy-gauge fishing line.

Most of the time they were dead already.

I focused again on Frey, who was busy pouring himself another glass. This time I joined him, while Joey watched on.

"So," I said to Frey. "Whatever happened to the investigation?"

He winked at me. "Seems like the police lost interest when they figured out who the guy was. There wasn't anyone losing their mind over a dead schmuck, so I guess they buried it."

They buried it because they knew who he was, I thought. *They knew they were better off without a guy like that running around.*

"And the world's a better place without him around,"

Joey added.

"Seems like the world's been getting a lot better lately," Frey said.

"You being poetic or cryptic."

"Yes?"

I sighed. "Frey, we really do need to know about Elizondo."

"Why?"

"Because I'm *asking nicely.*"

I wasn't trying to threaten him — that would just add to his suspicions and it would certainly turn him on the defensive, but I was starting to get tired of the games.

"You don't have to tell me your business," Frey said, "but I do want to know *why* you want to know about him. He's one of my best suppliers. Always on time, and always trustworthy. If anything happened to him…"

"We're trying to make sure nothing *does* happen to him, Frey."

Joey shot me a glance. I nodded, once.

"Why? Someone else have it out for him?"

"Something like that. What do you know about him? His shipping schedule, routes, daily routine?"

"Shit, man," Frey said. "He's not my wife. I don't know what he does day-to-day. But he's coming in Friday."

I nearly dropped my glass. "He's coming in *tomorrow*?"

Frey nodded. "Yeah, had a shipment coming in Sunday that I was going to intercept and help with — he told me he's bringing me forty barrels that I wanted to try packaging myself. I got set up with a —"

"Frey," I said, purposefully interrupting him. "Why's he coming in a day early? I thought the shipment was *scheduled* for Sunday?"

"It was," Frey said, nodding. "But haven't you been watching the weather?"

CHAPTER EIGHTEEN

FREY WAS REVERTING BACK TO his edgy nervous self the more he told us. Joey and I had leaned in a bit, once again ratcheting up the tension in the room, and it must have caused the poor guy to feel like he was on the hot seat.

"So there's a hurricane?"

Frey laughed, a violent, nervous hiccupy sort of thing. "Yeah — about four of them. You guys seriously don't watch the news?"

We both shook our head, but Joey spoke. "Doesn't really affect us much. People are in a good mood, they come here to celebrate. World goes to hell in a hand basket, they come here to commiserate."

I beamed. I'd told Joey that same thing verbatim the day he started working for me. It was true — people typically needed their vices more than ever when they were in a good mood, but they were just as loyal to their sinful desires when times were tough. Alcohol and hospitality weren't the fickle masters industry pundits would have us believe — both were in steady demand, it seemed. It had been that way in my experience behind the bar, and I had a feeling it would take a lot more than a slight recession to fuel a mass exodus from nightly haunts.

"Well, you boys are missing out," Frey said. "Cat-4, Joanna, is making her way here by way of the Bahamas, and it's expected to be a Category 5 by landfall. It'll back off some, they're saying, but it's going to be a doozy. And then there's a couple big tropical storms spinning up down in the Caribbean, and it's anyone's guess where *those* will end up."

This was typical talk for this time of year — hurricanes and tropical depressions were commonplace, but they were more common south of us. The locals and oldies talked about 'the big one' like it was only a matter of time, but the truth was we were pretty safe from anything devastating.

"It's going to get bad here?" Joey asked.

"Well," Frey said, "probably not terrible — nothing we ain't seen before, at least once a season, but for the shippers…"

I nodded. *This is starting to make sense.*

"It's heading straight across their main lanes. The bigger guys can wait it out farther east, but the smaller vessels and midsize lines can't do anything but speed up and try to beat it."

I nodded again. "They'll try to tie up somewhere in the bay, or maybe down in the sticks." It was common practice to bed down for a hurricane by letting the boat float, albeit in a place that was largely protected on all sides to break the wind. The natural rise and fall of the seas wouldn't do any harm to the vessel — it was the battering winds and possible rains that caused the problems. During hurricane season it wasn't uncommon to see dozens of small sailboats and catamarans poking out through the mangroves in the backwater areas and behind the larger islands.

"Right, but if Elizondo's ship does that, they're marooned out there for a week, maybe two."

"So he's hustling in, trying to beat it?"

"That's the idea, anyway. They'll at least be docked, so when it hits they can't blame the shipper for missing his target. Who knows if they'll get it all unloaded by then, or if they'll have to wait until after."

"What's on the boat, Frey?" Joey asked.

"Usual fare — like I said, I'm waiting on forty barrels so I can —"

"Forty barrels of what?"

"Oh, uh, rum."

"What else is on the ship?"

Frey frowned, deep in thought. "It's a typical run, I guess. I usually get rum — that's their main import — but I've seen tequila, Caribbean whiskeys, lots of wine, that sort of thing."

"Always alcohol?" Joey asked.

"That's what he does. He's a shipper for a company that trades in spirits and fine wines. Specifically from the Caribbean."

I was taking it all in meticulously, making sure I was repeating every word he was saying and translating it into understanding as it bounced around in my brain.

Rockford Elizondo was a shipper — that much was clear. I didn't know if that meant he was the captain or just a high-ranking crew member, but Jonathan Frey made it sound as though our pal Rockford was going to be on this boat when it arrived in port to deliver its wares. It was loaded down with barrels and bottles of alcohol and wines, and my guess was that there was quite a bit of it.

And it was going to be coming in a day early.

"Joey," I said. "We need to get up there."

He nodded, finally turning to the back bar area and grabbing at a bottle of bourbon. He poured himself a shot of liquor, neat, and down it in one sip.

"Yeah boss," he said. "I agree."

Frey looked at each of us once more. "Okay, boys," he said. "I've said my piece, and I have my opinions. Time for you guys to return the favor. What's up?"

I wasn't sure I wanted to bring him in, but it probably wouldn't hurt to let him know the basics. I looked at Joey for confirmation, but he was shrugging up a storm, looking like an idiot.

"Fine," I said, making the call. "You've been helpful, Frey. Thank you for that. We never would have known the boat was coming in a day early, and it could be life or death. Glad we know now — I'll drink to that." I raised a glass, and we all clinked them together over the bar.

"We're trying to track down this Elizondo character because we think he's in trouble."

Frey raised an eyebrow. I could tell he was trying to put things together, things like why we knew about Elizondo's trouble and what a bartender and his cook thought they were going to do about it. I didn't want to give him any wiggle room to make wild-ass assumptions, so I just told him.

"We think he's been targeted, and his life's in danger."

Frey nodded. "Right, so why not go to the cops?"

Joey jumped in. "Well, for one, we can't proved anything, and if we tried to it'd look pretty bad. We'd be under just as much scrutiny."

"And what else?"

"For *two*," I added, "we were sort of told *not* to go to the cops."

Frey laughed. "You guys probably know the same guys I know."

"Yeah," I said. "We know the same guys you said you *didn't* know."

"I don't know them," he said. "More like know *of* them."

"Anything about these guys neither of us know you'd want to tell us?" Joey asked.

Frey thought for a moment, nursing his melting ice cube, then looked up. "They've been trying to build a small importing empire for a while."

"Importing?"

"Yeah, liquors and stuff they can't easily make here without a ton of regulation and oversight."

"Which would explain why they would want Elizondo dead," Joey added.

"Eh, sort of," I said. "It would be helpful to not have someone as distinguished as Elizondo hanging around, hogging all the attention and new business. But it doesn't make sense just to off him. It's way too difficult logistically, too."

Joey looked straight at me. "Unless you got someone else to do it," he said.

I shrugged. "Well yeah, that makes it *logistically* easier — their hands are clean, then — but it still doesn't add up. What's the payoff? Why can't someone else equally as knowledgable and equally as experienced as Elizondo just head down here and take his place? It's a big company, after all. Why Elizondo *specifically*?"

Frey looked at both of us. "You — you guys really *don't* watch the news, do you?"

I frowned. "I have a feeling you're about to tell us something you should have told us about ten minutes ago."

"Sorry, I didn't know if it would be relevant then."

"What is it?"

"Well, Rockford Elizondo's sort of been a media darling, a poster child for small business in the area lately. He's a well-known philanthropist, and while he's pretty rich and out of reach for most of us, they've painted him as sort of an Everyman."

"And he's a *shipper?*"

"Well, yeah," Frey said. "That's the thing. He's *currently* a shipper. Everyone thought he was just a business guy. You know the type: fancy parents, fancy education, fancy everything. Basically a ticket to the top, doing whatever you want."

"So it's weird that he chose shipping," Joey said. "Not exactly a sexy career path."

"No, not really," Frey said. "But that's part of his appeal, I think. He's thorough. Studious, smart, good intentions."

"I'll bet he's good-looking, too," I said.

Frey made a face that said, 'yeah, pretty much.' "So he didn't just 'choose' shipping. He's making a move."

"Making a move?"

"Yeah," Frey said. "The local news did a thing about him a few years back, and they hyped him up quite a bit. He bought a country club or something not too far from here, but they gave him a lot of credit for how he did it: he bought the place, but only *after* working there for a year. Spent a month as a groundskeeper, then a few months at the pro shop, then finally the last few months tailing and shadowing the managers."

"So he could learn the ropes," I said.

"Exactly."

"Wow," Joey said. "I didn't know anyone was that patient."

"Well, money wasn't an issue with him," Frey said. "But it's a pretty ingenious, if labor-intensive, way to insure you're getting a good investment. And to truly understand the business."

"I'll say."

"So he's in shipping now?" I asked. "And that means he's making a move?"

"Well that *and* his announcement a few months ago."

I cocked an eyebrow.

"He told everyone he's going down to Jamaica, to source

rum for a new venture, and that he'd be coming back full of ideas and a 'new vision' for the enterprise."

"Wow," I said. "So he's back now."

"Yeah, coming in soon. But that's not even the best part. He *bought* the ship outright before he left, and made sure that everyone he worked with — myself included — knew that he was starting up a new venture, and that he wanted our loyalty to lie with him, not his previous distribution company."

"My god," Joey said. "The guy's been orchestrating a brand-new distribution chain? Publicly?"

Frey nodded. "Sort of. Most of the fanfare has been publicized — like I said, he's a media darling, so they're all eating it up. But anyone who cares, like me, is pretty much out of the loop. We all just knew he was leaving, then coming back, supposedly with a new batch of product and a new company."

I was finally starting to put all the pieces together, and I was finally starting to realize why the guys up in Charleston thought I didn't need any more information than they'd given me. They figured I'd already known about all of this — it was, after all, my industry.

I looked at Frey and Joey simultaneously. "So you're telling me that Rockford Elizondo is coming back to Charleston in a day, loaded down with brand-new product, a brand-new company, and that he owns all of it *outright?*"

Frey nodded. "Yep, exactly. And if I was going to target someone's business for a hostile takeover, that'd be the one."

"You got that right," Joey said. "And I think we're about to be dealing with a *very* hostile takeover."

CHAPTER NINETEEN

"LISTEN," JONATHAN FREY SAID. "I really appreciate you guys letting me help you —"

"You're not helping us out," I snapped. "You're just along for the ride. Just like we discussed."

He nodded, but I could see the smile still plastered to his face.

What we'd discussed was simple: we needed to get to that ship, if only to follow behind it and help guide it in. Joey and Frey did an hour or so of searching to figure everything out: they'd either have a state-of-the-art navigation system or, if it was an older vessel, which was likely, they'd be lucky to even have a mechanical barometer. Either way, *my* boat *did* have a top of the line nav and comm system, and Joey and I like to joke that if a nuclear submarine decided to park off the coast of South Carolina, we'd be the first to know about it.

Elizondo's vessel was a Handysize, a small freighting and cargo ship, capable of being loaded down with an impressive amount of transportable goods yet probably on the lighter side for this voyage. Their captain might know this area well, or they might not. We planned to go find out.

If we left early afternoon, we predicted we'd be able to intercept them sometime late evening or just after midnight.

There were a lot of guesses, which caused Joey a lot of grief, but I reminded him of my mantra: plans were made to be changed, because they *always* changed.

He tended to believe that because that mantra was generally true we should *over* plan, but I always won out and forced his hand. We'd go in just like we always did: ready for anything, expecting nothing. It was a dangerous game, but there wasn't much about any of this that *wasn't* dangerous.

The biggest wildcard, then, was Frey. Jonathan Frey had insisted on helping us out, and we eventually agreed to let him come aboard and play navigator while we worked out what to do next. Joey made the argument that he would, if nothing else, be someone else to talk to.

I didn't like having another life to worry about, but I made it clear to Frey that he wasn't there to help us with any fighting that might come our way. He was to keep our drinks full, provide assistance when it made sense, and, above all, stay out of our way.

He'd agreed too quickly, and I could tell he thought it was all just a speech I'd prepared to make him feel special. He probably thought we were just playing around, heading out into a literal storm to just throw a fist up at life and shake it around a few times, then head back in, drink and cuss like sailors, and laugh about the adventure.

I didn't tell him about Hannah, and Joey didn't tell him about Shalice.

Joey had done a pretty decent job hiding it, but I could tell he was pretty ripped up about it. He missed her, sure, but more than that was the guilt. It was heavy, like a literal weight on top of you, and I could see it pressing down on him. They'd killed people that way, back in the day. Put a bunch of weights, like rocks or something, on your chest, one at a time, until you just died. Quit breathing altogether, or your ribs were crushed and everything inside you just collapsed. I figured guilt was pretty much the same thing. Guilt had a weird effect on people, and I'd seen it and experienced it first hand more than I cared to admit.

So I didn't. I didn't talk about my past with anyone, not even Joey, even when he asked. I had never told him about my late wife, or any of the other woman who'd come and gone before or after her. I didn't talk about my family much at all, and Joey respected that.

I hoped Frey would stay off that topic as well.

He was back to his nervous self, but in a decidedly more giddy way. He was bouncing, literally jumping up and down just a bit as he walked onto the *Wassamassaw* and onto the deck. My reminder that he was just along for the ride seemed to have absolutely no bearing on his attitude.

I stepped into the bridge and started her up while Joey untied her moorings and prepared for the journey. We had her at a boatyard for the time being, but the plan was to come back in to Hannah's old place after our excursion, if the weather allowed. It was a larger dock, private, and it was far enough from any civilization that we could camp out there for an indefinite amount of time if the need arose.

My bar was closed, again. The oldies would be upset, but they'd get over it, and the other regulars would just head up to Charleston or down to Habor Island if they needed a fix that badly. We'd reopen soon enough, just like always, and they'd all come back and cash in their free drink coupons. The ones who hadn't gotten one from Joey would get a free drink anyway.

When Joey was ready and Frey had poured us all a round, I aimed the *Wassamassaw* toward the horizon and put it on autopilot. I set our speed at thirteen knots, hoping to get a good distance out into open water before we really opened her up.

I wouldn't have guessed there was a massive storm brewing. I didn't necessarily have an eye for the weather, but it still seemed like a beautiful, perfectly calm night. I wondered how many other vessels were heading directly into the mouth of the category 5 hurricane at this very moment, unknowingly.

As I joined Frey and Joey on the deck, drink in hand, I sipped the cocktail — a poorly made whiskey smash — and looked around.

"Beautiful, isn't it?" I asked, to know one in particular.

"Sure is, boss. Can't believe we're out here again on business. I'd sure love to just sail sometime."

"You got that right. I promise we will, too. Nice and long trip, you, me, and..."

I stopped myself before I said her name.

"I know."

I nodded. "I know."

I wasn't sure what I could possibly say next that wouldn't seem insensitive, and saying nothing at all felt wrong as well, so I was thankful that my phone starting ringing right at that time. I pulled it out of my pocket, wondering how long we'd have before my cell service ran out, and answered.

"Hello?"

'Dixon?' the voice on the other end asked.

"Yeah," I said, gruffly. I already had a feeling I knew who I was talking to. "What's up?"

'What's your location?'

"What's my — who the hell is this?"

'Dixon, we need to know where you are. Right now.'

I took a deep breath. Frey and Joey were staring at me, but I walked toward the steep set of stairs that led to the upper deck and ascended them. "I don't have to tell you anything. You one of the grunts I met up in Charleston?"

No answer.

"That's what I thought. Why the hell are you calling me? And why in the world do you think I'm going to just broadcast my location? It's not like —"

'We've been tracking your boat, Dixon,' the voice said. *'We just want verification that you're on it. Doesn't matter anyway.'*

"And why not?" I asked.

'We're calling you off.'

I frowned. "Excuse me?"

'You heard me, Dixon. We're calling you off. You're no longer needed. I appreciate you coming all the way up here, but —"

"Bullshit," I said. "You're not calling anything off. I know what this is all about, and you're not backing down. You want this guy taken out."

'Dixon, I'm warning you —'

"You just don't need *me* to do it anymore. Why is that?" I strained to understand, forced my mind to crunch the limited data I had into something that resembled a solution. The variables were all there, all the pieces of the story. They just needed to be rearranged into something coherent.

And the first place to start was with what had changed.

"It's the weather, isn't it?" I asked. "You're speeding things up, and since Elizondo's ship has been rerouted slightly to stay in front of it, you don't think you need me any more."

Another pause, this one longer. *'We have a — an asset — nearby. Yes.'*

So they've got someone closer to Elizondo now, and they're speeding things up as well. I felt my face squeezing together as I tried to figure out what it meant. *If I wasn't the guy who was going to kill Elizondo, then that meant someone else was.*

And it meant that Elizondo's guys would be coming after me *after these new guys got to him.*

Shit.

"No," I said.

'I — I'm sorry? Dixon, this isn't a —'

"Yeah," I said. "I know. 'Not a democracy,' or whatever you were about to say. 'Not up for discussion,' but let me tell you something: I agree. This is *not* a democracy, and it's *not* up for discussion. But it's *my* call. You call your dogs off Elizondo or I'm going to —"

The phone's connection terminated.

I yelled a curse. I wasn't sure if the disconnection had been due to the caller hanging up on me or the fact that we were well out from the shoreline by now, but it didn't matter.

I'm screwed.

I ran back to the stairs, only to find Joey and Frey looking up at me.

"What's up?" Joey asked.

"We're hosed. They're sending in another guy."

"Another guy for what?"

"To nab Elizondo."

"But how can —"

He stopped as he realized the same thing I'd realized while on the phone.

"They've got someone capable of doing the job who's closer to him now," Joey said. "Because he changed his course to beat the storm."

I nodded.

"Well, that really messes with our plan."

Frey, to his credit, didn't speak. But he seemed even more nervous now, and the drink in his hand apparently wasn't helping.

"What do you want to do?" Joey asked.

I shook my head. "Shit, I don't know," I said. "They're not just going to believe that we're backing down. That means they're probably preparing for us to get involved, even if we'll get there after their guy's finished the job."

"So, we need more guns," Joey said.

"And more guys."

"Right. But we don't know any. And even if we did, we'd completely miss our shot if had to go back in to get them."

"Right."

"And we don't have time to go back and find more guns. We've got what we've got."

I nodded.

Frey was rocking back and forth on his heels, looking around at the boat and the sea surrounding it.

"Frey," I said. "You all right?"

He looked at me, wide-eyed as ever, and nodded slowly. "Y — yeah, I guess. Crazy. Just crazy."

"What is?"

"It's — you guys — it's all real. I had a feeling you guys were in on something. I mean, I'd always had my suspicions, but…"

"Frey," I said, waiting for him to look up at me again. "Listen to me. You're in this with us, now. I don't want you getting killed any more than I don't want *me* getting killed. That means we need to work together, which means you need to do exactly what we tell you to do."

He nodded.

"Good. You ever shot a gun?"

He nodded.

"Well, that's good news. Here's the thing: I don't want you shooting any guns. You're here to provide support, like steering our little getaway vehicle when it comes time to —"

The sound of gunfire ripped through my head, and before I could even look up to see where it had come from, Joey was moving.

CHAPTER TWENTY

"GET DOWN!" HE YELLED. "MOVE inside, now!"

I jumped down the steps and whirled left, into the main cabin. A flurry of shots ricocheted off something on my boat, but a few rounds landed in the wall next to my head.

"You've got to be kidding me!" I screamed. *I just had her cleaned and fixed up!*

I caught a glimpse of the shooter as I dove to the carpeted floor, between Joey and Frey. A speedboat, long and thin, cutting through the water about a quarter-mile out. I hadn't noticed that the wind had picked up, and the gentle lapping of waves against the *Wassamassaw's* hull had grown in volume, preventing me from hearing of the boat's approach.

They were still a long way out, which meant that their first set of rounds was nothing but a lucky shot. Any luckier, actually, and one would have landed in the back of my skull.

But they're only getting closer.

The second stream of bullets soared toward us, but either landed short in the water or flew over the boat. I heard no sounds of impact, and I figured the guy shooting had been off-target thanks to the same waves that made it impossible to hear them.

The boat's engine roared into my consciousness next. It was loud, far louder than I thought it should have been if it was simply creeping closer to us at a normal speed.

Which was when I realized that it was certainly *not* creeping toward us at all.

It was *barreling* toward us, and it wasn't slowing down.

"They're going to hit, Dixon," Frey said.

"I can see that." I turned to Joey, still laying on the floor next to me. "You have a piece?"

He didn't, but he was closest to the case I'd brought along. There was another small armory in my room belowdecks, but I wasn't about to run out and get shot at.

Joey crawled over to the couch and grabbed the case. It was unlocked already, so he opened the lid and extracted two 9mm handguns. There was a third inside, but I was glad he hadn't offered one to Frey.

I grabbed the pistol and checked it, knowing already that it was loaded but going through the motions anyway out of habit. Joey did the same, and when I felt ready, I popped up and onto my knees.

I fired off three quick shots, only one of which landed anywhere near the boat.

Thankfully, however, the man who had been standing and firing at us ducked out of the way instinctively.

"Now's our chance," I yelled. "Keep him down."

"What about if they hit us?" Joey asked, still aiming toward the boat, waiting for the man to try to rise up again.

"It's a suicide mission if they do," I replied. We're bigger. We go down, they *definitely* go down."

I didn't wait for his response. I ducked and ran out the door again, heading for the stairs at the stern of the *Wassamassaw*. I could hear the engine of the other boat, still right on target, still threatening to collide. They hadn't slowed down.

Joey fired, two shots, but I'd already reached the set of stairs that led to the engine deck and the door to the cabins down below. It would have been faster to just run through the main living and dining room to the spiral staircase, but I wanted to try to stay behind the railing and out of sight as much as possible. I pushed the door open and ran down the hallway to the master suite at the end, my bedroom oasis on the seas.

It was a fantastic room, completely consuming the bow of the ship, with wide, stretching windows scattered around the front of it, just above the waterline. A king bed sat in the center of the room, with enough room on the sides of it to walk easily to the closet or restroom on either side.

A small office — just a computer and a desk bolted to the wall — had been installed at the back of the room by the previous owner, where I was now standing. No door separated it from the master bedroom, but a spiral staircase stood next to the desk, leading up into the bridge.

I loved how spacious the room felt, yet I also loved that the entire bridge and captain's quarters, including the office, could be completely shut off from the rest of the boat. It made for a secure space with enough room to move around comfortably. I'd never shopped for a yacht before, so I had little to compare it to, but I assumed I had gotten a hell of a deal out of it, and I had no complaints about the layout.

The gun safe I was aiming for was in the corner of the small closet, almost completely taking up the space inside. I wasn't much of a 'closet' guy, so I figured a hidden gun safe would be a better thing to have in there than clothes, anyway.

I reached the closet in two strides, but before I could swing the sliding door open I felt the *Wassamassaw* lurch sideways in the water. I nearly lost my balance, but I reached out and pushed against the wall for leverage.

I heard the roar of the speedboat's engine, then the *crack* of a few rounds being fired, and immediately afterward the deep thuds of the bullets landing inside my boat.

They buzzed us, I thought. They'd turned at the last second, not wanting to risk the chance that they would be worse off from a collision, but they'd taken the opportunity to get a couple great shots right where it would hurt me the most.

The fuel tank.

I knew we wouldn't be able to take any more shots like that, and I also knew that I needed to check the engine cabinet to ensure that nothing major had been damaged. The twin Caterpillar Supercharged 650HP diesel engines sat side-by-side, beautiful to even someone like me who knew next to nothing about them.

A few bullet holes wouldn't sink the boat, but a few bullet holes to a fuel line or tank would certainly, after a while, put us dead in the water. We couldn't risk that, and I was hardly a boat mechanic — there would be little I could do from here to fix anything broken.

That meant only one thing: we needed to fight back. I could hear Joey's pistol, firing at the speedboat that was now heading away from us, but I knew it would never be enough. We needed more firepower if we had any hope of winning this battle.

That was why I was down here in the first place.

I swung the closet door open and began unlocking the safe.

With a click, the lock disengaged and the heavy door fell open a few inches. I pulled it open farther and reached inside, already knowing where and what I was reaching for.

My hands closed around the weapon and I pulled it out

of the safe. I left the safe open for the time being, and quickly turned and walked back out of the room.

As I left the room, my mind went blank, then fired up again with a singular focus on my mission. It was like a computer that had been completely reformatted and booted up into a mode that allowed for only one program to run.

Kill the bad guys.

It was a cheesy program, I had to admit, but it was the thing that was going to hopefully keep me alive. Men I'd served with called it different things, but it was essentially a massive boost of adrenaline followed by a animal-like focus on nothing but survival. I'd developed the skill long ago in the service, honed it for years afterward, and still relied on it to this day.

As a bartender it wasn't so useful. But for my moonlighting gig — it was critical.

CHAPTER TWENTY-ONE

"YOU'VE GOT TO BE KIDDING," Joey said. "You bought an AR15?"

I nodded, checking the magazine and balancing the weapon on my shoulder, preparing for the speedboat's inevitable return.

"When?"

"Couple weeks ago," I answered. "Felt like it was time to upgrade the arsenal."

Joey whistled. "Well, I'd say that was a good investment," he said.

Frey was his typical wide-eyed self, and he hadn't moved from the carpeted floor. Joey and I were standing at the doorway that led out of the room to the main deck, and I looked down at our third passenger to see if he'd been shot.

He looked back up at me. "I'm fine," he said. "Just a little tense."

"Well, that's allowed," I said. "Why don't you head down below, away from the mess up here?"

He shook his head. "I'll stay close to the bridge. Just like you said, if you need someone to steer, I can handle that."

I nodded. "Thanks — I'm hoping we won't need a quick getaway this time. We can't outrun that thing, and if they make another pass and take some potshots at us again like they did before, we're probably going to have some real trouble on our hands, and steering won't help us at all."

"Still," Frey said, "I feel better at least seeing it coming."

I nodded, completely understanding. If I was going to die in a blaze of glory, I at least wanted to stare it down. "I respect that, Frey," I said. "Stay out of the way, then. I don't want to step on you."

He shifted, sliding backwards on the carpet until he was in the center of the room, then he stood up and walked over to one of the chairs. He sat down in it, peering out from behind me, trying to see the boat.

The speedboat had almost finished its wide arc and was now preparing to bear down on us once again. I nudged Joey with my elbow. "Ready?"

He nodded, not taking his eyes off the enemy craft. "Gonna have to be, I guess."

"Yep," I said.

The boat was coming straight at us again, and this time the shooter was standing on the back, his foot up against the seat in front of him for balance. It wouldn't do much if the boat hit a wave, but unfortunately it looked like the ocean was currently on their side. The sea stretched, long and flat, the distance between our two vessels growing smaller by the second.

"Get ready," I said.

The man fired, the shots fell wide.

"Not yet."

He fired again, and I heard one of the bullets land above my head, smashing into the doorframe.

"Shit," Joey said. "That was close."

"Hold," I said. "Three more seconds."

The three seconds ticked off like we were in slow motion. I saw every detail of the boat — the man driving, the man preparing to shoot at us, the engine behind it all, roaring and heaving them through the water. The boat grew bigger, and I could then make out the mens' faces. Both were unrecognizable, but they had a menacing, 'I've-been-here-before' look to them. They were stiff, but still relaxed, perfectly poised for fighting. They were prepared.

Hired guns, I thought.

The three seconds were up, and I knew our window had arrived.

"Now!" I yelled.

All three weapons — my AR15, Joey's 9mm, and the man's pistol — all erupted in gunfire at once. I was too committed to duck, and apparently all of us felt the same. Joey let off two shots, while my three-round burst sounded three times in quick succession. Eleven rounds from us, total, to the man's three.

One of the bullets zinged past my elbow, searing the top layer of flesh on my lower arm, and pounded the wall behind me. Joey was still standing.

The boat was still coming.

I suddenly saw what had happened. Their shooter was reloading, scrambling around for another magazine. His teammate, however, was hunched over in his seat.

The *driver's* seat. One of the bullets we'd fired must have hit the mark, killing their captain.

The boat was no longer being controlled, and the shooter had no idea. He was digging in his pockets for more ammunition, staring us down the whole time.

"They're going to hit us now," Joey said.

"Yeah," I said. "They are."

I had a dilemma. I could aim for the man who was still alive, possibly kill him, and we'd be safe from further attack, but there would be no way to navigate out of the way before their boat smacked dead-on into ours.

Or I could let him live and hope he noticed that his guy was dead.

Frey made the decision for me.

The *Wassamassaw* lurched sideways again, but this time it was caused by the beginnings of a sharp turn. Frey had rolled the wheel hard to the right, and we were nearly rocked off our feet. Our slower speed made it possible to turn sharply, and while we were still in danger of a collision, the movement of the boat apparently had gotten the shooter's attention.

I saw him look at us, on the *Wassamassaw*, then down at his own teammate. I saw the recognition in his eyes, and then I watched him look back up at me, fury on his face.

Please make the right call, I thought. *Live to fight another day.*

He raised his pistol, and I tracked him with my own assault rifle. There was no way he would get off the shot from there.

And the boat was still hauling toward us. Maybe five seconds until it hit.

Come on, man.

I was forced to wait him out. I couldn't shoot him — he was the only thing keeping *all* of us alive, and it was up to him to keep it that way.

"He's not going to do it," Joey said. "He's going to let it —"

The man suddenly jumped forward, landing hard on the passenger's seat. He leaned over, the gun falling from his hand. Then, in one fluid motion, he yanked the wheel hard to the left.

I watched as he just about lost his balance, but he held on. The speedboat surged up and out of the water, hitting a wave at just the right moment to send him, the dead driver, and the ton of plastic and metal screaming into the air.

But they missed us.

If Frey hadn't pulled us to the right, and our shooter hadn't pulled himself to the left, we'd all be scrambling to bail from two sinking vessels right now.

The man turned and looked at me when the boat hit the water again. It didn't slow down, and it didn't turn. He kept his hand on the wheel, but the driver's head fell sideways and onto the shooter's arm. Still he held on.

Joey pulled off a few shots, but all flew wide.

"You going to take a shot?" he asked.

I looked at Joey, then back down the barrel of my rifle. It was an easy shot from this distance, and even though we were pulling apart and increasing the distance between us, I knew I could make it.

So I did.

The three-round burst of fire sailed through the air, and I knew it was a direct hit even before it landed.

"You missed," Joey said.

I shook my head. "Look again."

He did, and I waited.

Suddenly a plume of smoke surged upward from the engine, and the boat stopped moving.

"You hit the engine?"

The man ran up onto the back of the boat and knelt down, fiddling with the motor, but another surge of smoke and fire caused him to recoil, then fall back onto the seats.

"He's not going anywhere," I said.

"Why not just finish him?" Joey asked. "Bastard tried to kill us."

"We don't need to," I said. "He's toast."

"You think he's taking on water?"

I nodded, then fired three more rounds. Two of them hit their mark. "Yeah," I said. "He is now."

The man was screaming, likely obscenities directed at us, but I couldn't hear a word.

"We just bought ourselves time," I said. "And I'd like to head over and see if he'll talk."

"He's not going to give us anything," Joey said.

"He'll either give us something or he'll die," I replied. "This way it's *his* call, not ours."

Joey nodded, understanding. "I'll have Frey turn around and pull up next to him, then."

"Thanks, Joey." I looked at him, then at the dead speedboat about a quarter-mile from us, then walked into the room. "We're going to get her back," I said.

"I know," he answered.

"But we can probably use a drink to clear our heads," I said. "Agreed?"

He forced a smile, a genuine grin of encouragement, masked by a set of genuinely concerned eyes, and nodded. "Agreed."

CHAPTER TWENTY-TWO

NO ONE DROWNS ON PURPOSE. It's like one of the major themes of humanity. If you're a relatively normal, well-balanced human, you don't drown yourself. You can't even do it on purpose without help from someone or something else. You need a weight, or a strong guy who's okay holding you neck down, or else an accident.

The guy in the speedboat had none of those things. He was *way* too far out to make a swim for the shore — hell, I couldn't even *see* the shore anymore — and there were no weights, strong guys, or accidents laying around on his boat.

That meant he *wasn't* going to drown himself. That meant he was ours. It was just a matter of time, really, and we weren't in a hurry. Technically, overall, yes we were in a hurry, but in *this* moment in *this* situation, I didn't give a shit about getting out to him really quickly.

Let him wait.

So I let him wait. I walked inside and let Frey steer and let Joey pour me a drink. Old Fashioned, just the way I liked it with a decent high-rye bourbon, a block of ice, a Luxardo cherry, and stirred slowly and deliberately with about five splashes of bitters that Joey had pulled from somewhere below the counter.

It was delicious, and I needed to keep my mind occupied while we waited for our enemy to sink a little bit, so I engaged.

"What's the bitters?" I asked.

"Homemade," Joey answered.

"You're making bitters now?"

He shrugged. "It's not hard. Pretty straightforward, really, and you can make it taste like whatever you want."

I swirled the drink in my right hand and stared at it. Tried to decipher it, to decode it. Took a long, deep sniff, then a small sip. Just enough to wet my tongue, and then swirled it around all over again as it splashed around in my mouth. I swallowed, then took a deeper swig, this time aiming for the bitters with my taste buds.

"Chocolate," I said.

"What else?"

"Clove?"

He nodded. "Close. It's a hint of anise, actually. But in such a small dose, and with the cinnamon added, I think it's pretty clove-y also."

"It's good. Really good. What's the base?"

"Michter's."

"Good choice."

We stood there for a minute, Joey behind the bar and me in the middle of the room, waiting. It was awkward, just pretending like there wasn't a guy who had previously tried to kill us slowly sinking into the Atlantic off our port side.

"He's going to shoot at us, you know."

I nodded again. "Yeah, probably."

"What's… uh, you know."

"The plan?"

Joey took a drink, stared at me the whole time. *Yeah, boss,* I could hear him thinking. *What the hell is the plan?*

I shrugged. "He's literally a sinking ship. Not going anywhere. We've got another two minutes at this speed before we're even close enough for him to attempt to swim over, and I'd bet he's willing to at least try *something.*"

"Something? What's that supposed to mean?"

"I mean he's not going to go for the kill right away. Put yourself in his shoes, Joey. He's drowning, knows his life is on the line, and the only thing — literally the only thing — that's giving him hope is that *we're* here. Coming toward him. Knows we're a couple minutes away."

"So what makes you think he won't just try and take over our boat?"

I looked at him. Smiled. This was an easy one. I remembered a time in my training, early on, when our commander took us out into the woods for a survival training exercise and we found a deer, trapped in a bear trap. It had been left and forgotten by a hunter, or my CO was a far better commander than I'd given him credit for. Either way, the deer was squealing, a small, tired bleating that made us all feel sorry for it.

'What's he thinking?' The CO asked. *'Why is he just laying there, not scared of us?'*

The answer, then and now, was simple: we were his saving grace. We were the only thing between him and the slow, desperate clutches of dying a painful death. The deer knew it, and the man in the boat knew it, too.

The man in the boat might have had a weapon or two lying around, and enough brainpower to use it, but he *also* knew that if he did use it, we'd simply turn around and hightail it out of there.

"Because he doesn't want to die," Joey said.

I took another sip. No need to give him the satisfaction.

"Because he knows we're his only shot," he continued. "He *will* try something, won't he? But not right away. He knows that. He's figured it out, same as us. He'll wait, bide his time, try to get us to board. Or to get him to board our ride, and *then* he'll make his move."

"He's hoping we take hostages."

"Yeah," Joey said. Then he looked at me with a strange expression. "Do we?"

I turned to the entrance to the bridge of the *Wassamassaw* and started walking. "Frey," I called. The man poked his head out just as I got close. "Pick up the pace. Let's buzz this guy once or twice and see what he does."

Frey nodded. "You got it, boss."

"Joey," I said, turning back around. "Pour our driver a drink. No reason he should be left out."

CHAPTER TWENTY-THREE

THE THREE OF US, WITH our three Old Fashioneds, made haste for the guy in his sinking speedboat. He was still standing, waiting. Patiently, even. Like he knew the play — we would come by, ask him to talk, maybe exchange a few shots, then we'd leave.

He had the same expression on his face: a combination of rage and confusion, as well as pure stupidity, but now I thought I could see a good bit of expectation as well. *He's got a plan,* I thought. Just as we'd suspected, this guy was going to try to make a move. For our boat, or our weapons, or both. He didn't want to die today.

Hate to be the bearer of bad news…

Frey had a good read on the *Wassamassaw's* movement. He was a capable boat captain, which surprised me, but I guess I'd never asked if he'd driven before. I had no idea if boats were his thing or not, but he seemed to have a strong, steady hand at the wheel.

Frey moved us out and around the other boat, now halfway submerged and sinking fast. He positioned us into the wind, so we'd float back toward the smaller boat on our own, but also so that if we needed to get away quickly we'd be able to without having to worry about the currents keeping us close together.

All the while keeping his right hand poised with his drink in hand.

Man after my own heart. Frey may have been an odd fish, but he had some likable qualities. I downed the rest of my own drink and walked out on deck to watch our progress.

The man on the other boat was unarmed. He knew the drill. He knew what was at stake.

Maybe he'll talk.

"How close are we getting?" Frey yelled.

"I want to smell his breath," I replied.

Frey didn't answer, but the boat turned inward and toward the smaller vessel and all of the sudden we were on him. The two watercraft bumped together, Joey leaning way over the edge of the *Wassamassaw* to grab the railing of the smaller vessel.

"Leave it," I said.

The boats moved back apart, first a few feet and then almost ten. The ocean is a curious beast, and I have always found it fascinating how we take it for granted. We're smarter, we think, than the great blue, but we forget how absolutely and unbelievably powerful it really is. Within seconds, the boats were so far apart again that Frey had to commandeer us closer.

"Need a lift?" I called out.

The man glared.

"Just checking," I said. "We don't want you to die out here, friend."

He yelled profanity back toward me. I'm not one to cringe at the use of curse words and foul language, but whatever he said made me hesitate.

"Listen," I yelled. "Come aboard. We can talk."

"I'm not telling you a damn thing," the man said.

"Fair enough. Frey, get us moving again." I said it loud enough for the man to hear, also knowing Frey was poking his head out the back door of the main chamber, far from the bridge. He looked at me, waiting.

"What do you want?" the man asked.

"I want answers, asshole. Not that hard to figure out, you know?"

"I'm just here because I was told to stop you."

Frey and Joey were watching on, intrigued. I stood there, the AR15 up and ready, just waiting — *begging* — the man to make a move.

"Well, you failed. What's your boss going to do about that? You got a comm in there?"

The man actually looked around, as if he hadn't thought about it before that moment. Finally he looked back up and me and shook his head.

"So… a rendezvous? Scheduled appointment?"

Again, a head shake.

"So you're out here alone. Sinking. Give it five minutes, you're toast. Treading water. Maybe less. What have you got to lose?"

"I can't tell you anything."

"Sure you can, asshole. You can tell me who you're working for."

He stared.

"Tell me who's going after Elizondo. God knows you're not making it to *that* meeting, am I right?"

Nothing.

"I'm coming on board. Want to stop me?"

The man just stared. Empty. No expression whatsoever. I'd seen this before — he was done, given up. Waiting for an opening in the bleak death of failure. And I knew exactly what that meant: he'd be *glad* to have me aboard, because it would mean he might have a chance.

It was a small chance, a sliver of opportunity, but it was a chance nonetheless.

He knew it, I knew it. I wanted information, he wanted revenge.

Joey gave me the eyes, but I ignored him. He took my assault rifle, trading me the 9mm. It would be a better close-up weapon, and the AR would be a far better mid-range choice.

Frey moved back inside while I threw my leg up and over the side of the *Wassamassaw,* heading down the ladder that led to the lower decks and, in this case, the water. The sinking boat was about five feet away, and the man's legs were soaked by now, but he didn't move.

He waited.

I climbed down, watching him the entire time.

At the bottom rung, I spun around and jumped. Made it to the edge of his boat, which didn't help the sinking factor at all, but both of us retained our balance. I sloshed through the rising water collecting in the speedboat's bottom, then trudged up to the man.

The dead captain was slouched over, still very much dead. I took a quick look at him to assess any possible threat, then turned back again to the man who had given us so much grief in the past hour.

"Who sent you?" I asked.

He clenched his jaw.

I raised my pistol.

"You going to fight back?"

He shook his head.

"Stupid move, asshole," I said. "I'm armed, threatening you, and I'm your only shot at getting out of here alive. So let me ask you again: *you going to fight back?*"

He stared. Reading me, or trying to. I didn't let him. I kept my face calm, not even upset. Stoic, even.

I raised my pistol, just a flick of my wrist to let him know that I meant business and I wasn't going to screw around with any tricks.

And that's when the tricks started.

He immediately moved for his back, reaching a hand behind and pulling out a pistol. I knew it was a gun before I even saw it. He'd done exactly what I planned on, exactly what I'd been trained to read. The way he'd been standing, amidst a sinking boat in the middle of the Atlantic, the way his face showed me nothing useful. It was all part of it. All a piece of the puzzle I'd been putting together.

His move is going to be to try to trick us. To lure me to his domain, onto his turf.

Sinking turf, but still turf.

I read it perfectly. He was still outnumbered, still underprepared. He didn't stand a chance.

My weapon was ready, his was not. The half-split-second difference made *all* the difference, and I raised mine and fired, sending a shot through the thigh of his right leg first, then twisted, readjusted, aimed and fired again. Sent another through his knee. *A little low, but that'll do the trick.*

He went down, fast. Splashed in the water and actually disappeared for a second before he came back up for air. The gun he had been trying to grab for had disappeared as well, so I took the third shot without worrying about retaliation.

Another shot to the leg, this time hitting his other thigh. Hitting the knees destroys a good leg, just about no matter how you crack it, but hitting someone in the thighs does something entirely different: it pisses you off. It's painful, but not enough to pass out, and it doesn't do enough damage to really put you out of commission forever unless you accidentally hit an artery. And while I'm a heck of a shot at this range, I knew I wasn't going to hit anything necessary.

But I did hit him where it *really* hurt: both physically and mentally. He now *knew* he wasn't going anywhere. He was stuck here, dead on the water, unable to swim even the three feet it would take to get to my boat.

I looked down at him, flopping like a fish out of water, except that half of him *was* in the water, and felt no pity.

"Who sent you?" I asked again.

He struggled, twisted around. *This is the moment,* I thought. *If he knows, he's telling me.*

"You taking me off this boat?"

I shrugged. "Depends on whether I like your answer or not."

The boat shifted, sunk down another few inches quickly, and then settled. I was once again amazed at the buoyancy of the wrecked craft. It was doing its best to stay afloat, fighting against the inevitable.

"You're just going to leave me here to die."

"Probably," I said, "but you get to choose whether to die from a bullet to the head or from drowning. Your choice." I raised the gun and held it up to the side of his head.

"You — you know," he coughed. No blood, but that wouldn't be far behind. "You know him."

"Yeah?"

"I thought you already knew about it. That's why we're all here, right?"

He was gasping for breath, but I wanted to keep him talking. Now that he *was* talking.

"Who sent you? Simple question." I turned the pistol at aimed it at the man's rear end. Not sure if he knew or cared where I was about to send the next piece of blistering lead, but he got the point.

"It's — it's obvious, man," he said.

"Nothing about this is obvious. Who sent you?"

He stared up at me as the boat slipped beneath the water for good. I sloshed around in it, hoping there wouldn't be any trouble getting back to the *Wassamassaw*. It was a few yards off, not anchored, so it would be moving with the swells of the ocean and the wind. If I was lucky Frey would keep us steady enough to get there with only a short swim.

This guy was giving me nothing, so I figured the least I could do was offer an olive branch, maybe see if that helped jog his memory a bit. I looked up at Joey, standing at the edge of my yacht waiting for the signal. We'd discussed very little before I'd jumped ship to this guy's boat, but I was clear about one thing, and I was ready for it.

"Now, Joey."

He gave me the thumbs-up and disappeared from view for a moment. A few seconds later he reappeared and threw down to me the object he was holding. I caught it, one-handed, then turned back to the bleeding man.

He cocked an eyebrow as he stared at it.

A life ring, with the words *Wassamassaw* painted on the side of it. A certified floatation device that was a requirement on all marine vessels, but most of the time ended up being nothing but a moniker-bearing decoration.

"You're saving me?" he asked.

"Hardly," I said. "But it's a conscious thing, you know? Keeps me happy, able to sleep at night."

"It'll be hours before anyone finds me."

"At least. But the water's warm. Maybe use the time constructively, to think about something cool to say to your boss if they do find you?"

He glared.

"Or just spend your time fighting off the sharks. I'm sure they're hungry."

I turned to leave, my legs now completely soaked up to

my thighs, but my feet still standing on the boat's floor. The edge of the boat was higher, to my left, and placed an unsteady foot on the top of it, six inches beneath the surface. It was like walking up a submerged staircase. The hull of the *Wassamassaw* was directly in front of me now, either by some expert commandeering on Frey's part or some serendipitous wind movement.

I grabbed at the built-in ladder on the side of the *Wassamassaw* and started up. Halfway to the top I stopped once again, turned and looked down. The guy was floating inside the tiny little ring, bobbing up and down. There was no sight of his boat.

"Give me *something*, man," I said. "Tell me who sent you. Just a name is all I need."

The man's glare didn't change, but I thought I saw something soften in his eyes. He'd given up. Resigned himself. They'd sent him on a suicide mission with the hope that he'd at least do some damage to us. He realized that now, and I could see it on his face, even through his glare.

"You should already know this, Dixon. Your father sent us."

CHAPTER TWENTY-FOUR

"WHAT DO YOU *MEAN,* IT'S your father?"

Joey was watching me towel off. I was fully clothed and dripping all over the brand-new floor in the main cabin, but I didn't care. I wanted to move, to figure it out, to take action.

I was feeling the heat rising inside me, both a boon and a curse. It would help me focus, keep me laser-targeted on my mission. But if I left it unchecked it would get out of hand and I'd devolve into a state of rage-induced panic.

One of the benefits of my Army life and post-Army training is that I know myself *very* well. I know my habits, my reactions, my emotional state. I'm pretty in tune to those inner workings most people just allow to come and go and not really think much about, and I'm pretty good about understanding them.

And right now I didn't know *what* to think. I was pissed, sure, but I also wasn't sure if I believed it. Hell, I'd started this mission with the expectation that I'd be avenging my murdered father, and now the dead guy who'd tried to kill us was telling me that my father was the guy who'd set it all up.

It didn't add up. None of it. The only thing that *did* add up was that if my father was involved, if he wasn't actually dead, he was in over his head.

And *that* sounded like my old man.

I shook my head and watched the last few remaining droplets of saltwater flick off my hair and land on the carpet. I'd jumped from the sinking boat and swam back to the *Wassamassaw*, where I was able to reach the ladder on the side of the yacht and climb aboard. The water felt good, but nothing else about this moment did.

"I don't know, Joey. I don't get it either."

"But he's *alive?*"

"I don't *know*, I said. I haven't seen him."

"But that guy said he was working for him. You think —"

"I have no idea what to think."

Frey popped out the bridge again and joined us in the cabin. He looked at Joey, then me, as if wanting to ask a question. Finally he walked over to the bar in the corner and started looking around.

I watched him for a moment, then turned back to Joey. "This sucks."

Joey nodded.

"We're going to get her back."

He nodded again.

"We're going to get her back *now*, and then I'm going to have a word with my dead father."

Frey walked over, carrying a glass of brown liquid. I raised an eyebrow, questioning.

"Rum," he said. "Flor de Cana."

I nodded. "Good choice. Mind pouring me one?" I asked.

"Me too," Joey added.

We waited for our drinks, Joey taking a seat on the couch

across from me, while I sat in one of the armchairs that had come with the boat. I liked the chairs, as they fit my larger frame well enough and didn't force me to sit up perfectly straight.

"Who are you getting back?" Frey asked. His voice caught me off guard, almost as if I'd forgotten he was there.

"She — she was with us before, last time we were out on the boat. Joey's girlfriend."

"They took her. I'm going to get her back."

Frey listened, taking this in, sipping his rum. I wondered if the anxious, timid man behind the bar was up for something like this. I wanted to bring him back, but he'd already proven helpful and we were already out on the water.

"I'll do whatever I can, guys," Frey said.

Joey nodded, accepting the help, so I made a silent agreement with myself that I would keep Frey at arm's length, away from anything too dangerous.

When our drinks arrived, Joey took a long sip and then stared at me intently. I knew what he wanted.

I sighed. "I don't know, Joey."

"Well let's come up with a plan together, then. No reason you have to do all the heavy lifting."

I nodded. Joey liked plans. I didn't. But in fairness to him I knew we'd need to at least come up with something remotely resembling a plan. It was safer that way, and it would force me to consider all the variables.

"They're racing in before the weather," I said. "That means we're probably not going to beat them in a head-to-head race."

"But they're coming toward us, right?" Frey asked.

"Generally, yeah. Heading north to Charleston. But we need to make sure we're aiming directly at them in order to intercept."

"*If* we want to intercept," Joey said.

I frowned. "What do you mean? What else would we be doing?"

"Why intercept Elizondo, though? He's going to have plenty of security there, on board at least. And what are we supposed to do? If he doesn't want us on board we're not getting anywhere close."

I nodded. *True.* "Okay, but then how *will* we get to Elizondo?"

"Why would we? We're not supposed to kill him."

He was right. Of course. *Of course.* I put the back of my hand on my forehead, enjoying the momentary respite from the heat. *When had the heat gotten here?* It was hurricane season in South Carolina, and out on the water it was usually even chillier. But it was hot here, now.

"It's hot in here."

"It's in your head, Dixon."

I looked at Joey. Then at Frey. I felt the heat, from inside. He was right, it was inside me. *Calm down,* I urged myself. *You're supposed to be a master of your own emotional state.*

But I was still confused and angry. Maybe even a little bit scared.

"We still need to get to Elizondo, don't we?"

"Sure, but there's not really any sense trying to get on his ship. Like I said, he'll be well protected. But we *do* need to keep him alive."

"Right," I said. "So how do we do that?"

Frey cleared his throat. "Maybe we try to take out the guys trying to take *him* out?"

It made sense. Really, it was the only way to do it. The guys who'd taken Shalice had done it as a threat: we were supposed to keep Elizondo alive until he'd made his delivery. If Elizondo was taken out, the implied threat was that they'd take out Shalice.

So the only way to play great defense in this situation was to play great *offense.*

"So we're going after my dad."

"Seems that way, if he's really behind it."

I thought about it for a moment, then nodded. I was still pissed, but things were starting to click into place.

"He needed me to be a part of this scheme. He knew I'd be able to get the job done right — to kill Elizondo — but he wouldn't dare just come out and ask me to do it. Hence all the cloak and dagger."

"And faking his own death."

"And that. Right."

"So he's really behind it?"

"There's a lot of money involved. So yeah, I can almost bet he's behind it."

CHAPTER TWENTY-FIVE

I GREW UP IN A small town in a small state. Technically the state isn't the smallest of them all — Virginia is far bigger than Rhode Island, Connecticut, and the two forgotten twigs of states up near Maine — but to an adventurous kid who longed for the *more* part of life, Virginia felt as small as anything else.

It was ironic, then, that I felt the immense expanse of land behind our Virginia homestead was my true home — it was just endless woods, creeks, and enough game to keep a family of four alive. And it had. My father and I hunted just about every weekend growing up. I didn't know about licenses and permits, lotteries, or any of the other stuff hunters are supposed to know about. We just walked out our back door, looked for a good direction to start walking, and then we started walking.

Sometimes my brother would come with us. Most of the time he'd stay at home with Mom, cooking or learning some of the what my father called 'more delicate' skills. He'd always been a momma's boy, but for some reason my father hated that. He'd always treated my little brother like shit, and the day he ran off with a chick he'd met at the mall was the last time I'd ever seen him.

In truth, my old man treated all of us like shit. I was a set of arms to help carry firewood, or to load his guns, or to fetch whatever it was he thought he'd just shot, even though I was a far better shot than him by the time I was twelve. He treated my brother like shit, accusing him of being gay all his life like it was some sort of criminal offense to be gay.

But worst of all, and probably the reason I've never been able to forgive him, was the way he treated my mother. The sweetest woman I'd ever met, she was the person in my life I looked to for structure. She was a rock, teaching both her boys how to clean and cook fish and wild game, turn anything we dragged inside into food, and how to take care of ourselves. She was the calm, balanced individual who knew she only had a set amount of time with her cherished offspring before we figured out the hell we lived in and made a break for it.

My little brother went first, heading out at the ripe old age of sixteen, and I suspect it had more to do with not wanting to be under the same roof as his old man as it did with the beautiful blonde he'd met at working the sunglasses kiosk at the local mall.

My mother never forgave herself, but she never let me know it. I took off a few years later, running for the Army as fast as my asinine youth could muster. My old man just about popped a hernia when I told him, and I thought that would be the first time he'd ever hit me. Maybe it was his own military training or it was the fact that he hadn't had a drink in a couple hours, but he didn't hit me then.

Instead, he started hitting *her*. My mother, the woman everyone loved and no one wanted to upset. I don't know where it came from — maybe he thought having a gay son and a deadbeat one was the worst offense God could give a man, even though neither were true: I was successful in the Army. *Very* successful. I was sent all around the world and trained by the best there was, and I liked every minute of it. I *didn't* like the Army in general, and that was part of the reason I got out as soon as I could.

The Army is the kind of thing you wear like a loose-fitting shirt. You can grow and change inside it, but it's always going to be the same. The fit doesn't change, you do. It fit me at first, then it didn't. I'm not a clothes, guy, but even I buy a different shirt every few years or so.

So I ended up vagabonding it until I made it out to South Carolina. I was thirty-eight years old and I had no idea what I wanted to do with my life. I felt terrible for not knowing, but I was too damn stubborn to admit to myself that maybe just getting a job to make ends meet wouldn't be the worst thing in the world.

I rented a tiny apartment in Edisto Beach, but I drove up to Charleston one afternoon and got a job bartending at a dive bar just south of the city. The shifts were terrible, but I found that I had a knack for service — I liked people enough, and I was good behind the bar. I also liked the owner, who let me sample the liquors after every shift, which made me a better bartender but a far worse driver.

I stayed there for five years, then opened my own place in Edisto Beach, and the rest is history. Seems funny to me that my old man, the man I'd sworn to push out of my life for good, had once again gotten his claws around my neck and was squeezing with all his might.

My old man was the reason we were all here, and in a funny way I respected him for that. He'd pulled me into this business of mine — the one *outside* what I did as a bar owner — and he'd lured us into his web of lies, still somehow controlling his kid's life even though we rarely spoke.

I was sitting in the cabin, on the armchair I loved,

thinking about him and Hannah and Joey and Shalice, and even thinking a bit about Frey. I was planning, which was uncomfortable to me, but I was coming up with something that I thought would work just fine. Best of all, if it worked it would culminate in a climax where, for once in my life, *I* got to win.

I took another sip of Frey's chosen drink, the Flor de Cana, and smiled.

I'm coming for you, old man.

CHAPTER TWENTY-SIX

"WAKE UP, DIXON," JOEY'S VOICE called to me.

I opened an eye. "I'm not sleeping."

"Good. What's the plan?"

I stretched, trying to hide the fact that I *had* been asleep for the past fifteen minutes. I shrugged.

"Really? You haven't been sleeping, and you *still* have no idea what we're going to do?"

I looked around, trying to get a bearing on where we were. As usual, in the middle of the day on the ocean it was damn near impossible to determine your location with any hope of accuracy, so I looked over to the bridge. "Frey," I called, "where are we?"

He walked out, still holding his drink, or at least the third incarnation of it, and shrugged back at me.

"Really?"

"We're… floating. That's about all I can manage."

I shook my head. "You got us out of that scrape back there, didn't you? You're a better pilot that you give yourself credit for."

"Th — thanks," he said. "But I was hoping we'd switch it

up now that we're not under attack." He stopped, his eyes rolling back in his head for a moment as he thought. "Wait a minute, you guys *do* know how to drive this thing, right?"

Joey smiled. "No, we usually just hang out at the dock. Makes for a great party, and we don't need to learn anything new."

I stood up, stretching again, my fingers brushing against the laminated off-white ceiling. I walked over to Frey and stuck my arm out, placing my hand on his shoulder. "Thank you, Frey."

He nodded. "Yeah, of course. I — I always wanted an adventure."

"You married?"

He shook his head.

"You have kids?"

Again, a head shake.

"Then I hereby recruit you as driver of this little dinghy, Frey."

He smiled. "I don't really know how."

"Frey, listen. Every time Joey and I have, uh, done whatever it is you think we've done, we've learned something. That's part of the adventure. We need a driver, and you're the right guy for the job."

"Why's that?"

"Well, honestly? Because you're here."

"I see."

I waited, not wanting to give him any other reason to back out, while simultaneously hoping he'd want to back out.

"I'll do it."

I smiled, wider this time. "That's the right attitude, Fr —"

"How much does it pay?"

My mouth was still open, and I left it there, stupidly. I wasn't sure what to think so I turned and stared at Joey. He had a stupid grin on his face as well, almost as stupid as my own face.

"Well, boss?" Joey asked. "What's this little mission pay?"

I scowled at both of them, then walked into the bridge. "Frey, your first lesson starts right now. We need to get you up to speed with this boat, and then we might be able to talk about compensation."

Frey followed me in and took a seat in the tiny chair mounted to the wall up against the corner of the stairwell and the wall. "Honestly, I just want to be able to help you guys out, get Joey's girl back." He paused. "And maybe drink for free."

I shook my head as I watched the horizon out the front window. "And when we're done here, I'm going to teach you how to negotiate."

He laughed, stepping up to the wheel. "Fair enough. Where are we heading?"

"We're turning around," I said. "Going north."

"What's north?"

"Well, I'm hoping that we can intercept Elizondo's ship."

"I thought we weren't trying to get to Elizondo any more?" Frey asked.

"We're not, really. But Elizondo is the target for the guys who were sent by my old man. So we get to Elizondo, we get to my dad's guys."

"Got it."

"And then we kill them."

Frey didn't speak for a moment, but he did grip the wheel and handle the wide, sweeping turn port-side. I stepped back and handled the throttle until he reached down and grabbed at it. *He's a natural*, I thought. Sailing was far different than piloting a 131-foot-long yacht. There were no lines, no tacking or jibing, or any other nautical thing other than talking in terms of knots and port and starboard, and making sure you didn't crush any tiny fishing boats just off the coast.

I'd found the *Wassamassaw* to be a very capable handler, and in no small part to the fact that it was a top-of-the-line craft, completely overhauled and reworked earlier this year, including the pair of brand-new twin C8.7 engines I was told were 'every bit as capable as the originals, but far more powerful.' As I said, I knew nothing about engines — I just wanted them to work. These, so far, had worked wonderfully.

I'd spent so many hours on deck of this vessel that it felt like my own home more than my apartment did. That probably wasn't a difficult thing, either, since my apartment was the stark contrast to this place: a single-room piece of work in the area just outside the town of Edisto Beach. It was owned by a commercial real estate agent in Charleston, and he had no interest in keeping it up, making it anything different than what it already was, or in answering his phone when I wanted to call. The maintenance that needed to be done I did myself, and the only time I ever heard from him was when the rent needed to increase — invariably every year, on the birthdate of my lease.

I had no decorations, not much furniture other than a second-hand couch and coffee table, and my dishes consisted of whatever it was I didn't sell when my late wife died and left our wedding shower gifts behind. In total, I probably owned about $2,000 worth of personal effects, not including my growing weapon inventory. My insurance policy didn't cover anything that low, so I was paying renter's insurance on as much as $10,000 of crap I knew I didn't have.

The *Wassamassaw*, on the other hand, was pure luxury. Completely redesigned after the debacle we'd had inside it a few months ago, and paid for by the United States government, I spent as much time as possible inside or on deck. The yacht had been given to me by Hannah herself, after realizing it was too strong a memory of her father, and since she had bailed and ducked out to Europe for some unknown amount of time, I felt no qualms about taking it out as often as I could.

It was the best boat in the fleet, hands down, especially since the 'fleet' consisted of mostly the yacht-club owners down south of us and a few of the lingering rich folks up north who lived around the islands. The Charleston crowd was generally more conservative, since anyone with enough money to make a thirty-million-dollar yacht purchase tended to not live anywhere near Charleston.

I loved the *Wassamassaw*, even though I wasn't terribly fond of the memories I'd made aboard it. I missed Hannah, but it was more out of friendship than love. We'd grown close, as significant life situations tend to force you to do, but the *Wassamassaw* wasn't a reminder of her as much as just a reminder of what it was that I did.

There was no mistaking it: I wasn't *just* a bartender. I wasn't just an upstanding, taxpaying citizen who owned a bar and wanted to pay it off.

I killed people for a living. It was a good living, and it allowed me to do two things I desperately wanted: to pay off my bar, and to rid the world of the types of people that needed ridding.

I wasn't surprised that Frey went silent. Until that moment neither Joey nor I had come clean with him, and until we had it was only speculation and guesswork on his part. We were clean about it, and we were careful. We'd been in a few scrapes together, but we'd always managed to keep things wrapped up tight when it came to the local police. Most of the time the local cops wanted the job done anyway, as we were exterminating the types of people they went home and told their wives and husbands needed to be exterminated, but were otherwise obligated by professional vows and oaths not to exterminate. We operated just below the line of legality, but I felt no remorse whatsoever.

Anything bigger than local police meant the Feds were involved, and then they were too small for the Feds to really want any part of it. Add to that the fact that I had some history with them and we were typically home-free. Not a care in the world, just doing our job and getting rid of the evidence by 'fish-baiting' them in the bay.

Jonathan Frey, of course, knew none of this. He'd probably made a few intelligent leaps of faith, but there was no way he understood exactly what it was we were into. So I wasn't surprised that *he* was surprised. We killed people, and we made a lot of money doing it. That wasn't something a guy heard terribly often, I would think.

"How do you do it?" Frey asked.

"Depends on what they order," I said.

CHAPTER TWENTY-SEVEN

THE *WASSAMASSAW* HAD NEARLY COMPLETED its turn to the north and Frey was coddling the wheel delicately, like a true pilot, measuring the winds and the waves with a single hand while nursing the throttle with the other.

"What they order?"

"I'm a bartender," I answered.

"So they come in, order a drink, and — what? You just *decide* to kill them?"

I shook my head. Didn't care if he saw it or not. "No, not like that," I explained. "I work with someone up in Charleston. They spend all the time and money researching, finding the people. Then they give them a little coin. I call it a 'mark.'"

"Then they come to the bar, right?"

"Yeah, exactly. They order a drink or three, and pay for it with this little coin."

"So that's how you know you're supposed to kill them."

I looked over at him. He was shorter than me by a lot, and a bit rounder, but he seemed like a fit guy overall. "Yeah, although I always verify it myself."

"How do you do that?"

"I talk to them."

"Really? What do they say?"

I thought for a moment. "Depends, I guess. I've always been good behind the bar, and the secret to bartending isn't in mixing a perfect drink or knowing what they want to drink, it's in asking the right questions. You want to get them talking about their own lives without their feeling like you're prying. If they come in with someone else, that's even more difficult. A simple question here or there could interrupt their thought process, or worse — it could ignite whatever emotion they were feeling from talking to their date in the moment."

I'm careful, but I'm not perfect. I've been at the receiving end of plenty of verbal blows over the years, and while I do pride myself on being able to pick up on the nuances of coupled attendees, I know I'm *very* good at prying out the important details from my marks.

Most the guys — and they're just about all guys — come in with a chip on their shoulder already. They expect something, and I can read it on their faces like they're a old-person book with the huge lettering. They want something from me, and they've driven a hell of a long way to get it. Most of the time it's a person — an actual human being, articulately described and requested by these schmucks — and they know that I'm the person who's going to give it to them.

Or at least they *think* that. It's always my absolute *pleasure* to explain to them that while I do have what they *deserve*, I don't have what they *want*.

What I offer them is simple: meet me out back, and I'll bring you what I think you need.

Every time, without fail, they follow me through the

kitchen, say hello to Joey working his magic at the griddle, and walk outside to the back alley with me.

And every time, without fail, I give them what they deserve.

The first few times it was a bit messy, as I was newer to the game and a bit out of practice. But I got it done, no matter what they ordered at the bar. A Screwdriver? Sure, I've got one of those, and it seems to fit *right there*, just beneath your eye and straight through the anterior cranial fossa into the frontal lobe.

A Whiskey Smash? I'd always pour them my worst bourbon — which was better than the best bourbon you'd find at a lesser establishment, I might add — muddle out some fresh mint, and add enough crushed ice to make the drink look valuable and my profit margin to soar. Then I'd take them out back and beat them to death with an empty bottle. People don't realize that Hollywood movie bottles are *very* different than real bottles. Thanks to shrinkage policies developed by professional whiskey manufacturing distributors, modern-day glass booze bottles are *very* thick, and therefore *very* hard to break. Sure, you can drop them from a staircase at a cheap motel and they'll shatter to pieces, but humans — including their skulls — are far softer, and you're far weaker than gravity from a second-story building.

It takes a lot of beating and a lot of effort to mash in a human skull using nothing but a booze bottle, but that's my job. A Whiskey Smash is ordered by a mark, and a Whiskey Smash is what they get.

Probably my favorite method was the Irish Car Bomb. A simple shot, nothing but Guinness and Irish cream and whiskey. Again, the cheapest I've got, but with a twist — I let the guy pour the whiskey himself, as sort of a 'last meal' ritual.

Then, with no fanfare or festivities, I walk them out back,

get them into their own car — I drive, as it's all part of the experience — and take them down to the beach. There's a place I really like, as it only takes about fifteen minutes of driving south to get to it, it's far away from even the small towns like Edisto Beach, and it gives me the time needed to verify the mark. When we arrive, there's a dock with a concrete gangway out to the water I can drive up to, get the mark excited about the rendezvous, and get everything ready.

They stay in the car, exuberantly awaiting that thing they 'deserve.' I walk around to the back, pull out a bottle of whiskey (Irish, as it's a much better fit for this sort of work), and bring it to them. We talk, they take a few shots, and I pour it over their head and light it on fire.

Simple, effective, and gets them going. Never in my experience have they had the foresight to unbuckle their seatbelt first, so they fumble around for a bit until they realize what's happening, but by then I've made it back around and have dumbed the lit match into the open gas tank. A lit match won't do a dang thing against a full tank of liquid, most of the time. The secret is to make sure you hold the match out to the *fumes* coming out of the tank — you have to let it really catch. It's a bit nerve-wracking, but it's very satisfying.

It's not an explosion really, not at first. It's more of an impressive slow-burn consumption, sort of like watching a fireworks finale in slow motion. Gives me plenty of time to get away.

I stand back, finish the handle of Irish whiskey, and watch as my mark is 'marked.' It's satisfying and sad, all at the same time. That person could have been a useful member of society, I sometimes think. But what's the point? Why waste the money and the time and the effort to rehabilitate? I push the car over the ledge, usually when it's still burning.

The job's done, I make it out to my drop point, collect the money, and I'm done.

Easy.

"So you decide that they're worth killing and you just... kill them?"

I nodded. "Pretty much, yeah. Based on the drink they order."

"Okay," he said. "What about a Sidecar?"

I frowned. "What do you mean?"

"If I was a 'mark,' and I ordered a Sidecar. How would you do it?"

I thought about it a moment. "Okay, I like this game. Cognac, orange liqueur, and lemon? Easy. I'd bash their head in with a bottle of VOSP next to their car."

"Very Superior Old Pale?" he asked. "Very specific."

I laughed. "VS isn't worth the bottle it's put in, and XO and Hors d'Âge is way to fancy to be breaking it over people's heads."

Frey frowned. "Really? That seems a bit... brutal. And too easy."

"Okay, smartass. Sidecar — directly named after the motorcycle attachment — one part each Cognac, orange liqueur, and lemon juice. I'm an Embury fan, so his recipe is *eight* parts Cognac to two parts orange to one part lemon. That means I'd do it the right way, the proper way."

"And that is?"

"I'd smash his head in with a bottle of VOSP. Hoping for eight times to do the trick."

Frey smiled, then laughed. "Okay, fair enough. Eight times the charm. And what do you do with the bodies?"

"Easy. Fishbait."

CHAPTER TWENTY-EIGHT

"FISHBAIT?"

"FISHBAIT. JOEY OR I will take them to the bay, dump them in, let nature take care of the rest. We bleach the bodies, but it's really about just letting time and nature do its thing."

"And do you *have* time?"

"Sure. The local cops don't care, and the Feds are happy that I'm taking care of it."

"You have their word on that?"

"Nope."

I waited for Frey to make a face, or to give me any impression that this arrangement wasn't proper. Instead, he stared at the horizon, a proper sea dog already, knowing that he was in over his head and not caring, or realizing that it didn't matter.

Or, I guess, maybe he agreed with it. On some level I wasn't sure how anyone could *disagree* with it, really. Frey seemed like the kind of guy who stayed out of the way, stayed to himself, tried to make himself useful but not so useful he was noticed.

It was odd he was here, so ready to jump aboard our little harebrained mission. He was nice enough, for sure, but it seemed strange to me the juxtaposition between his desire to help us in something so utterly dangerous it was near suicide and his levelheaded, stay-out-of-the-way mentality.

I liked having the help, but something about him didn't fit.

"Frey," I said. He turned and looked at me. "Who are you? Really?"

He frowned. "You've known me for a year now, Dixon. What do you mean?"

"You've known *Joey*, but I haven't really ever talked to you. What's your thing? What makes you tick?"

He struggled for a moment, silently chewing something while staring out to sea. "I don't know," he said. "I'm a distributor, been doing that for some time."

"Some time?"

"Enough years that I've forgotten most of them," he replied.

"You like it?"

He nodded, then shrugged. "Sure, yeah. Well enough, I guess. It's a job."

"But never exciting enough for you? You had to come down and ask us to recruit you for whatever you want to call this?"

"Yeah. I like the job, but my life's… boring, I guess. Joey always talks about you like you're some secret vigilante or something. Like Batman."

"Like *Batman*?"

"My word, not his."

"What did he tell you about me?" I was started to feel suspicious all over again, but I wanted to give him the benefit of the doubt. I didn't want to fishbait the guy.

"That's the thing," he said. "Not much. Really, very little.

Just said you were a good boss, liked whiskey, knew your stuff, etcetera."

"So why assume this kind of thing is what we do?"

"Because of what he *wouldn't* tell me about you. I'd always ask about you, how the bar was doing and everything, and he'd essentially shut down. Just try to change the subject."

"So you jump to the conclusion that I'm Batman."

"Well, you know… it always seemed so mysterious. Both you guys. Your bar's always closing at random times, on random days, for weird hours. I've made a couple runs down to you this year and have had to come back later. Then there was that report about old Marley's place. Seemed weird."

I waited for his explanation. Old Marley's place was a bed and breakfast off the main strip here in town, and had been the site of a pair of grisly murders earlier this year. Marley himself had been shot, and a younger man staying with his sister in one of the upstairs room had been found brutally murdered, a phone number etched onto his bleeding skin.

The papers and news reports kept things simple, surprisingly, only stating that the murder seemed to be one of vengeance, targeting the younger man only, and Marley had just happened to be in the wrong place at the very wrong time.

The full story was a bit more nuanced, and while it was still raw in my mind, it had ended well enough for those of us who had lived through it. The man who was murdered had a sister: Hannah. Joey and I had gotten into quite a scrape trying to save her from the same guys who had killed her brother, and though it was all over now, the spoils of war had given me a boat that served as a constant reminder of that past and had given Hannah the desire to escape everything and spend some time overseas.

"What was weird about it?"

"Just… nothing like that ever happens here. All the speculation, all the interest, then it just disappeared. Like the local cops were told to keep their mouths shut."

"Interesting."

"You have anything to do with it?" Frey asked.

I nodded. "Yep."

He looked over, but I wasn't about to give him details. Not yet. He was a good guy, but he wasn't a friend and confidante. Depending on how he performed out the gate on this little excursion I might consider throwing him a bone.

But not yet.

I watched his brow, furrowing and loosening, a man deep in thought and trying to be perceived as doing the exact opposite. He was a good captain, a capable sailor. Time would tell how capable he'd be when we got into our next scrape.

Then, and only then, would I be willing to make a judgement call.

CHAPTER TWENTY-NINE

JOEY INTERRUPTED OUR LITTLE MOMENT shortly after, stumbling in and making a racket out of it. "What's the plan, boss?" he asked. "I noticed we turned north."

"Yeah?" I said. "Quite the sense of direction you got there, kid."

I looked out the left-hand side of the wide, arcing set of windows in front of us and saw the South Carolinian coast in the distance. Frey did as well, then gave me a look.

"Give him a break," I said. "He's new to this."

"Not as new as you, captain," Joey shot back. He shifted and faced Frey's back. "He tell you I was a Navy man?"

Frey shook his head. "No, he left that out. So was I, back in the day."

"Really?" both of us asked in unison.

He nodded. "Spent a good chunk of my younger years chasing the tide. Did a few stints near Korea, China, Japan. Some up north in the Bering Sea."

"Nice," I said. "Didn't know that. Seems like there's a lot I didn't know about you, Frey."

He laughed. "Likewise. Happy to be here, and let's hope we can make something of this."

"What's in it for you?" I asked, finally. The words just shot out, as if they had been fired from whatever was controlling the word-cannon in my brain.

He didn't flinch. "I told you already. Looking for a little adventure. Distribution is a decent line of work, but I guarantee you it's not for the faint-of-heart, if things like 'driving 200 miles a day' and 'making lots of phone calls' is too exciting for you."

I wasn't sure if I bought it or not. At least not as-is. I couldn't help but feel as though there was something deeper in this guy. Something I couldn't quite put my finger on, even though I could feel my subconscious screaming to me about it.

"And when I heard about Joey's girlfriend," he continued, "that sort of sealed the deal."

"Yeah?" Joey asked.

"Yeah. Not a good situation. Figured I was here, ready for whatever it was you two had in mind, so I thought I'd better commit." He took a hand off the wheel and faced Joey. "Trust me, Joey, I'm going to help you guys however I can. We'll get her back."

Joey nodded solemnly, thanking him. Then he turned back to me. "Never answered my question, boss."

I raised an eyebrow.

"What's the plan? Elizondo's going to still be out on the bigger lanes, coming in hot from the southeast. Are we trying to intercept him, to beat him to Charleston?"

"Yes and no," I said. "We *are* trying to beat him to Charleston, but only because whatever's going to go down is going to be a lot easier to mess with if it's out on the water. We wait until they're docked in port and it's anyone's game."

"Whoever's got the largest army wins?" Joey asked.

"Sort of. The guys that talked to me up in Charleston, the fake detective and his two cronies, they're probably mafia. Or some sort of organized venture. The whole place stank of it, like they'd literally just put out their cigars and rolled up the hundred dollar bills into their suitcoats just before I got there."

"Mafia? In Charleston?"

Frey shrugged. "Not out of the question. I heard about a group making the rounds last year, trying to get a weekly payout from some of the bigger shops downtown."

"Wow," I said. "Seemed strange to me that they would be, but I guess it makes sense."

"Sure it does," Joey said. "There's money in Charleston. All sorts of it — clean, dirty, laundered, waiting to be laundered. You know that already, and I'd guess with the rise in cost of living in some neighborhoods it's brought in a lot more of a wealthy crowd."

"Yeah," Frey said, "and it's an untapped market. Not a whole lot of crime, per capita speaking. And certainly not a whole lot of *organized* crime."

"Okay, makes sense," I said again. "So that means we're messing with some big players, at least somewhere out there. Maybe we poked a small bear, but we poked it nonetheless."

"Your old man poked it, actually," Joey said.

I nodded. "Don't remind me. Whatever. We're in it, and we're in it until the end now. Elizondo's guys got Shalice, and even though they're better than the guys that want Elizondo dead, that still pisses me off."

Joey nodded along. I took a pause, sipping the last of my rum. "So we move toward Elizondo, but we focus on the guys moving on *him*."

"How do we find them?" Frey asked.

I smiled. "We don't have to. They called us off, remember? Whoever they've got now to get the job done is closer to Elizondo. That's why they sent out that little piece of crap to try to take us out. A small price to pay if they lost a guy or two, and if it worked it would have made their jobs way easier."

"So we're trying to beat their *other* crew?" Frey asked. "The ones gunning for Elizondo?"

"Correct," I said. "And there's no way we can beat Elizondo's ride, but I'd put the *Wassamassaw* up against any yacht on the eastern seaboard."

"Got it," Joey said. "So we try to get to Elizondo because *they'll* be heading for Elizondo. We catch up with them first, try to get them before they get to him."

"Something like that," I said.

"Sounds like a half-baked plan to me," Frey said.

I looked over at Joey, but Joey was already explaining. "He's not big on plans," he said. "They scare him, and he knows all plans get changed midstream."

"Well *I* like plans," Frey said. "So let me know when this one gets cooked. I'd sure love to know what we're getting ourselves into."

Joey laughed, patting Frey on the shoulder. "Sure thing, pal. When he finally comes around and sits down with a pencil and paper and writes out a full-fledged brief, you'll be the first to know."

CHAPTER THIRTY

IT TOOK LESS THAN TWO hours for me to once again realize why I hate plans. Plans are like a disease, slowly killing you from different fronts until you're completely consumed by it, then you aren't even yourself anymore. Plans require *planning*, but as soon as you begin to *act out* the plan, everything changes. So you go back, try to adjust things to make them make sense once again, and you lose time. You lose the serendipity of the moment, that small flitter of life just before you do something you know you can't turn back from.

Sometimes it fails, but most of the time — at least in my experience — it works out. I've learned to trust that flitter, that tiny spark of intuition that comes at the right time, somehow already worked out and mushed around into something salvageable by my subconscious.

That flitter of intuition is why I'm good at what I do. I don't plan well, and I certainly don't execute those plans well. But I know the job that needs to be done and I know I can do it. I go into it with those two ideas rock-solid in my mind, the quiet confidence giving me the hope that things will work out the way they're supposed to.

I don't turn back from a fight — I'm usually better at them than most men half my age — and I don't turn back from an opportunity for justice. I didn't with any mark that's ever set foot in my bar, I didn't with Hannah, and I wasn't going to with Shalice.

There was more on the line this time than with a simple mark or a single woman, but those things — just details in the plan I knew I wasn't going to create — could be dealt with later. My father, for instance.

I needed to see him, to actually look at his face and into his eyes and *watch* him react when I told him how I felt about his meddling with my life. But it was much worse than that. He'd dragged Joey and his girlfriend and now Jonathan Frey into it as well. That was crossing a *major* line, and I meant to share that with him.

But right now I was realizing we had walked into a trap.

We had 'planned' on there being one or two boats heading for Elizondo's ship.

Not ten.

But there were ten.

Ten speedboats, some larger than others, all of them tearing through the water about as fast as I was. I had Frey pushing the *Wassamassaw* as fast as it would allow, and it must have been for our larger frame and profile that we'd caught up with the convoy. The smaller boats had to maintain a slower pace to account for the larger, building waves. It wasn't much slower, but it was enough.

"On the horizon!" Frey shouted.

"Yeah," I yelled back. "I'm seeing it, too."

"Shit, Dixon," Joey said. "There's what — ten of them?"

I nodded. we'd both walked up to the top deck to watch,

sharing a set of binoculars between us. Frey had a better set in the bridge, so the three of us had been taking turns eyeing the horizon for the entirety of our trip north. Most of the time we saw a sailboat or a smaller yacht, and sometimes out east a larger contract vessel, but most of the boaters had listened to the weather report and were hunkering down for the rising storm chasing us all up from the southeast.

"Yeah, that's what I'm counting."

Ten boats, all traveling together and in the same direction, is not a normal sight. Not unless you were at a boat show, and I doubted that there was anything like that happening in the middle of the Atlantic. Ten boats, all *speeding* toward some unknown location, was even more abnormal.

"We're screwed," I said.

"We can't turn around."

He was right. If we'd spotted them, they'd certainly spotted us. While ten speedboats, heading straight north as fast as physics will allow, is one of the most unusual things I could imagine seeing in this part of the ocean, I also know that a multimillion dollar touring yacht, bearing down on its location *away* from the coastline and traveling even faster, is a close second.

They knew who was following them, and they'd planned for it.

Two of the boats on the flank peeled off and began a long sweep to the right.

"They're turning."

"They're coming back here," I said. "They'll probably just space out a bit, try to lure us between them."

"So what's our move?" Joey asked.

"We only have one." I looked at him, not wanting to go through with it but knowing it was our only option. "They're going to follow us back in to the coast, so either way we're getting into a skirmish."

"But what's our *move?* Do we try to outrun them a bit, maybe hope they'll run out of gas?"

"No," I said. "We play offense. Time to break out the big guns."

CHAPTER THIRTY-ONE

IT WAS GETTING DARK, AND was thus my absolute favorite time to be out on the water. The colors the sky is able to summon, to mix around with each other and spit out an absolutely stunning collaboration, is one of my favorite features of nature. Early morning on the ocean is my second favorite, but the sunset on a huge yacht, sailing on the open water, takes the cake.

But sailing at sunset while preparing for an open water battle against ten other speedboats is *not* my favorite time. I'd never done it before, so I guess I couldn't be terribly specific about my feelings toward it, but I knew I wasn't excited about it.

Joey wasn't, either. "What do you *mean,* big guns? I thought you had the AR and a bunch of pistols?"

I smiled. "Well I may have understated things a bit."

"Wait, really? Why?" he asked.

"Two reasons," I said. "First, the element of surprise. They know who we are, they probably know how *many* of us there are, and they know we're at least armed well enough to take out a boat or two, because we already did."

"Second?"

"Second," I continued. "Second reason is Frey."

"Why Frey?"

"Because I don't trust him."

"You don't trust anybody."

"Fair point, but that's only because I don't know them. I know Frey, at least a little bit now, and I don't trust him."

"He's a nice guy," Joey said.

"Never said he wasn't. And you can nice and untrustworthy at the same time, Joey. Ever met a politician?"

He chuckled. "Still, I'm not sure what you're seeing in him."

"I know," I said. "Me either. But it's a feeling, not really something I can put a finger on just yet. But I *know*."

"You know what, exactly?"

"That's just it — I don't *know*, but I know there's something about him."

"Could be that he's a dead shot with a pistol and we'll have no trouble at all taking out these boats."

"Could be. *Or* it could be that he's someone they sent to us, to try to get us on his side, and he's just going to kill us as soon as he can."

Joey looked out to the left, toward the sunset, and smiled again. He shook his head, an expression of disbelief on his face. For the first time that day we didn't have drinks in our hands, and I believe it was an unspoken acknowledgment of what we were about to get ourselves into.

"You disagree?" I asked.

"I do, man," Joey said. "I *really* do. I think you're wrong about him. I think he's a good guy, and I mean 'good guy.' Like us."

"We're good?"

"We're better than *those* guys," he said, pointing.

"Maybe. Maybe not. But I don't trust him yet," I said.

"So you didn't tell him you were packing more heat than just the pistol? What good would that do?"

I shrugged. "I don't know. Escalate things before they needed to escalate. Scare him? Force his hand?"

"You're crazy, Dixon," Joey said.

"You're just as crazy for going along with it."

"I'm not going along with *any* of your opinions on the guy. We need all the help we can get, and he's all we've got." Joey spit, clearing the edge of the yacht and watching as the tiny blob danced through the wind until it smacked into the surface of the ocean. "He's on our side, and we need him. You and I can argue all day about that, but it's the truth."

"Fair enough," I said. "Doesn't mean I have to give him any of the big guns."

He looked at me. "What, exactly, do you *have*?"

I smiled again, a wide, cocky thing that had never worked on anyone in my entire life yet still felt completely natural. "Remember that buddy of mine? The one in the FBI who helped out with Hannah's case?"

"Truman? How could I forget?" Joey asked. "He's the reason you got the *Wassamassaw.*"

I served with a guy named Truman who ended up flying up the ranks of government-style power. Not the political, whimsical kind, but real, bureaucratic power. The power of the pen. He'd helped me out of a few scrapes way back when, and he'd also helped after my stint with Hannah, ending with her foray into European travel with an unspecified end date and with my ownership of her late father's gorgeous yacht.

"Hannah's the reason I got her," I corrected, "but he pushed the paperwork through."

"He did you another favor, I presume?"

"A few, and I'm sure it was no small task, either. Lots of paperwork for this sort of thing, and most of the time it's so strictly enforced and tracked there's no sense even trying it."

Joey gave me an odd look. "What did you do?"

"I went back for that money. My father gave it to me, but I didn't want it, you know? It seemed tainted. Or dirty in some way."

"So you spent it on *weapons*? Jesus, Dixon, you're going to be America's Most Wanted."

I nodded. "Yeah, except that's where Truman comes in."

CHAPTER THIRTY-TWO

"HURRY," I CALLED BACK TO Joey, running down the stairs behind me. "We're going to be within range of them in a few minutes."

"*Our* range? Or theirs?" Joey asked.

We were heading to my private quarters, where I kept a couple of gun cases in the closet and another safe under the bed. The room was immaculate, as I wasn't much for clutter or mess, and I liked the feeling it gave me to keep at least one thing in my life in order.

I hadn't changed out the sheets or decor since Hannah Rayburn's father had owned the *Wassamassaw*, which Joey always thought was weird and a bit creepy. Thing is, I don't think the guy slept in the room much, and even if he had it wasn't like I hadn't *cleaned* the place. I'd gone over the entire boat with a fine-toothed comb, but that was after the FBI cleaning teams and upholsterers had finished with it. It wasn't easy to clean blood off carpet or walls, nor was it easy to fill bullet holes and dents from blunt-force impacts, so they'd done a fine job of essentially rebuilding the entire yacht's interior.

The comforter on the huge bed was brown, and the accents within the room were brown, too, giving the room a sort of feel that an interior designer had done some work here, making everything look nice, but stopped just before the point of applying real color. I liked the look of it, actually, since the white cleanliness of the space was offset by just a pop of not-white. It had an order to it.

Joey followed me to the closet on the port side of the room and waited while I swung it open and began working the lock on the safe. It clicked open and I let the heavy door crack apart from the case behind it.

I stepped aside and let Joey do the honors. He pulled at the door, revealing the contents.

"You — you've got to be kidding me," he said. "Right? You're kidding? These aren't real."

"Bushmaster M4A3 Assault Carbine," I said, proudly. "The Patrolman."

"I know it well," Joey said. "Sixteen-inch barrel, thirty round mag. And you've got *two* of them?"

I beamed. "Four, actually. Two more under the bed."

"What the hell, Dixon? How — how did you get these?"

"Ever heard of TOR?"

Joey's eyes widened. "You're kidding me. *You* figured out TOR and Bitcoin and all that?"

Joey was referring to the 'Dark Web,' a portion of the World Wide Web that was only accessible through special anonymizing software — the TOR browser. Constantly moving your connections through a maze of nodes and effectively making it impossible to trace anyone's identity, the browser opened up an entire world of internet sites that the general public has no idea about.

In about an hour of research, I'd learned that I could buy any drug I wanted, from prescription medications to black-tar heroine to pure Dutch crack. I could have it shipped through the mail and delivered to my door, or dropped at a mutually agreed-upon GPS-defined location anywhere in the world.

I could buy normal things, like I would on any shopping website, but through a securely untraceable means, or I could buy some of the insane, unbelievably dangerous items that most governments would jail you for even looking at.

Like weapons.

Lots and lots of weapons.

Most of the sites I came across were difficult, at best, to navigate, as they weren't written in English or any type of English I could decipher, and some of the sites made me feel about as safe as walking through south side Chicago at night with a sign on my head saying, 'I've got money.'

But thanks to a tip from Truman, and a go-ahead to purchase what I thought I would need 'to effectively protect myself in a sticky situation,' I learned quickly the inner workings of the Dark Web, enough to get a satisfactory usage of the thirty grand my father had donated to the cause.

I didn't press Truman on the details, like why he thought it was a good idea to be arming regular citizens, but I essentially got an answer from him anyway.

'People like you aren't just regular citizens,' he told me. 'We don't ever admit it to ourselves up here in our comfortable offices, but we need help. We can't go places sometimes, or we can't go places and get away with it.'

It was a conversation we'd had in this very room, Truman pacing the floor between the end of the bed and the stairs and me sitting in the office chair nearby.

'Why? Why me?' I'd asked him.

'It's obvious, isn't it?' Truman said. 'You're a known quantity to me, and you and I both know I'm not stopping you from getting yourself killed. Might as well give you the ability to keep yourself alive, you know? And you've got a serious knack for figuring out *exactly* the types of people we can't touch, but definitely need to be touched.'

I'd nodded, taking it all in.

When all was said and done, we'd signed a contract: I had to pass my purchase through Truman, so he could successfully 'FBI it,' a term I took to mean scrub it of anything that might come back to him. He was a good guy, and a rule follower, so I imagine the outcome of allowing a citizen to use perfectly good American dollars to purchase a storehouse of weaponry and ammunition, even though it was on terms that he agreed with, was something that bothered him.

But it was done, and I was thirty-thousand-odd dollars poorer for it. Joey was only finding out about it now because I hadn't really had a reason to *use* any of it yet. One of the things about finding yourself equipped with some of the best special forces gear on the planet is that you realize how *unexcited* you are to have to use it.

But today was a different day. I hadn't wanted to get into a firefight with ten enemy boats, and I certainly didn't want to do it while having to navigate a larger, slower vessel around them, but here we were.

Truman had given me one rule, I guess to add the final assurance that this wasn't the worst idea he'd ever had:

Let them fire first.

CHAPTER THIRTY-THREE

JOEY WAS PACING BEHIND ME, right where Truman had a few months ago. "You're telling me he was *okay* with this? Christ, Dixon, he seemed like he was one atom short of Hiroshima whenever he was around you."

"We had a strained relationship."

"What the hell does *that* mean? People have 'strained relationships' with their fathers. Or their brothers or sisters. Not with federal agents."

I shrugged. "What can I say? We were friends once."

"Close?"

"Couldn't be closer."

"And you're not now?"

I shrugged again. *I need a drink.* I was standing just inside the stairwell at the top of the stairs that led down to my room, so the bar was right behind me. I turned and made my way toward it as Joey scaled the last of the stairs. We'd each grabbed one of the Bushmasters and a box of ammunition. Fully-loaded magazines, organized and stored inside. We'd also grabbed three grenades each, all purportedly US-military commissioned and ready for war. The problem with grenades, of course, is that you can't test them. And buying explosives from a Russian-born (supposedly, according to the profile description) broken-English-speaking fellow using encrypted data streams and never doing any face time meant that I had no idea if these were grenades or snow globes.

I *hoped* they were grenades. They had the weight, the look, the feel. I was comfortable using them, and I know Joey had at least trained on them once or twice, enough to have a passing knowledge of their timing and force. With an explosive, that was about enough, since there's always an element of 'I don't know what the hell that was' involved with them.

"Did you hear me?" he asked again.

I nodded, reaching for the top shelf. "I did. Sorry. Been a long day, and we're just getting started."

"We've got two minutes, max," he said.

I agreed — the two boats that had peeled off were making a much wider circle to the southeast than I'd expected. They were trying to deep flank us, coming in very wide from the south, aiming for starboard side.

"Yeah, we're not now. Nothing happened, just time I guess. You know how it goes."

"Not really, not with friends."

"What friends do you have?" It came out harsher than I'd intended. Truth was I didn't think Joey *had* any friends. I had been more than surprised when he'd showed up with Shalice to the bar a couple months ago, but I figured it made sense that he wasn't spending *all* of his time at the bar or hitting marks with me.

He smiled. "I've got a couple friends. Unlike the Army, us Navy boys stick together."

I let the dig slide. I didn't have many friends from my Army days, and that was by design.

"Couple dudes from Florida and I are close. Call them up every few months, actually," Joey said, as if talking to someone once every few months for an hour at a time was a perfectly legitimate definition of 'close friend.'

"Well aren't you smug," I said. I poured from the bottle I'd grabbed — a Woody Creek, a decent rye that I'd recently discovered — and poured him one as well. I reached for a third glass. "Joey, you know me. I'm not really a 'friend' type of guy."

"No, I got that," he said, his smile growing. "I'm just trying to put it all together. You're cryptic, you know that?"

"Again, I'm not really a 'lay-it-all-out-there' kind of guy, either."

"Why did you and Truman grow apart?"

"It's actually just like I said. He wanted a different life, wanted to keep moving up the ranks and eventually got recruited. Turned in his gun for a badge and an ID card, then took up a pen and computer and makes his living telling other guys what to do."

"And you wanted a bar."

"I wanted a different life. Didn't know what that meant at the time."

"Do you now?"

I frowned. "Kid, you're getting awfully sentimental."

"Happens when you're about to wage war, I guess."

"Fair enough. Hey, go give this to Frey. I'm going to set up out here, try to get some semblance of a plan since I know you'll just complain if I don't."

"Sounds good," he said. "What should I tell him?"

I looked outside, saw the boats heading in toward us. They were side-by-side, which had benefits for both of us. For them it meant they were strong together, both shooting alternatively, so if there was a need to reload they wouldn't have to drop any fire.

On the other hand, it meant they were forcing their enemy — us — to focus their fire on a smaller area. We would have the higher ground, the proverbial hill to die on, but we would be able to aggregate our fire toward a singular area, which was certainly my preference.

The alternative was that they would hit us from both sides, hoping to draw our fire to one boat or the other that was straddling us. It was an effective strategy in old-school Naval warfare during the days of the pirates and buccaneers. Smaller sloops would face off against man-of-wars by flanking them, knowing that at least one of their sloops were going to sink. But in the barrage, the larger naval ship would likely take so much damage that in the end the opposing force would win.

Which told me two things: they either didn't know their naval warfare history, or they were really interested in keeping their boats alive.

Focus fire from a single location onto another single location. A viable strategy, certainly, and regardless of their interest in history, I assumed that wanting to stay together meant that they were most interested in killing us off with the smallest chance they'd lose a boat.

Which means they're planning on fighting a bigger battle later.

We were the secondary objective. We were the consolation prize.

"Tell him to keep moving," I said. "No matter what, keep moving. Nothing fancy, just give us a solid shot at them at all times."

Joey nodded, then left the room carrying Frey's drink.

CHAPTER THIRTY-FOUR

THE FIRST BOAT TO REACH us was the one on the left. It was moving slightly faster than its teammate and because of our own movement we were heading for a diagonal collision. The second boat was only seconds behind, but I already had a plan for that one.

"Joey, you back?" I hollered over my shoulder.

He was there, suddenly, holding one of the Bushmasters. "I'm here. What's the plan?"

"Shoot them," I said, pointing the barrel of my rifle at the first boat.

"Got it. Anything more specific?"

"Don't miss."

"Sounds good, boss."

He opened fire. The sound was deafening, even though I'd been expecting it. The Bushmaster was a solid weapon, fully automatic or burst fire for the military- and police-issue versions, around 700 rounds per minute.

The opposing team was not at all ready for the hell that broke loose. There were three men besides the driver in each boat, and each was armed with a small subcompact machine gun and holding it up toward us.

There was no chance — the distance was too great for their weapons to do any damage, and to make matters worse, they weren't expecting us to be well-armed.

The first burst ripped through the water and landed short, only one round hitting the hull at the front of the boat. The second and third bursts from Joey, however, hit their mark. The man standing at the front of the boat flew sideways, spun around by the shock of the impact, and fell off the side. The man next to him dove backwards as well, but it was unclear whether or not he was hit.

I watched the attack for another second, but then focused on my own skirmish. The second boat was now in range of my rifle, but I wasn't planning on taking them out with a rifle. We needed to conserve ammunition if we were hoping to go up against the other eight boats, so I was hoping for some luck from the grenades.

I grabbed one timed it, and launched it in the water, about as far out as I could manage to throw. It hit the surface of the water with a splash, about twenty feet in front of the speeding boat. *A perfect shot,* I thought. *Let's hope that thing still works.*

It had been years since I'd tossed a grenade, but the concept was simple: aim for the thing you want to kill, waiting the proper amount of time before you throw it. Don't hold onto it. Don't drop it. Throw it.

It worked.

The explosion was small, as could be expected from a grenade, but it was effective. The boat must have been on top of the thing when it blew, as a stream of water and debris flew upward from the center of the boat, two smaller streams ejecting upward from the sides. The boat itself lifted up and out of the water a few inches, but the water beneath it dispersed momentarily, which meant that the boat was now hanging about a foot out of the water.

It came crashing down, the new hole and the shock of the impact destroying the hull's integrity. The boat split in half down its width. Two of the men fell in the gap, while the other two fell into a pile in the center of one of the halves.

"Nice shot," Joey said between bursts.

"Thanks. You too."

The *Wassamassaw* was still moving, still plowing ahead toward the line of eight boats in the distance, and I was sure they were watching the proceedings. The two boats they sent were no longer moving — the first boat's driver was slumped over the wheel and the second boat had split and become two semi-buoyant pieces of flotsam. There were men in the water all around, some dead, some screaming at one another.

I couldn't hear what they were trying to say, and I didn't care. We were done here.

"Let's roll," I said. "Run and tell Frey to head for the horizon — we need to figure out what to do about the other eight boats."

Joey left without a word and I found myself staring down into a churning sea of men, equipment, and pieces of boat. I watched it for nearly a minute as it passed behind us and thought about the situation. Had it changed?

Whoever was behind all of this had a *lot* of resources on hand. Perhaps the mafia could be involved, though I still found that theory somewhat implausible. After my encounter with the non-detectives in Charleston I'd assumed it was nothing but a man with a lot of money and a couple friends, out to get this Elizondo fellow. They'd somehow tracked down my father, or he'd found them, and they'd come up with the elaborate plan to get his son involved in a coup so that they could reap the rewards.

They'd pay me off, my father — as usual — would play

me for a fool, and they'd be richer. Joey and I would go back to our normal daily operating procedure and no one would be the wiser.

And while *our* motive had changed when Shalice was taken, *theirs* hadn't. It still made sense that it could have been one or two people, teaming up with my father and stringing a yarn that I'd believe and be forced into action, but all that had now changed.

There were *ten* speedboats, all fully loaded and well-armed for what was supposed to be a simple smash-and-grab. Whoever could set something like that up was seriously connected, and seriously well-funded. My old man was connected, but I doubted he could have pulled something like this together.

The water was calm again, and we were tearing through it. The fleet up ahead had slowed down and I could now see individual silhouettes in each: three men and a driver, each holding a weapon.

This wasn't a one-on-one skirmish, the type of fight I was used to, it was an all-out war. Three men against twenty-four? Those weren't the types of odds I preferred. They were the types of odds *anyone* preferred.

I looked back at the destruction floating around in the water, saw a couple of the men treading water near each other, likely trying to figure out a plan. We were half a mile past them now, and putting distance between us. I stared up to the bridge, where Joey and Frey were now, and realized we needed another plan.

CHAPTER THIRTY-FIVE

"WE NEED A NEW PLAN," Joey said as soon as I'd entered the bridge.

"What makes you think that?" I asked.

"Frey does. His idea."

I eyed the guy. "Nice driving back there. Thanks for keeping us tight on them."

He nodded. "We do need a different plan."

"We didn't really *have* a plan. Just thought we'd start shooting and see what happens."

"Is that *usually* your plan?"

I nodded. Joey nodded as well, which sort of pissed me off, but I wasn't sure why.

"You guys need better plans."

"You got any ideas, Frey?" I asked. I didn't like that this guy was here, trying to tell me what our problem was.

"They're heading for Elizondo," he said. "They only sent those two back to see if they could get us off their tail easy."

"Yeah, so?"

"Well that means we just need to follow them in. If we instigate, we're screwed. There are at least twenty-five guys total in those boats, and there's no way we've got enough grenades and lucky shots to take them out."

"And then what? After we follow them in? What's the move?"

He shook his head. "No idea."

"That — that's is?" I asked. "We just follow them? They're going to get to Elizondo first, and —"

"And what?" he said. "Elizondo is on a *ship*. A hundred times the size of these little things —" he pointed out the front windshield — "and he's going to have his own convoy as well."

"Still, we have to do something," Joey said. "They've got Shalice with them."

"We don't know that," Frey said. "She was taken from you guys on a smaller boat, right? Who knows if it went to Elizondo's ship or not. She could be anywhere."

Joey was seething. I could see it in his eyes. The fear, the hatred, the acknowledgement of defeat. He knew Frey was right. He knew Shalice was gone, and there was nothing we could do about it. If we were going to get her back, it was going to be either because we lucked out or because we had a rock-solid plan. Possibly a good amount of both.

"There might be something," Frey said.

Both Joey and I stared, waiting for him to explain. He focused on the wheel for a bit, slowing down as well, then turned to the table set up along the far wall.

"I was looking at the maps over here," he said. "The *Wassamassaw* is here." He pointed at a spot on the wall map, tracing a line with his finger. "We're heading up toward Kiawah now."

I watched the line he was tracing, following the coastline as well as Kiawah Island. Kiawah Island was an upside-down boot-shaped stretch of land with the toe of the boot kicking out into the Atlantic.

"That's it over there, actually," he said, pointing this time out the windshield. "I think we'll be following the coastline pretty closely, since the storm's following us all in and Elizondo's boat eventually has to dock in Charleston. They'll have to swing wide to miss the jetties, of course, but they'll come in through the jetties. It's the only way in."

The jetties were a pair of artificial rock ledges that extended eastward from the mouth of Charleston Harbor, where the Ashley and Cooper Rivers meet. Constructed over seventeen years shortly after the end of the civil war, they served the purpose of creating a shipping lane as well as deepening the mouth of the bay for larger ships to use.

It was also a hotspot for fishing, the natural expulsion from the rivers providing a sort of nutrient gravy train throughout the miles-long chute between the jetties. All manner of fish, crustaceans, and sharks came out to feed on both sides of the north and south jetties.

"So we catch them at the jetties. See what's up then?" Joey asked.

"No," I said. "Too many fishermen. Even in this weather, there will be way too many people around, trying to bring in a catch before everyone hunkers down to ride it out."

"Mason's right," Frey said. "Those guys up there are going to try and intercept Elizondo *before* he starts through the jetty, as it will give them enough time to do whatever it is they're going to do out in open water, yet still close enough to land that they aren't in any real danger from weather."

He drew it all out on the map in front of us, pointing at the mouth of the harbor and the mouth of the jetties, extending it like pursed lips another few miles east and slightly south. I knew the area well, as Joey and I had fished it numerous times in the past few months, and we had also taken the shipping lane into Charleston twice for a restocking run that we had both decided would be more fun by sea than by land.

Joey was nodding, holding his chin with his right hand. "Makes sense," he said. "So what do *we* do? Those guys out there aren't going to just let us leave."

"We're not leaving, really," Frey said. "We're following them, making them think they're dragging us along into a big skirmish, but we'll tear off to the west at the last minute. Hang out *here*." He smacked the map with an outstretched finger, landing it directly on top of the northernmost point of Morris Island.

"Morris?" I asked. Like Kiawah, and Folly Island situation between them, Morris Island was a long stretch of land that was actually a thousand smaller islands and marshy areas with rivers and streams crisscrossing and weaving together over the area. The islands were great fishing as well, both for freshwater and saltwater species. Small boats and canoes could travel around all of the interlocking rivers, effectively making them the perfect vehicle for intra-island travel, while yachts like the *Wassamassaw* were mostly relegated to the outskirts — the big waters of the Atlantic and some of the larger river mouths.

"Morris Island is where we set up. Wait for them to come in."

I saw his point — Morris *was* a good vantage point, a great lookout if you were a lighthouse or a fort. But we were neither, and we certainly couldn't be waiting around for *them* to come to *us*. If what Frey had just explained to both of us proved to be true, all of the action would be long over by the time anyone came down the channel.

"It'll all be over by then, Frey," Joey said. "If they're heading out to intercept him, the fighting will all be at the eastern side of the jetties, not the western side. We can't camp there and wait for them because there won't be anything to wait for."

Frey shook his head. "No. Trust me. There will be."

I stepped back from the map and looked Jonathan Frey up and down. He was still staring at the map, working it all out again and again, convincing himself it was the right play.

"How do you know that?"

"Because," he said. "They can't win against Elizondo."

CHAPTER THIRTY-SIX

"THEY CAN'T WIN AGAINST ELIZONDO?" I asked. "What the hell is that supposed to mean? There are eight of them, armed to the teeth, and —"

"Elizondo's prepared for them," Frey said.

I stared at him. Honestly had no idea who this guy was. When I'd met him I'd sized him up, decided he was exactly who he said he was — a man wanting some adventure in his life, ready to have a little fun. We were here to help him feel young again, or something like that. His job was terrible, he had no family or hobbies, I don't know.

But now, I *really* didn't know. He was a completely different person. Jonathan Frey wasn't a distributor. He wasn't a nervous wreck, shy and slightly off-kilter. He was something else entirely. I could see it in his eyes now, just like I caught a glimpse of it a minute ago when he was detailing his plan up on the wall. He had a fire in him, something raging just behind his eyes, and it was contagious. I felt puffed up by it, just watching him draw it all out for us.

"Who are you, Frey?" I asked.

His eyes widened slightly, then shrank. All of him, in

fact, shrank. He just sort of melted down into himself until he was the nervous weirdo that I'd met in my bar not so long ago. I watched him do it, like it was something he'd forgotten to do and was just now realizing it.

Joey, too, seemed to notice. "Frey," he said. "What's up, man?"

"I — I don't… what do you mean?" he asked. "I'm not sure what —"

"Save it, Frey," I said, interrupting. "I get it. You're undercover. Sent to us to figure out what game we're into, right?"

The eyes widened again. I stared at them, boring into his soul to try to figure who had played us, and why.

"My old man send you, Frey?"

"No — he… I don't even —"

"Frey," I said, bringing my voice down again. "Jig's up. You're not leaving this boat until you give me something that actually makes sense. I'm going to ask you again, man. *Did my father —*"

"I'm ATF," he said quickly.

"What?"

"Alcohol, Tobacco, and Firearms," he said. "*Federal* Bureau."

I squeezed my eyes shut. *Shit. Here we go again.* "Okay. What does that *mean*?"

"I work for the ATF, undercover policing division. We try to find the runners, the big players, get them off the map."

Joey was pinching the area above his nose between a thumb and a forefinger. "Shit, Dixon, I had no idea. I'm sorry. I didn't —"

"*Save it,* Joey," I said. "Let me think."

"We don't have *time* to think," Frey replied.

"I wasn't asking for your opinion, *Jonathan*. That your real name?"

He nodded. Reached into his back pocket for a wallet and pulled it out. Flipped open the folding pad of leather and flashed a badge. Metal, real, not worth faking.

"Okay, fine. Jonathan Frey, of the ATF. We in trouble?"

He shook his head. "No. Not at all. On the contrary, you're helping out with a federal case. Rockford Elizondo has been shipping illegal wares into the United States for some time now, deflecting the taxes and waving off the import fees."

I groaned. "You've got to be kidding me."

"Wish I were. We've been tracking him for some time, but he's been smart about it. Staying offshore, usually in Cuba or the Dominican Republic. Only coming in when there's a shipment, which is only once or twice a year."

"So you're trying to bust him?"

"Well yeah, but we can't just rush up to him and ask him to come with us."

"Why not?"

"For one, he's better armed than we are. You think it's cheap where you got those guns you were using, you should what they cost in Cuba. And for the same price you paid, I'd bet they throw in a guy to use it as well."

"Wonderful," I said.

"That's not all," Frey said. "This gang he's up against — the one your dad's fallen into favor with — they're no joke, either. About a million bucks yearly short of being considered an 'organized crime detail worth considering,' as they call it in my office."

"So we're stuck in the middle of a massive three-way turf war," I said. "Even better."

"No joke," Joey said. "Why didn't you tell us?"

Frey looked genuinely concerned. "I wish I could, really. But we couldn't take the risk. You and Dixon were already involved, and for me that was *massively* helpful. I no longer had to come up with something random and try to sell it, nor did I have to figure out what team to set up and how to resource us. We're not the CIA, guys. We have a budget, but it's laughable."

"So you thought you'd stow away on a yacht with two psychos, hope to get lucky and get a shot at Elizondo?"

"Actually, yeah," he said. "And you're far from psycho. I'm connected as well, Dixon, and I've heard some talk that you're the real deal. You're the one who could get it done, they told me."

"Who told you?"

"You know who. I believed him. I watched you work, saw how you handled yourself against the boaters from earlier, knew how well-equipped you were. I think we can do this."

I shook my head, growing more frustrated. "Do *what,* exactly? Now we're back to killing Elizondo? What about Shalice?"

He sniffed. "That's the one part I haven't figured out." He turned to Joey. "I — I'm sorry, man. I still want to make sure we can —"

"We're getting her back. Non-negotiable."

Frey nodded. "I get it. I really do. But my job —"

"You don't *have* a job on this boat unless I tell you you do," I said. The words came out harsh, pinched and staccato. But they were true, and the two men in the bridge with me knew it.

Frey clenched his jaw, then looked at me. "Fine. I get it. Thank you, for helping me."

"We haven't done anything yet. And I'm not entirely sure we *are* going to do anything."

"You helped me get this far, and for that I'm grateful. But I can't do the rest alone, either. I'm understaffed and this is going to be the last time we can hope to get to Elizondo before summer of next year, so for me this is *it*. This is his biggest drop as well, so there may not *be* a next time. It's now or never for me."

I sighed. "What's the plan? How do we take him out, then?"

"That's the tricky part," Frey said.

I looked at Joey, made a face that I knew wouldn't take him much to decipher.

"We can't take him out," Frey said. "We have to bring him in."

CHAPTER THIRTY-SEVEN

I COULDN'T BELIEVE I WAS doing this. The plan was the wildest, stupidest thing I'd ever taken part in. It didn't even make sense, really, but it truly was the best we could do. If I was honest, I was a little excited. Scared, but excited. The best cocktail of emotions.

I had a cocktail now, actually. Joey had made up a batch of whiskey sours, fresh from some lemons I'd packed in the fridge a week or so ago. They were perfect, just tart enough to wake you up but with the sweetness that was required for it to go down smooth. I wasn't sure what he'd used as the base, but it had to be something with a high rye bill, perhaps a Wild Turkey 101 or something a bit higher end.

I sipped it, enjoying every drop as if it was my last, because, hell, it may have been.

As of now the plan was simple. Stupid, but simple. Shalice would be somewhere in Elizondo's fleet, perhaps by now even on the ship itself. The ship, according to Frey, was the smallest class of cargo vessel, something called a Handymax, specifically a 'Handysize,' and it carried up to 20,000 DWT — deadweight tonnage. Elizondo wouldn't have a full load, but it would be close, somewhere in the neighborhood of 15,000 and 18,000 DWT. The ship was called the *Rummer*, which seemed rather fitting for a man like Elizondo and his calling in life. It had the typical raised overlook-style bridge, a slightly raised bow deck, while the main cargo deck was flat and rose only about twenty feet higher than the surface of the water.

In addition, Rockford Elizondo would be on board, as Frey's research had determined that the man was brutally efficient, a natural control freak, and was a borderline schizophrenic. He was terribly worried about just the sort of thing we were planning to do, which only made things worse.

To get to Shalice, we had to know which boat she was on. We couldn't know that, but we could assume that any of the boats Elizondo sent to attack us would *not* have her onboard. We could further assume that Elizondo would only trust her care to himself, so we'd unanimously determined that she was somewhere on *Rummer* itself.

Frey's goal was to wait out the fight between the opposing forces, Elizondo's men on one side, the gang on the other. Frey was adamant that the gang's boats weren't going to be enough to even slow Elizondo down, but I wasn't so sure.

Nothing in my life had ever gone according to any plan I'd made or been given, so I had no reason to suspect things would be different now.

Joey, for his part, was even less satisfied. He'd fought Frey the entire time, wanting to rush in and get to Shalice immediately. I felt his pain, but I agreed with Frey on that one — Elizondo wouldn't risk his only bargaining chip, so if we could sit back and let them battle it out for a bit, it would only help our case.

We'd get into position off the coast of Morris Island and

from there watch the convoy come in through the jetties. Frey's prediction was that the *Rummer* would be accompanied by whichever of his smaller protective boats had survived, and none of the eight gang boats we'd encountered would be afloat. So far, we would have kept up our end of the bargain to keep Elizondo alive, so Shalice would be safe. At that point, Joey would take the inflatable dinghy from the *Wassamassaw* and head north and duck behind the *north* jetty for the *Rummer* to pass. He'd work in near it, then swim to the side of it and hope to climb aboard undetected.

From there, it was all hands on deck. All four remaining hands, firing my guns. I had more than enough ammunition if we were careful, and we still had plenty of grenades if any of the boats got close. Frey's idea was to lure the *Rummer* protector boats toward us while Joey worked his way around the ship, looking for Shalice. If things went according to plan, the bulk of Elizondo's forces would be on boats, attacking us, and Joey would have little to no resistance.

The major problems were quite major. Nearly impossible to overcome, no matter what any of us could come up with. First, Joey would have no weapons. Even if he took a Bushmaster with him in the dinghy, it wouldn't be reliable if he needed to take a swim to get from the dinghy to the *Rummer*. The pistols would fare better, but again it was a reliability issue. He planned to take one just in case.

Second, we had no idea what Elizondo's men would do. Would Joey run into interference? Would their team, however large it was, split and move to straddle the *Rummer* on its way through the jetties. Or would they all throw themselves toward us and kill Frey and me, then go after Joey?

Finally, and most importantly, none of us knew Elizondo. To Frey he was a dossier, a piece of paper or ten describing his actions over the last few years. But none of us actually *knew* him. Was he a loose cannon? An uptight planner? Something in-between.

There were too many variables

I wasn't convinced that this 'plan' of Frey's was anything but a harebrained suicide mission, but I had nothing better to offer. We poured drinks and headed north, hoping that for once in my life we would be able to make things work.

Then, as if the universe was answering my questions with a very definitive, 'no, you will not make things work,' the *Wassamassaw* listed sideways and righted herself, a great, giant groan emanating from belowdecks.

"The hell was that?" Joey asked.

I swallowed the sip of whiskey sour I had been rolling around in my mouth, my eyes closing and squeezing shut, trying to block out everything happening.

I had forgotten about that. I completely forgot.

"It's the fuel tank," I said, muttering under my breath as Frey and Joey watched on. "I didn't check it after our first little rendezvous with those bastards."

The *Wassamassaw* sputtered, stopped, and suddenly the silence of the ocean — a gentle crashing of waves that foretold the coming of a massive storm — overtook my ears.

"We're out of gas."

CHAPTER THIRTY-EIGHT

THERE WAS FUEL EVERYWHERE. THEY hadn't hit a line, but the actual tank. Somehow. From some miraculous stroke of luck on their part, one of their rounds had pierced the plastic hull of the tank, and there was now diesel leaking out and filling up the entire engine compartment. I could smell it as soon as I walked in — surely not a good sign — but I could also *see* it — *certainly* not a good sign.

I looked at the reserve, two ten-gallon jugs I'd never messed with that sat full in the corner of the tiny room. It would be enough to get us into Charleston, possibly enough to get us back to the *Wassamassaw's* home port at Hunting Island, but probably not near enough to mount a high-speed chase and full-on assault against faster and more agile boats.

Shit, I thought for the tenth time.

I trudged through the inch layer of gasoline on the floor toward the tank. It might be possible to plug it, but I'd have to find it first. If the hole was somewhere on the top of the tank, the fuel would have spilled out only down to the hole.

But we'd run out of gas completely, which meant there

was a hole in the tank somewhere *below* the intake line to the engine. Even worse, I doubted it was going to be on the side of the tank I could access — the bullet had come in through the ship's outer hull, so the hole would be on the outer side of the tank, flush up against the side of the *Wassamassaw*.

This was getting even worse. I screamed. Just a quick, empty fit of rage. I wasn't really *feeling* angry as much as frustrated, pissed that I'd gotten myself and Joey and Shalice — and now this ATF guy named Frey — into this mess. I screamed again, realizing how *massive* of the mess this was. We were sitting dead on the water, an inch of fuel covered the floor of the engine compartment, and the twenty-odd gallons of fuel we'd kept on reserve would only fill the tank up to the hole in its side — which would only empty again onto the floor. Even trying to start up the engine again afterward could be disastrous. If any of the fuel fumes had found their way into the line of fire from a spark…

Shit.

Okay. Think, Dixon. You've been through worse. I thought about it. *Had I?* Honestly, I wasn't sure. I'd gone into battles in places I'd rather forget, but I'd been armed better, well-prepared, and briefed by professionals who spent their days writing briefs and studying the best ways to do things like that. I'd been in few sticky situations with Joey, but again we were in our element — on land.

Out here, on the water, we were dead.

"Dixon," Joey called. "You down there?"

"Yeah, why?"

"We have company."

I squeezed my eyes shut and cursed again. *You've got to be kidding me.* "What is it?"

"You — you'd better just come up and see," he said.

I sighed. *Yeah, that's probably about right.* If it were good news, he'd have just said it. 'Dixon, there's a dozen Navy Seals up here who want to help us get Shalice back,' or, 'hey, man, turns out Elizondo's ship just sank and Shalice is on her way over in a paddle boat.'

But it wasn't going to be anything close to that. I didn't have to hear it in his voice, hear it in his hesitation. I just *knew.* My mother used to say that bad luck came in threes. Three funerals of people you knew in one season, three divorces of friends or family members, three financial crises.

I thought about it. If I really tried, I could have made just about everything that had happened today an instance of bad luck, but I had to admit that all the bad luck had happened in major themes. First the guys had come and shot our fuel tank, then we'd run out of fuel. Then Frey told us he was working for the federal government and that this was nothing short of a major sting operation he wanted to play sidekick on, since he didn't quite have the resources to do it the right way.

So whatever news I was about to receive was *not* going to be any good.

I trudged back to the set of steep, ladder-like stairs leading to the compartment and jumped up onto them. I could smell the gasoline swirling up from my shoes. They were soaked in it, and my socks were already starting to squish around inside them.

At the top of the stairs I could hear voices. Frey's, and then Joey's. They were talking to someone, not to each other. I rose the rest of the way out of the engine compartment and made my way to the main deck. Another half-set of stairs and I was at the top and could Joey and Frey arguing with someone, both men leaning out over the deck rail.

"Who is it?" I asked.

"Our buddies from earlier. Three more of the boats," Frey said, turning to me. "They started shooting from farther out this time. Nothing hit, but we took cover and then they were on us."

I looked over the edge and saw that he was correct. Three more boats, each identical to the ones we'd put out of commission earlier. Two of the speedboats were hovering nicely out of range of our pistols, but I could have made a shot with one of the Bushmasters. They were armed, though, the same subcompacts we'd faced earlier, and there were three on each boat, plus a driver. The driver of the third boat had grabbed the side of the *Wassamassaw* while two men aimed up at Joey and Frey, and now me. The fourth man was doing the talking.

"Mr. Dixon," he said. "Welcome. Elizondo's not going to be happy to see you."

"We weren't planning on seeing him until *after* you guys had your turn."

"We figured that out," he said. "Makes for a decent plan. Perhaps Elizondo would honor his end of the deal in that case. He's still alive, he lets you live. But the deal was that you were to protect him, no? And sitting back here while all the fun happens isn't what I would call *protecting* anything."

"That was the deal with Elizondo's men, yes," I said. "But that's not the deal we had with you."

The man nodded, fifteen feet down and standing on the front of his boat. He bobbed up and down like a cork in a bowl of water. "Quite the conundrum, then," he said. "You were supposed to take out Elizondo, you failed."

"You didn't even give us a *chance*!" I shouted. "You just came after us, while we were —"

"You were *called off,* Dixon. We had a better team in place. There was nothing more we needed from you."

I glared at him. "Well where I come from that's now how we do business."

"Yes, that's why we're making you an offer now."

"An offer?"

"Yes. We noticed you had some appropriate weaponry for the kind of thing we —"

"No."

"Dixon…" the man smiled, almost laughing, then turned to the driver, still holding the handle on the *Wassamassaw* to keep their boat flush against its side. He nodded. The driver let go of my yacht, stepped back, then moved over to the covered canopy part of the speedboat's rear end. The two men aiming up at us shifted as the boat did, but kept their aim steady and true.

The driver walked over to the canopy and pulled off the cover with a flourish. The poles keeping it upright groaned and split, breaking and falling into the center of the boat. The greenish brown canvas material snapped and folded in on itself, then fell backwards off the side of the boat.

I watched the proceedings, now thoroughly confused. The tarp was gone, and there was a fifth man sitting in the center of the area the canvas flap had previously covered.

No…

"Mason?" the man called out. "Mason, that you?"

I dropped my head. My eyes closed. *No.*

"Who is it?" Joey asked. "Mason, do you know —"

"It's my dad."

"Mason," the man said. "You up there? I can't see anything with the light. Listen — don't trust anything they —"

The driver kicked, his foot lashing out quickly and knocking over the man. He grabbed his side, groaning. He fell off the seat he had been cramped up in and then sprawled out on the floor of the boat. He pushed himself up, but then the driver kicked again. I could hear the air leave his gut from all the way up on deck, and I tensed up. I wanted to pick up Joey's gun and fire. I wanted to retaliate, but then… I didn't.

It's my father.

It was him, no doubt. He was handcuffed, his hands behind his back and his face smashed up against the carpeted side of the bilge pump enclosure and live well, and I was immediately torn. I wanted to fight back, to kill the bastards, but then again — it was my dad.

There's something weird about family. You can run away from it, you can abandon it, you can deny it, but it's still blood. In some cases you can even overcome it, but for me, for my entire life, I'd *wanted* to run away. I'd *wanted* to overcome my childhood, to deny it, to ignore it and become the exact opposite of what it had been.

But I had never been able to.

Call it most egregious irony in the universe, but I *wanted,* at that moment in time, to make sure my old man was okay. It was like all of the things in my life that had happened that I'd sworn to hate to him for were culminating in one final test of familial love. Like he'd been testing me my entire life, trying to measure the depths of my manhood, and I'd always come up wanting until now.

I hated myself for it, but I felt something in that moment. I truly did. I felt shame, and hatred, and grief, and the stomach-wrenching burn of injustice, all at the same time. I felt remorse, and the want for revenge, and the desire to just turn around and float away, as slowly and as quickly as the tides would allow.

But the tides *weren't* going to allow that. The universe had caught up with me, and so had my old man. The same old man who'd pushed out my little brother, hurt my mother, and then sucked me into this nightmare reality.

"Mason, I didn't want — I didn't mean for this…" my

father's voice trailed off, but the guys in the boat didn't kick him again.

"Dixon, your old man would like to come aboard and say hello. That okay with you?"

No. "Yeah," I said. "Head to the stern, I've got the deck open."

CHAPTER THIRTY-NINE

I WALKED DOWN THERE MYSELF, Joey and Frey following behind. Joey sped up and took the stairs directly behind me, then came up next to me as we made our way to the back of the *Wassamassaw*.

"What's the plan here, Dixon?" Joey asked. "We can't fight them off."

I didn't want to think. I didn't want to do anything. "You know how I feel about plans."

I turned to look at Frey. He was wide-eyed, but I didn't get the sense that he was scared. He'd completely duped us, so the man was likely trained well enough to fit in here. Instead, he looked as though he was surprised. Surprised that I wasn't fighting back. Or making a plan.

Or doing anything at all.

The first man, the one we'd been talking to came aboard. "The *Wassamassaw*," he said, then whistled. "Quite the ride, Mr. Dixon."

"Yeah," I said. "Thanks."

The next man came up with my father and both stepped onto the deck at the same time. My father righted himself, steadying his frame on the much sturdier boat. He looked up at me. “Mason.”

“Dad.”

That was it. Two words spoken, two men worlds apart crashing together again in a way neither of us wanted. I wanted to just kill him right there, to get it over with, but that feeling once again returned. He was my father. I couldn’t do it.

I followed the first man into the living room, only half-listening as he examined every corner of the space. I’d forgotten the effect it had on people — the *Wassamassaw* wasn’t a particularly luxurious yacht compared to some of the outrageous ones I’d seen, but to someone used to boating around on a speedboat or fishing barge, my ride seemed downright garish. Even though it had been refinished, the interior completely redesigned, I’d opted for a very simple design and decor — since I was neither interested nor good at choosing interior decorations of any space.

“You going to pour us a drink, bartender?” the man asked.

“I usually get a name first,” I shot back.

One more man came aboard, and I assumed it was the over gunman, leaving the driver to keep an eye on their boat. The man followed my father and the man holding his arm, his subcompact hanging by his side in his other hand.

“You can call me Jet.”

“Chet?”

“Jet.”

“Like an airplane?” I asked.

“Like — yeah, like an airplane. Now how ‘bout that drink?”

“What’s your drink?”

“Damnit, Dixon, I don’t care.”

I reached beneath the counter and rummaged around

until my hand found the top of a plastic 1.75L bottle. I pulled it out, keeping the label to myself.

"What is it?" he asked.

"I thought you didn't care." I poured a glass of the liquid and shoved it his direction. "Shouldn't care if it's on ice either, then."

The man sniffed it, held it up to his lips, and took a sip. He didn't spit it out, which was surprising, but he certainly didn't think it was very funny.

"Taaka. It's a vodka. Runs less than ten bucks for a handle of it."

"It tastes awful."

"Well, you should have been more specific," I answered. "Now, if you don't mind getting to the point of why you're here, I have a ship to track down."

The man nodded. "I already told you. We can work together."

"How's that now?"

"We need your guns."

"And I already told you no."

The man holding my father lifted the butt of his subcompact and slammed it into his gut. My dad groaned and collapsed on the floor.

"Knock it off," I said. "I already thought he was dead. Why not just kill him now?"

The man stepped over to my father, pulled out a pistol he'd had in his belt, and held it up to my dad's head. "Sounds fine with me," he said. "Makes it easier, even."

He pressed the safety. I tensed. Unfortunately he was watching me.

"That's what I thought, Dixon," he said. "Even for a schmuck like your old man, you can't watch me do it."

"Try me."

The man laughed. "I don't need to, Dixon. I know men

like you. Known you all my life. You're though, but you're not an idiot. You know there's nothing gained by offing your old man."

I glared at him.

"Kill him now, and you retaliate. Maybe you can get that weapon out from underneath the bar top and get off a round or two. But my guys have a bit of an advantage over your guys."

He was right — his weapons were *made* for this sort of close-distance combat. Far faster and more agile, like their boats. Plus, I didn't *have* a gun underneath the bar. *Note to self.*

"Let him live, and you might just find out what it is we need from you."

"I thought it was my guns," I said. "You could have just shot your way up here, taken them yourself."

The man looked like he was deep in thought for a moment. "I could have, sure. But that would have killed the three of you, and *you're* really what I want."

"We are?"

"You are. The guns are nice, but I seem to remember coming out here with a few more men. I think *you* took them out, so I'll need *you* to replace them."

"I see," I said. "No."

He laughed, amazingly took another sip of the vodka, and walked closer to me at the bar. "Dixon, here's the thing. We have that cute little girl of your."

I cocked my head sideways. "What girl?"

"Oh, you know. You know *very* well. Dark hair, dark skin, beautiful eyes. Pretty good body, too."

Joey's jaw clenched twice, but he didn't move. Just stood by the railing, just outside the door to the living room all the rest of us were in. Unguarded. Alone.

Don't. I hoped he was watching my face, but then again I

wasn't even sure if my face was sending the proper signal. For all I knew it could have been saying, 'go for it, kid.'

"How'd that happen?" Frey asked, suddenly a part of the conversation.

The man — Jet — turned to look at him, and I saw on his face the confusion, as if he'd not even noticed Frey was in the room until just now. "And who might you be?" Jet asked. "We were briefed that there were two of you. You don't strike me as much, so I'm still willing to say there are only two of you, but — it would be poor form to completely ignore you, now wouldn't it?"

Frey coughed. Took a step back. "I — I'm Jonathan Frey."

"Ah, right. Whoever the hell that is."

"How'd you get her?" I asked.

"We just took the boat while it was heading back to the *Rummer*. Simplest thing, really. Couple of shots to the engine, couple to their hull, and they were sinking fast. Just kept a bead on them while one of my guys nabbed her."

"So where is she?"

"Safe, for now. With my team."

So she's on one of the boats heading to the Rummer.

"But I want to be clear, Mason. I am *not* opposed to having a little fun with her before we put a bullet through her head. Not sure if you're a 'save the girl before she dies' kind of guy or a 'save the girl before we have a little fun with her' kind of guy."

"Both."

"Well. In that case, here's your play. It's all you've got, so be thankful you're getting it in the first place. You help us get to Elizondo's ship, get inside, and get him, we give you Shalice back. Alive. You help us but make it difficult, you get her back alive, but after we're done with her."

"Option three?"

"I shouldn't have to spell it out. She dies, you all die, everyone dies. Except Elizondo, and that's the whole point."

I nodded. *This isn't getting easier.* "Okay, well, can we talk about it?"

"No. I've already decided for you, so it's time to move out. I will accompany you to wherever it is you keep those pieces we're so fond of, and you will carry them back up. As many trips as it takes."

"I've got three Bushmasters, that's it."

"Fine, and two of them are sitting against the chair there, so we'll go ahead and start with those." He motioned to his teammate and the man ran over and picked up the weapons. He did it fast, like he'd practiced it, and within seconds he was holding both M4A3s under his left arm while still aiming at us with his subcompact.

"Any other goodies you want to bring along? Remember, you're the ones using these. Elizondo's guys won't be able to tell the difference in the dark, so I'm sure you'd feel better being well-armed."

"I had grenades," I lied. "But I used them against your boat."

The man nodded. "I wondered how you pulled it off. Don't have any more?"

I shook my head.

"Fine. Well we don't have time to check, and they're useless out here anyway. Let's go."

He waited, no doubt wanting me to lead the way to my quarters and give him access to my safe. I thought about it for a moment, looked over at Frey, and then over at —

Joey.

I heard a yelp, a quick groan, and then a splash. All of it was louder than the sound of the speedboat's engine, which the driver had smartly left running, but I knew that I'd heard it, they had, too.

"What the —"

No.

I ran out from behind the bar, Frey by my side. My father and the man guarding him followed, then the two other men inside the living room. We all raced over the deck, dodging the deck chairs and furniture that sprawled out over the top of it.

We were all too late. The boat's engine revved up, loudly, and I saw the silhouette of the driver as he sped away. *Joey.*

One of the men opened fire, but Joey was smart about his escape, turning rapidly and serpentine at random intervals. It was only a matter of seconds before he was completely out of range.

I looked at my father, his head still hanging. I looked at Jet.

"Well," I said. "We're only going to need *two* of those M4s now."

CHAPTER FORTY

THEIR BOATS WERE FAST. I had a hard time getting comfortable while sitting on the edge of the bow of the speeding watercraft. It was curved upward slightly, convex, making it even more slippery and difficult. I clutched the rail with my right hand, but prayed that a rogue wave wouldn't hit beneath me and rip me straight up and into the water.

Frey was doing the same thing opposite me on the port side of the boat. The guns were between us, but neither of us was going to dare letting go of our railing and try to fire on the men behind us.

The boat Joey had taken had had one man on it, the driver. The other four, including my father, were on the *Wassamassaw* when he'd stolen it and taken out the pilot. One of the two remaining boats that had been hovering a quarter-mile away took off after Joey's boat, so that meant that the four-man load of the last speedboat was now holding ten men. It was cramped in the back, and it was nearly impossible to hold on in the front.

Still, the boat was impressively fast, and within minutes we were near the south jetty, aiming for the point we'd previously identified as a good chokepoint. The boat shot through the gap between Morris Island and the south jetty and out into the open waters of Charleston Harbor. We turned right, aiming at a spot slightly northeast, where the *Rummer* would have to be coming from.

"They're coming, just in front of the storm," Jet said from somewhere in the back of the boat. "Guns up, get ready. Shoot at anything that moves. There shouldn't be any civilian vessels out any more, but that's not our problem."

I looked over at Frey. He gave me a shrug. *We're in it now,* I could hear him thinking. Also: *what's the plan, Dixon?*

I was thinking the same thing. I had no idea what we were supposed to do now. I didn't know if Joey was long gone, or if he'd been able to outrun the heavier boat and get to the *Rummer*. Or if he'd gotten through whatever forces Elizondo had thrown at him.

I looked out at the water. An overcast sky, thick cloud cover, and the city was behind us. I couldn't see anything. It was pitch black, the line between the sky and sea completely smudged into a congl'omerate painting of blackness. Our speedboat, not surprisingly, was operating without running lights. They'd planned on a night attack apparently, and I wondered if Elizondo's men had as well. If so, we were in for a long night — neither team would be able to see the other, and we were all racing around between two three-mile-long lines of rock trying to shoot at each other.

We needed to do something. We needed to do something *fast*.

I scanned the horizon, or what I thought was the horizon, once again. A thick layer of fog had settled now, further masking anything that may lay in front of us. I stared at it for a good three minutes, none of the men in the boat with me speaking.

Finally, about a mile out in the distance, I saw a twinkle.

A yellowish light, pale against the fog and smeared outward in all directions by a phenomenon of light. It grew, and then was joined by a few other lights. All were off the horizon a bit, raised up from the surface of the water slightly. They grew and rose, grew and rose, and suddenly I knew what I was seeing.

The Rummer. It was directly in front of us, bearing down, steadily creeping along in the night. We were right in its path, and in another five minutes it would be on top of us.

Then I heard it. Not the *Rummer*, but the boats it was traveling with. A steady roar, a gentle rising in volume, a low, dull note that sounded like the combination of a saw wave synth and a bass drum roll.

"They've got a fleet coming toward us!" one of the men behind me yelled.

"How can you see who it is?"

"They're all coming our direction," he replied. "And they're not shooting at each other."

I knew what he was implying. They were *all* Elizondo's men, his entire fleet, bearing down on us. If the *Rummer* was going to be on us in minutes, these guys would be on us in seconds. We had very little time to do anything, and once again I realized my predicament was multifaceted: I was on an enemy's boat, coerced into working for them, trying to fight off a navy of armed boats, and Joey was nowhere to be found.

Frey would have been helpful if we were on our own turf, but out here, stuck between *two* hard places, he was little better than useless. *I* was useless.

"What's the play, Dixon?" Frey asked.

"I was just going to ask you the same thing," I said.

"I'd suggest getting those weapons ready," Jet said from behind me. "They're going to be firing back, hard and fast."

And they *did* fire, but they didn't wait for us to fire first.

The sky just above the horizon lit up like a pop concert and I could almost *feel* the energy flying our way. There must have been a thousand dots of light, all dancing on and off like Christmas lights on narcotics. The muzzle flash of the guns was followed shortly after by the sound, a terrifying wave of noise that totally consumed me.

The shots were wide and short, hitting the water in front of us in a field that spread about a hundred feet wide and maybe twenty across. It was covering fire, the type used to tell us to get the hell away.

But it didn't stop. It advanced, as if ammunition was no concern for these folks. The rectangular field of bullet impacts on the water's surface shrank, narrowing at the sides and growing smaller still on the horizontal, all while pushing closer to our boat.

And I was going to be the first casualty.

I did the only thing I could think of.

"Frey, get off!" I shouted. I didn't wait to see if he'd heard me. I rolled sideways and off the edge of the speedboat just as it took off. My head bounced against the silicon bumper behind me, but I barely felt it.

I hit the water. Colder than I'd remembered from earlier. I wondered if the storm had anything to do with that, if it could change the water temperature that quickly.

I opened my eyes underwater, but my head quickly broke the surface and I saw Frey there, across from me, wiping the saltwater out of his eyes.

"You okay?" I asked.

"I'm not dead, if that's what you mean."

I treaded water, looking for the boat that had just taken off without us and with our guns.

"What now, Dixon?"

"Hey, we're alive."

"And we're sitting in the middle of the ocean with a hurricane about fifteen minutes away."

As if on cue, the skies opened up and a burst of lightning cracked around us. I saw the storm, even more evil and far larger than I could have imagined, coming in from the southeast. It was close. *Too* close.

"Yeah, I'm not exactly sure about that."

The boat that we'd jumped off of was heading toward the fleet, a last-ditch suicide effort that would undoubtedly end in all eight men, including my father, dead.

The fleet was now interspersing their fire, taking potshots in three-round bursts from whatever automatic rifles they were using. I couldn't see if any of the shots had hit, but it was only a matter of time before they turned their single competitor into one of the hundreds of lost wrecks, forever interred beneath the waters.

Another lightning blast, another crack of thunder, and another boat. *Another boat.*

"Frey," I said.

He looked at me. I pointed to the north, toward the jetty.

"Who is it?"

It was a speedboat, just like the one we'd been on before. Just like the two we'd sunk, and just like the one Joey had stolen.

It had a single driver, and he was heading directly toward us.

Joey.

The kid was a maniac, heading directly for us full speed. I wasn't sure if he'd seen us or not, but I raised my hands up and yelled at the top of my lungs.

Suddenly the air and water in front of me blew up in an explosion of daylight. I winced, covering my eyes, and saw that it was a light. The guy on the boat had pointed a huge flashlight at us, slowed down, and was now making an approach.

"That you, Dixon?" I heard Joey ask. "Damn, that was lucky."

"Lucky that you found us, or lucky that you didn't slice our heads off?" I shot back.

"Yeah," he said. He offered no other explanation. "Here, let me help you guys up."

We swam to the back of his boat and let him pull us up and over the edge onto the back deck. It was colder now, not just from being wet but from the tempest building in the air. I knew it was here, maybe minutes away, and I knew it would be bad. Unlike many storms that come up this way, this hurricane had been building and building and had not yet had landfall, meaning it was raging for some destruction.

I was about to ask what had happened, how he had fared, when a crackling sound came from the tiny speakers near the wheel. A voice came through, asking for support. Gunshots punctuated the distress call, which came through the speakers just after I heard them in the distance in real life. The battle was raging, and there was no telling how long Jet's single boat would be able to fend off the fleet of Elizondo's men.

"That's the radio," Joey explained. "They were all chattering on it when I took this boat. Then I heard a bunch of gunshots and more calls for help. It was kind of surreal, actually. I think their entire force is gone."

Frey and I nodded simultaneously. "We jumped ship when we figured that out. Jet's guys are the only ones left. My dad's with them, but they're facing a massive onslaught from Elizondo."

"Yeah," Joey said. "I heard each boat going down. They called in their position, then said something to the effect that Elizondo's got way more firepower than they were prepared for."

"I knew it," Frey said. "I knew it."

"And I heard something else, too," Joey said.

I raised an eyebrow. Joey's face was lit up with a grin, but it looked terrifying in the flashing lightning happening all around us.

"I heard one of them say 'they've got the girl,'" he said. "It's Shalice. She's alive. And she's with Elizondo's men."

CHAPTER FORTY-ONE

WE FLOATED FOR A BIT, taking a brief respite from the wild insanity that was playing out just to the north of us. The speedboat my father was on was somehow still alive, judging by the sporadic back-and-forth shots I could hear between the bursts of thunder. I still couldn't see anything at all, save for the moments of brightness from the flashes of lightning now surrounding us.

I wanted out, to head into Charleston and then home and just make it all go away. I wanted to ignore the fact that I was worried about my old man, if only to know what his fate was going to be. And I wanted to not care at all about Joey and Shalice, and the fact that she was still in very real danger.

And then there was Frey. If we stopped, he would continue. He'd all but told us that, but I knew it intuitively as well. He was on a mission, and there was something deeper to that mission than he'd told us. I could guess — he was part of a small team that had been given an impossible mission, and there hadn't been enough budget to go around *before* they'd been given their task. There might be three others, four max, working with him in the office, but he'd likely be the only field agent. He had no partner, and he had no police force he could call for backup.

So he'd go in, guns blazing, just like Jet and the team he represented had. A suicide mission, for sure.

I sighed. That meant I was still in it, still fighting. I'm not one to toot my own horn, and I certainly am not one to think that I'm good at everything I do, but there are two things in this life I know I can do well: scramble in a difficult situation and make drinks.

Making drinks wasn't on the agenda tonight. But I had been trained in the Army and by my father growing up and later through private channels, and — most importantly — I was naturally gifted in the art of battle. One-on-one, perfectly matched in weaponry, I'd bet on myself every time. Even two-on-one and sometimes three. Hand-to-hand combat wasn't a specialty, but I'd won my fair share of scrapes. I preferred to do things the easy way, the way they made sense to me: to run in and figure things out as I went along. That way I could adapt and roll with the punches as they came, keeping everyone involved on their toes.

That was where people made mistakes. On their toes. I thrived in those moments, though.

So that's what I knew we were doing. Running in, trying to get to Shalice. Somehow, some way.

"Any idea?" I heard Frey ask.

Joey shook his head. I troweled off using a tiny hand towel I'd found in a seat compartment. It smelled of gasoline and oil, but I didn't care. It was drier than my hair and clothes and it was only getting colder.

"Storm's coming in," Frey said. "That could be good for us."

"It'd better be good for us," I said. "We'll use it to our

advantage. Go in quiet as possible, but use the storm for cover."

"That means we have to wait until there *is* a storm."

That moment the heavens opened. The sky split like someone had just gutted the bottom of a universe-sized water tank, and gallons of water began spilling around us. It was an *absurd* amount of water, and for a moment I was worried that the boat would fill up and sink. But there wasn't enough space in the boat to hold water, and the entire front end that Frey and I had been sitting on earlier easily provided the buoyancy it needed to stay afloat.

Still, the water was annoying. The rain fell in cold, hard sheets, both piercing and chilly, and within seconds my hand towel was soaking wet and useless. I tossed it into a ball into a corner of the boat and looked up at the pitch black sky.

"This ought to work," I said.

The noise was deafening, and I knew it would be more than enough cover for the volume of our engine, even at full throttle.

"Yeah," Joey said. "It'll be more than enough. Let's do it."

Frey walked between us. "I'm all for moving in on Elizondo guys, but can we get some idea of a plan?"

I shrugged. Joey smiled. "This is definitely Mason's area of expertise."

Frey looked at me, the surprise not hidden on his face.

"He's kidding," I said. "Obviously. But I think this is one of those times when it'd be best to just follow my lead."

"And what's that look like?" he asked.

"Just roll with it. Whatever happens, happens. Try not to die."

"Wow," Frey said. "You should write a leadership book."

I smiled as Joey sat down behind the wheel of the speedboat. We'd drifted to the west a bit and were now facing the shoreline of Morris Island. It was a blacker black against the already black nothingness of everything else, and the only reason I could see that it *was* land was the gentle haze of the city lights thrown upward far behind it.

"It's worked for us before," I said. "Just trust your gut and don't get shot."

CHAPTER FORTY-TWO

THE PLAN WAS SIMPLE: WAIT for Elizondo's ship to pass, get behind it, and come alongside the Handysize vessel. From there we'd attempt to get onboard. We didn't know how.

Even I was feeling rather pessimistic about this plan. There were still gunshots, but they had receded into the distance quite a ways, or else the rain was so pounding that everything seemed to be miles away. The *Rummer* was in front of us now, still a quarter-mile away and inside the jetties, while we sat in the spot we'd originally decided upon, right off the northeast coast of Morris Island at the mouth of Charleston Harbor.

The speedboats were either silently lurking near the *Rummer* or they were all out chasing Jet and whoever was still alive on his own boat. We didn't care, because we didn't know. Worrying about it would get us nowhere, so Joey and I had decided to just go for it. Frey hadn't argued, so I took that to mean he didn't have a better idea.

"What are we waiting for, exactly?" I asked.

"The *Rummer* needs to get fully inside the harbor," Joey replied. "That way we'll have the best chance of getting in unseen."

"They have radar, Joey," I said. "They already see us."

"True, but at least this way it's *only* radar that can see us. If we're lucky. If we went in before them, so we're sitting right in front of them, then they get a heads-up view of us, clear as day."

"So you're hoping they're not going to be able to tell who the little green dot on their radar screen is and just let us through?"

He shrugged. "Yeah. Something like that."

"Great."

The lightning and hazy cast of greenish-yellow light spilling into the harbor from the city showed us the location of the *Rummer*. It was a half-mile away, broadside with the stern of our own boat, and moving fast. There were no speedboats near it.

"I'm also hoping he's true to his word," Joey said. "His guy told you that we were supposed to protect him, remember? So if they see a single boat heading in, they'll hopefully assume that it's you. No one would risk opening fire on a ship while they're in a speedboat, you know?"

"Sure," I said. "I guess. Let's hope you're right."

"Okay," Joey said. "Almost."

The *Rummer* turned to the northeast, just a bit, and continued plowing forward into the deeper waters of the bay.

"Now!" he yelled to himself. He threw the throttle forward and gunned it for the backside of the *Rummer*. The force threw me backwards onto the hard floor the boat. I hit my head against the engine compartment but decided to stay down, lying on my back on the floor of the boat. It was far more comfortable than trying to fight the rain and wind and waves at the front of the vessel or try to stand in the middle of it.

Our journey lasted thirty seconds. I could sense the side of the great ship even before I could really see it. It was black, just like the sky and the water and the horizon, but it had a very definite absoluteness to it that I could feel. The rain sounded like it had gone away, but it was just one of my ears playing tricks on my mind — the *Rummer* blocked out a majority of the thunderous weather.

And just like Frey had described, the Handysize carrier rose about twenty feet — maybe less — from the surface of the ocean. It almost seemed close enough to jump to.

"Grab the anchor," Joey said. "There should be one in one of the compartments. We can swing it up and over, maybe climb up that way."

I nodded, started rummaging through the cases of equipment onboard. There wasn't much — the gang that owned these boats kept them sparse for whatever reason. Likely they had just purchased them for this mission, not caring much that they were lacking some necessary gear for legality.

"I'm not sure there is one," I yelled back to Joey. "These guys didn't really —"

An amazing blast of light hit us and lit up everything on deck. I froze, still crouched over the open compartment.

The sound of a voice crackling through a megaphone reached my ears next. '*We are sending down a ladder,*' the voice said. '*Mr. Elizondo would like to speak with you.*'

A rope ladder immediately unfurled and fell down the side of the ship, landing just in front of the pilot's seat on the convex front of the boat. I looked over at Frey and Joey. All of us were unarmed. Unprepared. Soaked to the core, ready to give in to anything. But the two men stood still, stoic. They just looked up at the shadowy figures leaning over the edge of the *Rummer*. Three men, two of them pointing rifles at us.

More than enough to shut me up.

"Well," Joey said. "I guess a ladder will be easier to climb than a rope."

CHAPTER FORTY-THREE

ROCKFORD ELIZONDO WAS A WALKING contradiction. Dark, deep-set eyes, brown hair, and South American features, his skin was stark white. He looked more Italian or Spanish than American or South American, but his accent was pure New England. Like a rich frat boy, smooth-talking but quick.

"Welcome," he said. "It's good to meet you face-to-face."

I gave him a single head-dip nod.

We were standing in the bridge, high above the rest of the ship, and for the third time that day I was toweling off. My shoes were still wet, my socks still squishing with every step I took, and I knew there would be a couple blisters forming on my toes. To make matters worse, my socks and shoes still reeked of fuel.

There were six people in the room — Joey, Frey, and me, as well as two of Elizondo's men, each armed and standing near the two doors. Elizondo himself stood at the center of the bridge, his back to the wide set of windows. He stood with his hands behind his back, a proud leader ready to address his subjects. His mouth was a small line, straight and empty and dead on his face, not a smile but not a frown. The men he had employed as guards tried to imitate their boss' pose, but their guns gave away their intensity. Each of them carried a modified AK47, the most popular assault rifle available on the black market, which also told me something about the type of men we were dealing with.

These guys were hired on to fight for Elizondo, to protect him and his product. And the product was massive. I saw the front end of the ship out the window on the bridge, completely covered with stacks of square crates. I imagined each of the crates held four or five fifty-three gallon barrels, and within those barrels, aging rum.

I wondered how he was planning to get it all into the country unseen.

"You failed."

I frowned. "You're alive, aren't you?"

"I believe I am. But that's thanks to my men, and my boats. Not you. You sat back, waiting for everything to end."

"Seemed like a good way to stay not dead," I replied.

"And it was," Elizondo said. "But it was not what I requested of you."

"Oh," I said. "I didn't realize it was a request. It sounded a lot like an order. And I'm not really one to take orders."

"I figured that," Elizondo said. "Which was why we took some collateral."

"Shalice," Joey said. I saw his fists clenching at his sides.

"That her name?" Elizondo asked. "She wouldn't tell us anything, not at first. I had my men remove her clothes, one piece at a time, until she was just wearing that cute swimsuit you must know."

Joey took a step forward, then stopped himself.

"Of course, by then we didn't *care* for her name. I just needed to know who you two were."

"And?"

"And I was satisfied. Navy, Army, you two had a decent service record. Sort of washed up now, though? Just running a bar in a city no one lives in."

"Something like that."

"But it was *this* person I was most interested in." He took a few strides forward and ended up in front of Jonathan Frey. Frey was back to his distributor self, nervous and shifting his weight from foot to foot.

"What's your name?" Elizondo asked.

"F — Frey. Jonathan Frey."

"The *distributor.*"

"Yes."

"And what do you *distribute,* Mr. Frey?"

"Uh, well, I have all kinds of —"

"Liquor, I presume?"

"Y — yes."

"Well, in that case," Elizondo said. "We're competitors."

He lifted his head just a bit and motioned to one of his men. The man at the port-side door turned ten degrees with his upper body, lifted his rifle, and fired.

Frey was too slow. He lurched forward but the bullet caught him right in the side. He fell to the floor, the blood already falling out of him.

I started running, making my way toward Elizondo, but the guy at the *other* door was tracking me. I noticed it out of the corner of my eye and at the last possible moment changed my strategy. I dove straight down to the floor, just as the man's rifle coughed, the bullet flew over my head and smacked through the glass, and I hit the hard laminate floor.

The wind left me, but I refused to stop. I crawled forward, then rolled sideways, keeping instruments and desks on the bridge between me and the two shooters in the room. I heard Joey scuffling, his deep grunts telling me he was engaging one of the men. *Good,* I thought. *That leaves one guy with a gun and Elizondo.*

Suddenly Elizondo was there, in front of me, looking down at me. With a gun.

Never mind, I thought.

"Get up," he said.

"No, I'm good down —"

He kicked at my head, missed, and hit my side. It didn't feel any better than if he'd have hit my head.

"Get up," he said again.

I picked myself up and straightened out my damp pants. Smelled the whiff of fuel emanating from my shoes once again. The smell had always made me feel nauseated. I sniffed, then exhaled through my nostrils to try to push away the awful aroma.

"Follow me."

He didn't wait, didn't care to make sure I was following. He just walked toward the port-side door, the man standing guard near it shifting sideways as his boss strolled through. I stepped over Frey's body, seeing that he was alive and breathing, but holding his bleeding side as he lay on the floor. I wanted to stop, to help him, but the man at the door tracked me with the barrel of his rifle and I knew what he was implying.

I nodded and stepped over the threshold and started down after Elizondo, down the same stairs we'd scaled a few minutes earlier. I wasn't sure why Elizondo had made us come all the way up here, other than some odd power play.

I remembered Frey's words. Elizondo was a borderline schizophrenic, a control freak. Perhaps the man just had to do things a certain way. I'd met people like that before.

The guard followed behind me, then Joey and finally the last guard. *Great. Three on two.* And the odds were *not* in my favor: we were still unarmed. And wet, which just made things worse. No one liked fighting in wet clothes.

CHAPTER FORTY-FOUR

WE FOLLOWED ELIZONDO ALL THE way down to a floor below the main deck. If the crew slept in their own quarters on some level of the ship, this deck wasn't it. I followed the length of hallway that out to the main floor and was stunned. The level was the height of two floors, with at least as much floor space as the main deck. And stretching from floor to ceiling on both sides of the massive room were barrels. Oak. The liquid inside some of them seeping slowly out between the tight cracks.

"My supply," Elizondo said.

"Rum barrels?" I asked.

"Mostly. Some brandy as well, and a few are the barrels from experimental whiskies my partners are working on."

"They're all full?"

He smiled. "*Quite* full. Each of them has fifty-three gallons in it. Checked just this morning by my team."

I made a face, still admiring the massive space.

"And each of the crates on the top deck holds four more barrels."

"How do you sneak it all in?" Joey asked.

"Sneak?" Elizondo turned and faced us. "I don't understand."

"All of this is illegal, Elizondo. Isn't it?" I asked. "Not to mention your security force out there, shooting up anything that moves."

He laughed. An odd, giggly chuckle. "I see. I understand what you think. Yes, I can see how you would believe that. But you might be surprised that I have an import license for everything that you see."

"Bullshit."

"Well, believe what you will. You may have noticed the lack of coast guard vessels outside, as well as port authority. My business has always been in question, but I can assure you that I am nothing if not a law-abiding citizen."

"Yeah? Then why go through all this trouble, Elizondo? Why hire these grunts to shoot at us and protect you and bring you in safely if you've got the entire United States government at your back?"

His eyes glistened, widening. "Ah," he said. A long, slow drawl on the end of the word. "That's just it. I do *not* have the United States government behind me at all."

"I'm sorry?"

"You know who is in charge of what comes and goes into and out of this country?"

"The government?"

"Yes. And do you know who decides *specifically* who gets those import and export contracts?"

"Uh… the government?"

"Indeed. And do you know who *pays* the government for that privilege?"

"I'm going to say, 'people like you?'"

"Yes," Elizondo said. "But *not* me. Other people, sure. But not *me*. I have been working in this field for *years*, and I'm *good* at it. But I haven't gotten the contracts I need to get the *one-hundred percent legal* products I carry into the United States."

Joey scoffed. "Then it doesn't really sound *legal*, Elizondo."

He glared at Joey. "Well, it would *seem* that way. But there is not constitutional limit on the total gross amount of product that can enter or leave the country, except in times of declared famine or embargo. So what you're talking about is called an oligarchy. A collection of a few suppliers that are in tight with the government, forcing them to keep the little players like me out."

"You don't seem so little." I was hoping a small compliment like that would keep him talking, as he seemed to be enjoying this final bad-guy-tells-all scenario. It would end — this wasn't a movie, after all, but I was determined to figure out where he was keeping Shalice. At this point I assumed it was either in his private quarters, which would be somewhere near the bridge, or in a brig, which would be belowdecks somewhere.

That meant we had a *lot* of searching to do, and we didn't have a lot of time to do it. And I was quite sure Elizondo wasn't going to just let us snoop around his boat.

"You don't understand — little isn't a number on a balance sheet. It means that I'm not 'in' with the bigwigs that are playing the game in Washington. The American alcohol industry has been highly regulated since its inception, and to this day it is one of the most difficult to get into."

"Yeah, I know. I run a bar."

At this he actually laughed. I wasn't sure if he was making fun of me or confiding in me, from one business associate to another. I decided to take it as an insult.

"This is my way of telling the industry what I think of them," he said. He turned back around to face the storage space, leaving his two guards to do their jobs, which they performed admirably, keeping their rifles low and pointed our way.

Joey looked over at me, a slight frown on his face. *He seems weird,* I could hear him thinking.

I agreed. *Definitely off.*

"What are you showing us this for?" I blurted out. "Why now? If you're going to kill us, just —"

He laughed again, but this time it fell into the enormous room and echoed throughout the space. It was a bold, hearty belly laugh, completely out of context for the man who'd done it and the situation. "*I* am not going to kill you, Mr. Dixon. *Why* would I do *that*?"

"Look around, asshole," I said. "Your men killed how many guys today? My father was one of them."

"The man who wanted to kill *me*," he said, under his breath. "Seems ironic."

"And yet here we are. Joey and I got into this because we were lied to. Whatever you're going to do to us, I'd sure like to find out."

"And you shall. All in good time."

"But?"

"But I thought you'd like to see your little prize first," he said.

"Shalice?" Joey asked.

"Follow me."

Elizondo started off again, walking through the natural hallway formed by the towers of barrels that had been stacked on either side of the room. Each tower was strapped down using an interesting combination of buckle straps and cordage, holding the barrels upright and against the walls at the same time.

I'd never been to a rickhouse before, but I knew enough about the methods of moonshining and making whiskey from my research into the subject. The distillate was mixed, usually cut with a bit of water to a certain proof that aged well, and stored in fifty-three gallon barrels resting on their side for years. For straight bourbon it was four years and up in virgin American White Oak barrels — The Federal Standards of Identity for Bourbon is a jokingly real government entry in the Code of Regulations stipulating what can and can not be called 'bourbon.' — while other aged spirits were kept in their barrels for differing time frames.

The point of a rickhouse was twofold: first, by storing the barrels on their side, the barrels could be moved and sloshed around easily, allowing the distillate to interact more with the oak wood and help with the colorization and imparted flavor profile. The second reason was temperature: the higher a barrel was in a rickhouse, the higher the temperature swings between day and night. In bourbon country, temperatures at the top of a stuffy, non-climate-controlled rickhouse could reach 130 degrees Fahrenheit in the summertime, then plummet in the winter months. By rotating the barrels from the top of the house to the floor level, the distillate could benefit from the expanding and contracting of the wood at different times of year. Sunlight, temperature, and regular contact with the wood it was stored in were all major variables for aging a great spirit.

This 'rickhouse' seemed nothing like what I would have expected. It seemed that the barrels had been put in here and on deck not for proper storage and aging technique but to try to cram as many as possible inside.

Odd. Just like Elizondo.

We were at the other end of the room, toward the bow of the ship, when Elizondo made a hard right and walked us through another open door and into another hallway. This hallway stretched from bow to halfway back to the stern, following the starboard side of the hull. Individual rooms with simple, narrow doors were spaced on both sides of the hall.

The crew's quarters.

The rooms were numbered in descending order, the odds on the left and the even numbered rooms on the right. We were between rooms 13 and 12, so we were close to the front of the ship. The end of the hallway was about fifty feet ahead of us.

"She's in room 2," Elizondo said.

"We can see her?" Joey asked. I could hear the elation building in his voice. Hesitant, but present.

"Indeed you can," Elizondo said. "In fact, I'd suggest you spend as much time with her as possible."

He stopped in front of room 2. I listened, but couldn't hear anything from inside the room.

"Why's that, Elizondo? What's this all about?"

Elizondo stepped forward, knocked on the door, then stuck a key in the lock and turned it. The door fell open into the room. It was a sparsely furnished room. A chair, a desk, a bed. A mirror on the wall, a small toilet behind a curtain. No shower or bath.

Shalice was on the bed. She sat up when Elizondo opened the door. She was in a swimsuit, just as Elizondo had said.

Joey pushed past him and rushed in. "Are — are you okay?" he asked. "Did they hurt you?"

She was crying, but she hugged him back. She shook her head. "No. Not really. They roughed me up a bit. Scared me. They — they took my clothes, to get me to talk. I didn't know what to say."

I looked back at Elizondo. The man's small, thin, mouth was back to its nonchalant shape. "You're going to pay for this, Elizondo."

He nodded, almost reverently. "I'm sure I will. But we're

running out of time. I'd like you to stay with Shalice, to keep her company."

"Where are you going?"

"I have an appointment."

He turned and walked out the door. I followed, but was met by the end of the mens' weapons. "What's this about, Elizondo?" I asked again.

He turned around, faced me. "It's about money," he said. "It's always about money. Your father, I hear he was told there was money involved. 'Take me out and take over my business,' something like that?"

I nodded.

"He was right. There *is* money here. But it's not as easy as they think. I told you a bit about that. You don't just walk into this business, or steal your way into it. It takes *time*, and even then — even when you've paid your dues — the big guys cut you out because they can. Because you're competition to them, and they've got the government on their side."

I was shaking my head, not understanding. I wasn't sure if Joey was even listening. "I don't get it, Elizondo. *What's this about?"*

He smiled, but just shrugged. "I tried to make it work," he said. "But I've got a nice life for me down in Cuba. Great house, plenty of servants. I wonder why I even ever wanted to work up here. I should have just stayed down there, just focused on the Caribbean."

"So go back," I said. "I'm not stopping you."

"I know," he said. "You certainly aren't. And I will. But like I said, I have an appointment."

He rolled his wrist out and checked a watch he wore with the face on the wrong side of his arm. It was gold, gaudy and probably real, ugly as it was. He shook it, it disappeared into a sleeve, and then he walked away.

One of the men with the guns slammed the door in my face while the other pointed it at me to discourage me from any funny business. I heard the first man fumbling around with a key, then the lock sliding into place.

I waited until I assumed they'd left then slammed my shoulder into the door.

CHAPTER FORTY-FIVE

THE DOOR WOULD GIVE, JUST a bit, but it was going to take some work to break it open. It was a simple construction, just a couple sheets of plastic with a forming layer of aluminum or something lightweight sandwiched between them. Like a cooler lid, or a screen door without the screen section.

Odd, again, that he would leave the three of us in such an unsecured room. He knew it was easy enough to break out, and it was a wonder why Shalice hadn't already figured out how.

"What are we going to do?" Shalice asked.

Joey hugged her again. "We'll figure something out," he said. "We always do."

"We're going to get out," I said.

"But the men," she said. "They'll shoot us."

"Those two goons?" I asked. They're not worth the scruples he's paying them."

"No," she said. "All the other guys. There were at least forty of them. All over the place, in the rooms around us, on deck. Everywhere."

Joey and I looked at each other. I shook my head. "Those guys are gone, Shalice. There wasn't anyone else on board. Maybe three guards. There were only two with us once we got up to the bridge."

She frowned. "Where'd they all go, then?"

"Could be that they were on the boats," Joey said. "He had an army with him."

"A navy, more accurately," I added.

"Maybe," she said.

We sat there a moment, thinking. Trying to figure it out.

"This is weird," Joey said.

"Yeah. I picked up on that."

"What's his move? I mean, what's the point of all this? Grab us, stick us in here with Shalice, then leave. Why not kill us?"

"Maybe he plans on killing us later."

Shalice's eyes were wide, but I didn't care. She'd been through the worst of it, so a few words weren't going to hurt her.

Joey shook his head. "That wouldn't be an intelligent use of his resources. And it sounds like everyone's leaving the ship. It was ghost town out there."

"Yeah, you're right," I said.

"And all that rum," he added. "Just… sitting there. He's floating a ship full of hard liquor into Charleston, all —"

"It's not liquor," I said. I realized it just when he said the word. I heard *liquor* and something clicked. Or, rather, something *didn't* click. It hadn't added up, and I suddenly knew why.

"It's not?"

"Joey," I said. "You ever seen a rickhouse?"

He shook his head.

"I've seen pictures. It's where they store whiskey for

aging. Distilleries use them, and they're just warehouses full of barrels."

"Like the one out there?" Joey asked.

"With a major difference. You store barrels in a rickhouse on their *side,* so you can easily roll them and stosh around the insides. All the barrels out there are stacked, and the towers are at least three deep on each side. Probably so you can fit more in, but there would be no way to move any of them around, ever."

"Maybe it's just for transport," Joey said.

"But he said they were *full*, remember? Fifty-three gallons each, checked them this morning."

"Yeah?"

When you age liquor, there's something called the 'angel's share.' It's a percentage of distillate that's lost to seepage, then evaporation."

"So the barrels wouldn't be full?"

"Never. *Maybe* they'd be close to full when they were first filled, but if that were the case we'd see a lot more of them seeping. The black lines where the planks of wood touch each other. There would be bubbles and slow, sugary distillate seeping out of every one of them."

"What are you saying?"

"I'm saying he's *not* transporting rum," I said. "Or any other spirit. If the stuff was brand new, each barrel was full, he'd leave them in Cuba, or wherever he'd first filled them. It's way cheaper to store it down there than try to transport it here, get it unloaded and transported to a rickhouse, and that doesn't even include the land cost. If he was bringing rum into the States he'd be smarter to bottle it *there*, then bring it in."

"So what's inside the barrels?"

"Who knows," I said. "But it's not going to be any good for us, whatever it is. Help me with this door."

Joey walked over to the chair, a utilitarian piece of metal and cushion, and lifted it over his head. "I think we can just break the handle off," he said. "This isn't the most secure room."

"You can say that again," I said. I watched him do. He lifted it higher, aimed for the handle, then swung down with a solid amount of force. The loud crash rang throughout the room, but I wondered if it could be heard out in the hallway.

Or maybe they've already left, I thought.

Joey hit it again and the handle popped off, crashing to the floor and bouncing around a few times before it came to rest against the curtain separating the toilet from the rest of the room.

He tried the door, but it was still locked. "Damn," he said, "I thought that would work."

"It *did* work, Joey," I said. "It's just stuck. Here, move over."

Joey stepped to the side and I stepped back a few feet from the door. I focused on the area just to the right of where the handle had been a moment ago, then pulled my foot up and back. I kicked as hard as I could, careful to land my foot flat against the door. The door popped open easily, and I was staring at the room just across the narrow hall.

"There," I said. "Let's go. Help Shalice."

He was one step ahead of me, holding Shalice around the waist. She was able to walk, but she was tired and weak, and she didn't turn down the help.

We stepped outside and turned left. I hoped we could get back upstairs without any trouble, but I had no idea what was happening down here in the first place. If Elizondo had wanted us locked up, he hadn't taken a lot of pains to ensure we were. That meant we were either not important to him or it didn't matter anymore.

Because no one's left on the ship, I suddenly found myself thinking. *Because they're all gone already, because…*

I smelled another whiff of fuel as my squeaky shoes hit the floor. The open passageway that led to the large interior storage space must have wafted some air up and into my nostrils.

"Smells like gas," Joey said.

"Yeah, it's been like that the whole time I've been here," Shalice said. "I've had a headache since they brought me here."

I froze.

Voices.

One was over a handheld radio, the other was from the man operating the radio. "Yes sir," he said. "Confirmed, four minutes thirty-seven seconds. Over."

I listened, then crept forward. The voice was right around the corner. Inside the warehouse of barrels.

What in the world?

I listened another few seconds, trying to determine whether the man was alone. I couldn't hear any other voices, or movement whatsoever. I turned back to Joey, brought my voice down to the barest whisper. "I'm going to see who this guy is. Probably one of the guards. Stay here with Shalice."

He nodded.

I walked out into the warehouse, knowing that the tower of barrels to my left would keep me out of sight for another few seconds. I slowed, crouched, then leaned sideways to get a look at the man.

It was one of the guards who'd accompanied us to the bridge and then back down here with Elizondo. His rifle was sitting on the floor next to him, but it was on his right side, away from me. He was kneeling on the floor and holding something in his hands, like a tablet of some sort. I couldn't recognize an iPad from a graphing calculator, but I knew this was some sort of touchscreen apparatus. The screen glowed bright, lighting up his features. It was encased in a thick rubbery rectangle, and I imagined it would be capable of surviving a fall from the top of one of these towers without much trouble.

Time to make my move, I told myself. The guy was busy, programming in something related to what Elizondo had told him over the radio. '*Four minutes thirty-seven seconds.*'

He finished, frowning once and then nodding to himself. He held the device in one hand while gripping the radio in his other. He brought the radio up to his mouth. "Sir, we're live. Give me the signal."

CHAPTER FORTY-SIX

I HEARD THE VOICE — ELIZONDO'S — crackle back immediately over the radio. "Good. Five seconds… three. Two. One. Set."

"Set."

The man pressed a button on the screen that I couldn't see, then hit another sequence of things with a fat index finger. Finally, he put the radio down and used both hands to press the device flat against the front of one of the barrels. It held in place, but he watched it for a second to be sure. Another nod.

Time's up, buddy.

I rushed him. It was easy, really, since he obviously had no idea I had even been standing there, and he was only five feet away from me. I tackled his head, holding on with the crook of my elbow around his neck, and gave him a perfect wrestling move to the ground. He fell on the gun, which was even better. I threw one of my long legs over his torso and squeezed, holding him tight, and tried to grab at the rifle with my free hand.

I realized quickly that he was stronger than me and a bit

more fit. He writhed sideways like an alligator, trying to spin me off of him, but I held fast. I wasn't hurting him though, and that was a problem. I could hang onto him as long as I wanted but it would do absolutely no good if he wasn't going to pass out.

He tried to bite at my arm, but I had it below his chin. He tried kicking me with the back of his boot, but again my legs were safely out of the way. It was a standoff, and neither of us was going to get the upper hand anytime soon.

Joey was there. He must have heard it, or been expecting it, but he was suddenly standing over us. I watched him step right up to the guy and look down at him, then at the tablet stuck to the barrel wall, then back to me. He kicked, a quick, tapping thing with just the point of his shoe.

But it worked. It hit the guy right in the eye and he howled in pain. I felt him weaken a bit and I took advantage of it by tightening my own grip on his neck. He coughed, trying to breathe, and I knew then that I had him.

Joey kicked again, this time for the other eye. The man was defeated now, and he knew it. He stopped struggling, just laying there for a moment. I refused to let it alter my approach, and I tightened around his neck even more.

Another fifteen seconds passed and he was out. No breathing. No movement.

I groaned.

"You okay, boss?"

"Yeah," I said. "But I wanted to take him myself. You ruined it."

Joey smiled and held out a hand, helping me up. Shalice was there in the doorway, watching, her eyes wide.

"It's okay," Joey said. "We're okay."

She swallowed, looked from me to the dead guy to her boyfriend and then nodded quickly. Then she looked at the tablet on the barrel.

"Four minutes and some change," Joey said. "I'd be willing to bet we don't want to be anywhere near here when it gets to zero."

"I won't take that bet," I said. "Let's go."

I grabbed the man's rifle while Joey reached for his radio. I held the assault rifle in one hand while I rummaged around on his belt with my other hand. I was looking for anything that might be helpful to us, keys or information or anything.

I found handcuffs. I took them and stuck them in my wet pocket and then stood up and nodded to Joey and Shalice. "Back the way we came. Run."

They didn't need any more encouragement. Shalice looked awkward wearing nothing but a bikini, but she was fast. Joey had to hustle to keep up, and they made it through the interior of the barrel storage area twenty paces before me.

"Head up one level," I said. "Main deck. Find a way to get off the boat."

"Where are you going?" Joey asked.

"I've got an appointment."

CHAPTER FORTY-SEVEN

I TOOK THE STAIRS TWO at a time and made it to the bridge about thirty seconds later. I walked in the same door I'd been through twice already, looked to the right, and saw Elizondo fiddling with something on a console.

I shot him, twice. Right in the back of his left leg. No hesitation.

He crumpled to the floor, coughing and seething. He scrambled around looking for something to fight back with, but I rushed over and stepped on his arm. I looked down at him. "What the hell is this, Elizondo?" I asked.

He sputtered. "I — I told you…"

"This is your little way of telling everyone else what you think of their system, isn't it?"

He glared up at me.

"This is just a little toddler acting out, huh? A rich kid who didn't get his way?"

"It's not… like —"

"It's *exactly* like that. Except you're richer and and crazier than a toddler."

"You're not going to kill me," he said. "You can't."

"I could," I said. "You'd better believe I could. I *want* to. I've done it before. Guys like you are better off dead. Really. No sense waxing philosophical about it."

"Then do it."

"Well, you know, I've had a little time to think. About thirty seconds on my way up here from down below. Here's what we'll do."

I grabbed his wrist and yanked it, hard. I took the handcuffs from my pocket and slammed them onto his wrist and then onto the metal post that held up one leg of one of the consoles. It had been mounted into the frame of the ship itself, so I knew it would hold just fine.

"Wha — what are you doing?" Elizondo asked. His deep, brooding eyes glistened in the darkness, reflecting the blinking lights and dim glows of the apparatus and consoles I couldn't even begin to understand.

"I'm making sure you get to lay in this bed you've made, Elizondo."

I looked out the front window. Saw the ship stretching out in front of me, the black waters of Charleston Harbor in front of that, and the lights in the city off in the distance. We were moving fast, heading right for the port.

Heading right for a group of ships clustered around the dock. There were Handymax size, ranging from just smaller than the *Rummer* to about twice the size.

"No — you don't understand," he said, nearly whining now.

I nodded. "But I do. I've got about three minutes to figure out how to stop this ship, buddy. You want to help me out?"

He glared.

"That's what I thought. I'd recommend just sitting there quietly, then. Could be a long three minutes."

I looked around. The wheel, the thousand buttons and knobs and levers. The throttle.

The throttle.

That was easy enough. I didn't know if a ship like this could be stopped properly by simply cramming to throttle back, but it didn't matter. I wasn't too worried about breaking anything. This ship would be on the bottom of Charleston Harbor inside an hour.

I yanked it backward. The ship groaned, creaked. I thought I heard popping sounds, either from the flexing of tons of steel working against physics, then de-stressing into their new locations.

The ship slowed immediately. We were floating, so we were still moving, but we'd slowed considerably and still were.

Next step.

I looked around, trying to find a button or a knob or something simple. I found it near the wheel, right off the right side of the console everything was mounted on.

Anchor.

I punched it, hard. Didn't hear anything at first, but then a louder, deeper groaning sound.

Come on, I thought. *Two-and-a-half minutes.*

I was guessing, but I figured I had at least that long. I *hoped* I had at least that long.

The anchor was descending, or so I hoped. It sounded like *something* down there was moving, so I figured that was good enough. I hoped it was good enough.

I looked once more at Elizondo, staring up at me. Helpless.

I saw Frey in the corner, no longer breathing. Felt the twinge of useless loss washing over me, but I pushed it to the side. That would have to wait.

There was a front door on both sides of the bridge,

leading out to a white staircase that descended down to the main deck. I took it and walked to the side of the *Rummer.* I looked over and saw nothing but blackness.

From the other side of the ship I heard the sound of an engine starting. One of the speedboats. I ran over to the starboard side of the *Rummer* and peered over the edge.

"Let's go, man!" Joey yelled. "Hurry up."

I saw the rope ladder they'd used to get onto the boat and the rope that was holding the smaller boat to the *Rummer.* I undid the knot and took the ladder down. As soon as my feet hit the deck, Joey threw the throttle into forward and then full. I lost my balance but fell into the center of the boat, right where I had been before. Laying down, stretched out, my head uncomfortably but securely resting on the carpeted side of the engine compartment.

"How much time?" Joey yelled down to me.

"No idea," I shouted back. "Just keep driving until we can't see the *Rummer* anymore."

He nodded, then focused on a spot where the harbor narrowed into one of the rivers that spilled into it. We were safe, we were heading away from the ship, and we were in the home stretch.

That's when the *Rummer* exploded.

CHAPTER FORTY-EIGHT

THE DETONATION OF THE SHIP happened in stages. The flames seemed to arise first, then the powerful heatwave carried the pressure to us, rocking the speedboat while we raced away from it.

The sound was next, but it wasn't a singular explosion. The blast ripped upward into the rain and thunder, adding even more confusion and hell to the mix. It was impressive, honestly. We were safely away from it and Joey killed the engine and we just watched it.

The hurricane was parked just off the coast, as the rain was still intense but the winds were bearable. It was cold, freezing even, and I shivered there with the two of them as we watched on and waited. We would need to get inside soon, as the hurricane would get bored of this spectacle soon enough and resume its course into the coast.

The explosions continued for a whole minute, then the entire fiery mess just sat there on the water and steamed and smoldered. We could hear the rain hissing as it hit the burning hulk of metal and evaporated. Lights of a Coast

Guard boat flashed in the distance, and then another set came in from north of us.

"They'll want to talk to us," Joey said.

I nodded. "I think we'll be okay. We've got Frey's testimony, about Elizondo's business and what he was really up to."

"Will they believe that?"

I shrugged. "Does it matter? The guy *also* brought a thousand tons of gasoline into Charleston Harbor and aimed it at the port. He would have taken out everything in a half-mile radius."

"The other distributors," Joey said.

I looked over at the port to the south, the ships collected in a bundle near one of the docks. They were all owned by one of the major distillers, no doubt. Frey had been right when he'd said that they were all trying to come in before the storm hit, to at least have their products unloaded and ready for overland shipping before the hurricane.

"How did he get it?"

"The fuel? He made it, I'm sure. Corn fuel is just like un-aged whiskey, just stronger. Usually up in the 180-190 proof. And it wouldn't need to be refined much or chemically altered since it was never meant to be used in vehicles."

"And he just wanted to blow up all these other ships?"

"They're the other *distributors*, remember? They were all coming in this weekend, trying to beat the storm. They probably all have to use the same port and docks, so it was a perfect plan. Get them all at once, where it really hurts."

Joey closed his eyes, taking it all in. "Wow," he said. "*Wow.*"

"Yeah," I said. "That's pretty much what I've been thinking."

I heard the sound of a large engine heading our way,

turning wide around the smoking and flaming hull of the *Rummer*. It was a Coast Guard vessel, speeding toward us.

The boat pulled up alongside us and shined their floodlights down into the speedboat. Shalice ducked away from the light, but Joey and I stared straight up into it.

A man leaned over the side of the boat, holding a megaphone. It wasn't necessary, even with the noise of the rain, but he had it turned up all the way. "You all have anything to do with this?" the man asked.

I nodded.

"You know what happened here?"

Again, I nodded.

"We're also looking for a man named Jonathan Frey. ATF agent. You seen him?"

I nodded. "Yeah, we've seen him."

"Will you come aboard our boat? We'd like to discuss it."

I looked at Joey and then at Shalice, still wearing almost nothing at all. Then I turned back to the huge Coast Guard yacht and yelled back up at the man. "Yeah, I think we'd like that. But we'll need something to eat."

The man turned to someone I couldn't see and negotiated for a moment.

"And a drink wouldn't hurt either."

CHAPTER FORTY-NINE

MY FATHER'S BODY WASHED UP on the shore a few days later. It was bloated, but the coroner determined the cause of death to be a single gunshot wound to the head. Not execution-style, but likely from one of the thousand stray bullets that had been flying around just before Frey and I jumped ship.

I had to confirm the body, which I did without feeling or emotion whatsoever. *Dead body. My father.* That was about it. I didn't care what they did with him, and I wasn't about to pay any money for a burial service or funeral, so as soon as the police and Coast Guard and coroner were happy with my confirmation I turned and left.

Joey and Shalice were taking some time off up in Charleston, staying in her place. She was going to be fine — Elizondo was a zealot, but he had no stomach for personal torture. None of his men had touched her, and even the incident about removing her clothes turned out to be nothing more than forcing her at gunpoint to strip. Not pleasant, but a bit more palatable than what I'd originally thought.

Still, the case against Elizondo had turned it into a national affair. The ATF was involved, but only to evaluate and determine the truths behind the rumors of Elizondo's illegal importing. The FBI and CIA was fighting for territorial control over the case, with the balance leaning heavily in favor of the FBI. Truman himself called me and asked about the case, but he assured me it was off the record. I wouldn't testify, and according to the Feds building the case, I would remain an innocent bystander who happened to be out on the *Wassamassaw* at the wrong time. Our involvement was listed as 'kidnap victims' and our subsequent escape deemed lucky.

Fine by me.

The furthest I could get from all of this the better. My bar had been closed for the better part of three days, and probably would be closed for another three until I felt I had a handle on things without Joey around.

Jonathan Frey's funeral was small, and it was in Washington, DC. I didn't attend. Joey mentioned that he'd try to get up to it, but I wasn't going to ask about it. His death was listed on the ATF website, but few details were given. The most surprising thing about the man was that he was, in fact, a distributor as well as an ATF agent. I didn't understand how that worked, just that we now needed to find another supplier in the Charleston area.

It had been a stressful week, but I felt good. I was alive, and I had done the job. The ever-changing nature of plans suggests that by not having a plan in the first place, things go more smoothly. My new philosophy, after thinking about it long and hard for some time, was that having a plan was a necessary distraction. A necessary piece of a long-term mission. If only to put my mind at ease, to know that there was *something* I could rely on, even though I knew it would change mid-stride. Having no plan at all was planning to fail, or something like that. I now understood what that meant.

Those three days I thought a lot about morality: was I doing the right thing? Did I even *care* if I was doing the right thing? Like I'd always thought, morality is like death. You can fight against it, but who you are is always going to come through. Death will always find you. So will morality.

I don't know if I'm good or bad, or if there's really a difference, but I do know that whoever I am, that's it. That's what I've got, and there's not much sense in really fighting it. I'm good at fighting, but I figure that's a fight that's not really worth fighting at all.

MARK MY WORDS

PREVIEW CHAPTERS

Continue the fun! Turn the page for a preview of the next Mason Dixon novel, *Mark My Words!*

CHAPTER ONE

There comes a time in every man's life when they wonder to themselves whether it was worth it or not to kill all those people.

Okay, fine. Maybe not *every* man's life, but at least in mine, that's where I'm at. Wondering, deciding, convinced that I've made a mistake once or twice over the years. Killed a guy — or gal — who wasn't bad.

I'm good at two things. Making drinks is one of them. Killing bad guys is another. I prefer one of them, but I would never admit that to anyone.

I mean, how do you know? Were they all bad? And if all of them weren't bad, were the ones that *were* bad all bad? Or were they only *partly* bad? And was the bad part of them worth killing them? I've definitely offed some of the genuinely all-bad ones, and I've made the world a better place because of it. That's a fact.

But I've got a sense that maybe there should have been more to it. Perhaps they just hadn't ever been faced with their own mortality before. Had they had that opportunity like I've had many times over, might they have changed their ways?

Not to wax philosophical, but that's the kind of crap I think about all the time, and I have plenty of time to do it. I own a bar (well, the bank owns a bar, and they let me put my name on it), so it's a good thing I'm good at mixing drinks. I can pour like a pro, but my real passion is mixing up a fine concoction of delectable nectar and nailing the presentation.

Most of the orders that hit us, however, are the typical I'm-not-sure-but-my-old-man-used-to-drink-these drinks that I can make with my eyes closed and my hands tied behind my back, so I've got plenty of time to think through my own opinions about the meaning of life.

Joey, my barman, manager, cook, and all-around worthy sidekick, knows when I'm in a particular moment like this and usually allows me to finish my thought. But he *also* knows — somehow — what it is I'm thinking about, and more often than not he even knows my opinion about that thing I'm thinking.

Happened last night. We were in the bar. I was waiting and serving, and Joey was in the back whipping up his now-famous (at least in Edisto Beach, South Carolina) breaded catfish nuggets (more breaded than nuggeted), and I was thinking about the reason I'd done the things I'd done, and trying to figure out what I thought about all of it.

Joey came out with an order, slid it down the bar and gave me a wink, which meant the order was on the house, intended for someone he knew, and then started to turn away.

“Something on your mind, boss?” Joey asked, just before he had whirled away and started back toward the kitchen.

I grunted — my usual mechanism of mid-thought verbal self-interruption — and nodded. "Just… you know."

“Trying to figure out if it's all worth it? If those guys

didn't deserve it after all?"

I made a clicking sound with the insides of my cheeks, squinting down at him — he's almost a head shorter than I am — and he smiled.

"How the hell you do that, Joey?" I asked.

"Do what?"

"Knock it off. You know exactly what I'm talking about."

The order was still on the bar, and I usually wouldn't have allowed it to get more than thirty seconds of cold before it reached the designated eater. But since this one was a 'winker' and that designated eater was his girlfriend, Shalice, whom I'd spotted in the corner earlier, I let it pass and turned my attention back to Joey.

He made eyes at Shalice, who gave him a glance that could only mean, *hurry up with my food.*

I smiled, wondering when these two lovebirds were going to tie the know. After everything they'd been through, I figured they'd be inseparable. I didn't realize that meant she would be in the bar just about *every night* Joey was working.

He shrugged, wiping his hands on the sides of his apron. "I guess I'm just really in tune with your most intimate thoughts, man."

I made my squint squintier, adding in a nice Clint Eastwood-style lip turn (another trademark of mine), and shook my head. "You wish."

He sniffed. "Look, brother, I think about that stuff too. All the time. It's not that strange, you know. What we do — you know, it's not exactly *light* on the mind."

"Right. So what do you make of it?"

"Just… maybe that it doesn't matter."

"Joey, that's probably the single most *un*helpful thing you've ever said."

"No, hear me out boss," he said. "I'm saying it *matters,* but once it's done, it doesn't. It *can't.* We vet, we wait for a mark, then we move. That's it. You do your due diligence, I do mine, and we trust each other. You're a good guy, and — I think — I am too, so that's that."

I turned around and grabbed a bottle of Hornitas Black Barrel, a new favorite of mine, and poured two lowballs. I'm not generally a fan of tequila, but there was a certain and delicious whiskey-ness to this one, as it had been aged in charred oak barrels and had that wonderful caramel and vanilla flavor I can't get enough of. Joey sidled up to one of the two stools we kept behind the bar for just this purpose, apparently done with his bread-nugget orders.

We both took a slow, long sip — another reason I love this tequila: it demands slow drinking, and shooting it is more wasteful than trying to sip through a sieve. He closed his eyes and smiled.

"So you're saying that *we're* the good guys, and since we're good, they were all bad."

He shrugged again. "Maybe. I guess. I don't know. I just think that since we're *not* the bad guys, anyone trying to do us in, or screw with us, probably ain't good enough to worry about."

"You're making a lot of assumptions."

"You're thinking a lot of assumptions."

"Fair enough," I said. "But still — how can we *know?* How do I know that when I'm dead and gone, I'll be able to stand in front of those pearly gates and say with all honesty that I've done okay down here?"

"Didn't ever strike you for the religious type, boss," Joey said.

"Didn't ever ask," I answered. It sounded harsh, so I added a bit of clarity. "I grew up Catholic. Mom was devout, but Dad was a bit... unrefined. He never really took to it, and then with my brother..."

I didn't need to finish. He knew the rest of the story —

that my little brother was a bit more eccentric and artistic than my old man thought necessary for a young man, and often accused him — with no attempt at subtlety or understanding — of being homosexual.

For what it's worth, it never bothered me in the slightest whether he *was* or *wasn't* some thing or another. He was my brother. He was family.

Dad, on the other hand, wasn't so easily smitten with the idea. The verdict was still out, but Dad had essentially written off his second son as worse than the proverbial prodigal one. The verdict *also* was still out whether this prodigal would be received with open arms, should they ever had the unfortunate opportunity to reunite.

"You think this place shouldn't belong to you?" Joey asked.

I looked at him oddly.

"I mean, you're not one to really give a hoot about your *own* life, but when it comes to your bar..."

He was right. I didn't give two hoots of a damn about myself most of the time, but as soon as you crossed me on *my own property...*

"I guess," I said. I thought about his question again. "Yeah, I think you're right. I feel like I — *we* — worked tooth and nail for this little slice of paradise, and yet sometimes I wonder if it was worth everything we gave. If what we had to do to protect it was... right."

He nodded slowly. "Yeah, probably best not to wonder about things like that."

"Can't help it."

He stopped me, waited for me to look at him. "Look, Mason. I think life is important and all because it was given to us. It's *necessary*. But there's little reason to *enjoy* life if there's nothing to enjoy about it."

"So owning a bar is the *reason* for my life?"

He laughed. "Maybe. But probably not. I just think that protecting this place, putting what you've put into it to make it *yours*, working every day in here to make sure it was *you*. It's a part of you now. It *is* you now."

"Nice sentiment, but the bank owns it."

"True. But that's just the game — you have to play the game. The point is, this place is worth fighting for. No matter how you feel about yourself, or the rest of your life, it's worth it."

I nodded. "I'm just thinking a lot lately, that's all," I said, feeling the awkwardness that had been suddenly injected into the conversation and wanting to disappear it. "It's nothing. Just trying to sleep at night."

"You've never in your life had trouble sleeping at night," Joey said.

He couldn't have been more wrong, but for all he knew of my private life I had always been Sleeping Beauty. Since I'd met Joey, he'd taken it upon himself to give me grief for the number of hours I sleep, even though he knew they were solid and sound. Around four hours on weekdays, five on weekends.

When you're my age, you just don't need that much sleep. I don't know, science I guess.

"Well let's just say I've been thinking a lot about the choices I've made. Wondering if they'd be any different if I knew who they all were, each time. Like *really* knew."

"Probably," Joey said, as unhelpful as ever. "If we knew everything about everybody, we'd probably tear ourselves apart just trying to figure out how to *talk* to them, much less how to —"

"Get a drink down here?"

The voice came from my left, and I involuntarily stood up and walked over. "Sorry about that," I said. "Didn't see you come in."

CHAPTER TWO

It was a lie, of course. I see *everyone* who comes in.

But I didn't want to let on that aside from the little bell above the door that alerted us to new arrivals, I had a multiview security monitor set up just beneath the bar. I had watched the tall, slightly overweight guy open the door, look both directions, and then walk straight toward the bar.

He wasn't alone, either. He'd entered with another guy. Smaller in every way, even his eyes were beady and scared. He turned to his left immediately upon entering my space and found a seat that was not only empty but not close to any other guests. He was facing the door, kind of, but the look on his face told me that he wasn't facing any particular direction for any particular reason.

The thing about people who visit bars like mine — small-town, out-of-the-way dives that fall somewhere between hole-in-the-wall mom-and-pop setups struggling for rent payments each month and your local neighborhood chain restaurant bar — is that people don't come in for no reason.

They're here to see a friend, or they're here because they

want some real, live, human interaction they're not getting in their lonely bungalows where they spend the rest of their lives. These are the locals, the ladies and gents who know me or Joey and like us enough to patronize our establishment because, hell, their friends are bartenders. Most people fall into one of the two categories, but there's a third when it comes to bars like mine: tourists.

Tourists are easy to spot anywhere, but especially in Edisto Beach, South Carolina, since it's a small enough place that everyone knows everyone's dog, and it's only a matter of a quick phone call to get the owner to head over and pick it up. Tourists, however, stand out like a raised pinky on a wine glass. They think they have to act elegant, or gawky, or at least surprised by every little thing that's not the exact same way that thing is like from whence they've come. They smile at me like they're watching their two-year-old niece mash Play-Do through the teeth of a comb, and they order drinks like I'm a shiny, shirtless Bora Boran on the white sandy beach resort they *wish* they were at.

Pina Coladas, Mai Tais, Bahama Mamas, anything rhyme-y and fruity-sounding. 'Rum and Coke with a lime, because oh-my-word my neighbor Marjorie went to Aruba and that's how *they* do it there.'

...It's called a Cuba Libre, Susan, and it's how *everyone* does it.

Anyway, this guy who came in and walked up to my bar was clearly *not* a tourist, and his little buddy sitting scared in the corner wasn't, either. The bigger guy didn't have the fanny-pack gut or the overpriced camera-strap neck. He'd looked around like he already knew the place, but I'd never seen him before and in a town of 800 people (on paper), I'd seen *everyone* before.

So when he'd walked straight toward the bar, waiting until he'd sat down and gotten settled, ignoring everything in the world except for my conversation with Joey and waiting until the perfect moment to interject his question.

"Got it, boss?" Joey asked.

I nodded, already facing toward the new arrival and away from Joey. "Why don't you check the fryer?" I asked.

Joey nodded. I didn't see it, of course, but I knew that he did. It was code for, 'we got a mark, and you need to get the shotgun.'

If I haven't mentioned it yet, I'm out of the business. After my old man got us involved in a high-speed boat chase and subsequent freighter explosion off the coast of Charleston, I'd decided — finally — to throw in the stained bar towel.

I was done.

Joey was done.

Shalice, the girlfriend still waiting for her now-cool fish nuggets and chips, had been nabbed from my boat, the *Wassamassaw*, which previously had been her father's boat, and then her boat, and held captive on the aforementioned soon-to-be-exploded cargo freighter.

If it wasn't for the shitty life and questionable way of making a living, it would have been for her. And for Joey. And before them, it would have been for Shannon.

But deep down it had been for *me.* I alone had decided that I was done, and I'd decided it long before my father had roped me back in.

So now, whenever there was a person who fell into that small, niche fourth category of visitor to my bar — the *marks* — trying to lure us back into the game, Joey and I had an understanding. He'd watch the second camera bank on the monitor in the kitchen, wait for something to happen, then rush out with the Remington and start acting like the badass I knew he was.

I had my own piece under the bar top, so I was prepared

at all times for such an occurrence, but so far hadn't needed to use it.

I gave him the slight head-lift worn by the more youthful hipster bartenders — the, 'sup, whatcha want?' back-nod — and waited. No sense being overly polite to this joker, since I'd pegged him as trouble the second he'd stepped over the threshold.

He could have been a mark — he fit the bill, physically — but I knew my old man was not operating any longer. He wouldn't have sent a mark to me.

Because it was impossible to send a mark to someone if you were dead.

So this guy was something else, and that terrified me. He was an unknown, and in my lines of work — bartending and killing bad guys — fear of the unknown is a major cause of anxiety.

And sometimes a major cause of death.

"Whiskey, on the rocks."

This was interesting. I put the comma in there for him, but he said it. 'Whiskey… pause… on the rocks.'

'Whiskey on the rocks' was a drink ordered by a guy who knew how he liked it. He was confident, sure of himself, understanding of my job and the nature of what it meant to order something strong but discerning enough to want it chilled and diluted just a bit.

'Whiskey, *comma*, on the rocks,' was a different drink. It was a drink meant for someone who wanted something quick, to get the drink-ordering business out of the way and get on with the important stuff, the task at hand. It was whiskey, because the guy probably liked whiskey enough to want it or it was at least something easy and quick to think about and say, but it was… pause… on the rocks. The *pause* part is what, ironically, gives me pause. They're deciding how they want their *whiskey.*

If they know what liquor they want, they probably already know how they like it. No one orders Jack Daniels and *then* decides they want it the way they always have it: on the rocks, neat, with a twist, whatever. They already *know.*

So for a *'whiskey, on the rocks,'* it meant the guy wasn't here for a drink. I'd pour him a whiskey from the deepest well I had, throw in two 'rocks,' and slide it across. I'd serve him, of course — I'm not a barbarian — but he wasn't here for the drink.

I nodded and turned around, careful to check his spot in the long, narrow mirror that stretched horizontally across my back bar area while I iced the glass and poured from a thick plastic 1.75 that I hadn't even bothered to add a Quickpour spout to.

"Whiskey," I said. *Pause.* "On the rocks."

He tried a smile. It didn't work.

"What are you here for?" I asked.

He frowned. "Odd question."

"Maybe. You a tourist?"

He shook his head.

"Local? Must've just moved in, then, 'cause I haven't seen you around before."

Again, a head shake.

"Okay, than you're waiting for family, who *are* l locals. Briggs? Richards'? They've both got a son-in-law 'sposed to be in town this week."

"Nope."

I sighed, not trying to hide the eye-roll. "All right, buddy. I played the game. Guessed. Three 'no's,' so I figure you're here for me. I figured it right away, actually, and I've got my friend back there with the shotty, ready for whatever game you're *actually* here to play."

Finally, a *real* smile.

"*There* we go," I said. "What's worth a cheap drink and a

long trip with a buddy who doesn't look much like anyone's buddy?"

"You. Just like you said."

"Fine. I get that a lot."

"Just want to talk."

"I doubt that."

"I want to *start* by talking," he said quickly.

"We're talking now," I said.

"Maybe somewhere more *private*?"

I cocked an eyebrow. "Maybe you two bozos can get back into your jalopy and head back the way you came?"

He let out a huff. "Fine. Whatever. Your bar, your rules."

"Damn right," I said, wiping off the stain of water his drink had just left on the bar when he'd set it down right next to his coaster. "So let's play."

CHAPTER THREE

Playtime.

One of my favorite moments of pre-negotiation. Finding out just what exactly is 'for sale,' and what exactly the 'currency' we're paying with looks like.

The man smiled again. He wore glasses, but they weren't real. No one buys coke-can goggles and wears them earnestly unless they're in a movie about the 1970's or actually *in* the 1970's. His hair and shirt screamed 'IT support,' but the clock on the wall said, 'too late for his type.'

"We're here for you," the man said again.

"I got that already. What *flavor* of me were you hoping to get?"

"The kind of flavor that tastes bitter."

Okay, point his. That was a good one.

"Done. That's my perma-flavor."

His smile shifted to one that seemed almost genuine, and he let out a little chuckle. "Good to hear. Mason, I'm here to warn you. And to ask for your help."

I frowned. No sense playing the fool — the guy knew my name. "Okay, I'm listening, uh..."

"Fellows."

"Your name is Fellows?"

"It is." Nothing more. Just 'it is.' *Okay, point two — you're a fine player, Fellows.*

"Fellows, then. I can work with that. What are you here to warn me about, Fellows?"

"They're coming for you. I'm here to let you know."

"They *who*?"

"The guys you pissed off up north CHECKPOOP when you blasted Elizondo off the face of the earth."

Elizondo was the dead guy in a million pieces who had owned the shipper — a rum-runner — and was hoping to use my father to take over a massive liquor importing operation. The legality was still questionable, but he'd done something that wasn't — he'd taken Shalice and threatened me and Joey.

"Elizondo's not someone I worry about anymore," I answered.

"Elizondo's not someone *Elizondo* worries about anymore," Fellows said. He took a brutal sip from the 'whiskey, on the rocks,' his nose turning upward. "Listen, Mason, I'm just here to warn you. These guys… they're not messing around."

"I see. That whiskey, apparently, isn't messing around, either."

He actually laughed at this, pushing the drink away. "I'm not a drinker, believe it or not."

"Why order a drink, then?" I asked. "I'm still going to make you pay for it."

He slapped a twenty on the table. "I know. I figured it's the least I could do. You own a bar, after all."

I wasn't sure if that meant he felt for me because he was here to warn me about some super-scary bad guys or because I owned a bar, as if that was bad enough in itself.

"You're here to warn me about something. Some*one*, I'm guessing. Why do they care about Elizondo? And what exactly do they want to do to me?"

He shook his head. "No, it's not about Elizondo — they don't even know about him, outside of knowing that you did him in a few —"

"I didn't *'do him in,'* Fellows. He was on a ship that *happened* to be filled with freshly distilled explosives, and I just *happened* to drop the match."

"Either way," Fellows asked. "They've got your mug plastered on their wall. You're the target. Or 'mark,' I guess. If you're still using that term."

I frowned down at him, taking advantage of the fact that he was sitting at the barstool and I was standing, my side six or so inches higher than his. "I'm not doing much of anything these days, besides pouring drinks and trying to make a living."

Fellows nodded, second-guessing his choice from before, grabbing his glass and taking another sip. He squinted through it, the pain clear on his face. "Pouring drinks and floating that yacht of yours. What's it called? The *Seesaw* or something like that?"

"*Wassamassaw,*" I said. "And I only just got her back. She was run up onto a bank and had quite a few bullet holes in her gut after the Elizondo incident. Sent her up to Charleston to get fixed up."

Fellows nodded. "Guy I'm here with — back there? He wants your help."

It was a sudden shift in the conversation. I'd expected something like that, a quick question or statement that reminded both of us what we were *actually* here for. He wasn't a friend, or a confidant, or a tourist hoping to strike up a conversation. There was a job to do, and he wanted my help with it.

"What's your friend want?"

He shook his head. "Not my friend. Brother-in-law."

"Sorry."

"You and I both," Fellows said. "He's a banker, pretty high-roller, too. Does well with real estate deals, but he's sharp enough to have his hand in plenty of honeypots."

"Interesting choice of words."

"Yeah," he said. "It is. He's in some trouble, and I thought you might be able to help."

"Why's that?"

"Well, because you're already involved."

"Like hell I am."

"He bankrolled Elizondo."

Shit. Elizondo had been (emphasis on the *had been*, since Elizondo was now in a million pieces, settling on the bottom of Charleston Harbor) a bigwig importer, working against the corporations to build his own empire. He'd been savvy, but even savvy types can't survive a few hundred thousand gallons of ignited gasoline.

I'd always wondered where he'd gotten his money. Guys like that rarely used their own fortunes to deal — it was far safer, far easier, and far more rewarding to use OPM: Other Peoples' Money.

"So he's pissed because he thinks I killed him?"

"Nope. He knows what happened, and it actually worked out well for him. There was a contingency in his contract for reversion rights — Elizondo croaks, my bro-in-law gets a nice payday."

"So it's the *other* guys who are pissed. Elizondo's guys."

"Right," Fellows said. "The guys who wanted Elizondo's business to work. They had a massive stake in seeing it through. And, well, thanks to you, that all went up in flames."

"So they're probably not too happy with me."

Fellows drained his glass and coughed, wiping his mouth with the back of his hand. I raised an eyebrow — *want another?* — and he shook his head.

"You're a cop, aren't you?" I asked.

He seemed surprised at first, then he relaxed. He hesitated, but then gave in. "What gave it away?"

"Couple things. First, your eyes. The way you won't stop looking around, even when you're not looking at anything. You're staring at the mirror behind me, keeping an eye on your banker brother, but also on everyone else in here. You got a quick look around when you came in, and I saw you reach to your side — nothing holstered there tonight, though — then relax. You've got a piece, I bet, but it's in a chest holster or something. But your eyes are the main thing. Shifty, but not in a drug dealer sort of way. More of a checking things out and making sure you're comfortable with them sort of way."

"Good eye."

"It's gotten me out of a few jams."

"I suspect it has." Fellows sighed, then relaxed again. He was like a worn cushion, slowly giving way to the pressure and weight of the years. "I've been on the force longer than I haven't, and I'm ready to be done. But there are few guys in my department who are more crooked than a crazy eye, and they've got their sights on Billy — my brother — since they're bankrolled by his enemies."

"Got it. So you figured you could hide him out down here?" I asked.

"Well, uh…"

I looked at Fellows. Waited for the tell, for the thing that would alert me to what exactly was going on. He was a cop, so it wasn't easy to spot.

But then it was.

A simple, honest, smack of his lips. He was *sorry*. Apologetic.

"No. Fellows, you've got to be kidding me."

He looked down at the bar, then back up at me. "I'm sorry — they were already moving on him, and I — I couldn't just let them..."

"You brought them *here*?"

I suddenly felt the bar's walls closing in around me, becoming much smaller and weaker than the concrete-walled enclosure I'd purchased years ago. I wanted Joey there, and I wanted his girlfriend Shalice to *not* be here.

"I didn't *bring* them, Dixon," Fellows said. "They were already onto Billy, and I just... I mean I had nowhere else to go, so I —"

"Literally *anywhere* is somewhere else to go, asshole!" I shouted. "Your cronies are coming down to *my* bar, in *my* town, looking for *your* brother. You made this *my* problem?"

"I wasn't trying to, I just needed to get him somewhere I could — "

"What? Get him somewhere *what,* Fellows?"

"Somewhere safe?"

"You're a cop. Don't you have safehouses, support staff, *anything*?"

"No."

No more explanation than that. I suspected as much — this guy was risking his neck to save his skeevy-looking brother-in-law, and it was possible — probable, actually — that his shifty buddies on the force wouldn't take too kindly to his subterfuge. Cop or not, Fellows was on the wrong side of the law, even though he was on the *right* side of it at the same time.

This was getting confusing, and I needed a drink.

"How long?" I asked, pouring myself something from a

shelf I could barely reach. It was mostly there for decoration, as no one had the guts to order it.

Also because I charged $250 a shot for it.

"How long until what?" Fellows asked. He shifted, I poured, his brother squirmed in his seat in the corner.

"How long until I'm picking up shards of your brother's torso and my broken pint glasses from my floor?"

Fellows sighed. "They chased us out of Charleston. Didn't see me, but they know Billy was in the car. We lost them just outside the city, but they know which direction we were heading."

"So maybe they don't know where you are now," I said, hoping.

He shook his head. "I wish. Soon as I got here I got Billy out and kept him out of the light, but I saw a car parked across the street, watching your building."

"One of yours?"

"Undercover, but yeah. It was Mayes. He's one of the ringleaders. Big guy, looks like a crooked cop from an old TV show."

"And Mayes was scoping out *my* bar?"

"Yeah," Fellows said.

"Understood," I said. I turned to leave.

"Understood?" Fellows asked.

"Yeah," said. "*Understood.* I heard you, I acknowledge you, whatever."

"So where are you —"

"Give me a minute," I snapped. I strode to the kitchen, walked inside, and immediately caught Joey staring at me.

"News?" he asked.

"News," I answered, nodding. "This guy — Fellows — he's a cop. Not crooked, but knows plenty of ones who are. He dragged his brother-in-law down here because the guy got himself into a sticky deal."

"What's that have to do with us?"

"Nothing," I said. "Except that he's afraid some Charleston thugs are going to *make* it about us."

"Gotcha. So what's our move?"

I sighed. "Nothing yet, I guess. Things are moving along, but I'm not about to get us tangled up with something if we don't need to. And Shalice..."

He smiled. "She'll be okay. Isn't her first rodeo."

CHAPTER FOUR

"Ain't that the truth." I took a glance over at the corner of the kitchen, where there were about six or seven five-gallon buckets stacked up on one another, and a few six-gallon glass carboys sitting in front of them. "How's the whiskey coming?" I asked.

He shrugged. "You tell me, boss. You're the moonshining expert."

"Distilling. 'Moonshining' makes it sound illegal."

"It *is* illegal."

He wasn't wrong. Distilling alcohol for *any* reason was still a federal crime in the United States, even though it was typically a very safe, very easy to control hobby. Hobby brewers were allowed to brew an absurd amount of gallons each year for personal use, but home distillers hadn't been allowed to cook their own liquor since before Prohibition.

From what I'd read, the whole mess was related to taxes — the government wanted their cut, even if it was a stupid reason. So they taxed professional distillers into oblivion, making it damn near impossible to get a distilling license unless you had a *lot* of money, and then made home and hobby distilling completely illegal.

The irony was that every distiller I knew had started by learning how to distill liquor on their own — illegally. There weren't many classes, training courses, and resources to teach newcomers the age-old craft.

We were hobbyists as well, as getting into distilling was something I'd always wanted to do. Now we had a stack of five-gallon buckets full of the homemade moonshine, and three carboys each with liquor in its different stages of completion. There was a sour mash I'd been working on, a fresher all-corn bourbon, and a fancy rye, corn, and barley mixture that I was hoping would turn into a smooth, spicy brew.

The five-gallon buckets were holding the first batch of the penultimate step in the process: turning the high wines CHECKPOOP into fully distilled and ready-to-drink alcohol. The high wines were high ABV alcohol of somewhere around 90% purity. It was quite literally rubbing alcohol, nearly undrinkable and totally unenjoyable.

The high wines needed to be cut with fresh, crisp water, then stored at a slightly lower proof in charred oak barrels for months or years depending on the size of the barrels, until the wines had earned some color and flavor and turned into what we in the business called *money*. Or, more likely (since I didn't wanted to get arrested for selling illegal spirits), "good drinkin' shine."

I like to consider myself a whiskey connoisseur, which is evident in the fact that I own a bar and in the way I spell "whiskey" with an "e." I'm American, so whiskey has an "e" in it. The way it should be. But I don't necessarily consider myself a *distilling* connoisseur. The thing about producing great spirits is that it's a lot more science than it is art, but the art is absolutely crucial if you're trying to produce something anyone wants to drink.

Beer is different — anyone who drinks a lot of beer gets the itch to make their own, citing trumped-up charges like "buying beer is too expensive!" and "what else are we supposed to do with the basement closet?" and then they buy an inexpensive carboy and some fancy tubes and thermometers and they're in business.

I've had — and made — plenty of delicious home-brew beer. It's easy to make, a bit harder to make well, and overall approachable as a hobby.

Whiskey and other distilled spirits is a trickier thing to get into. Once you get past the "I'm breaking the law" issue, you're in a realm of pseudoscience masquerading as real science and real science masquerading as southern rednecks who talk with a drawl.

I love art *and* science, so I figured I'd try my hand. It was enough to get started, but part of the frustration is that it takes a *long* time to let the spirits mellow and earn their colors and flavors, only to discover that every first batch — and typically the first twenty batches — is crap anyway.

As such, I'd decided long ago that I needed a partner. A man I could trust, who could help with the chore of it all and, most importantly, be my official taste-tester.

I looked Joey up and down, wondering if he really was as gullible as he seemed to be at the moment. "You're my partner, Joey."

"What's that supposed to mean, boss?"

"It means I trust you. You're a good guy."

"And…"

"And I want to get your opinion on this before I age it."

"On the whiskey?"

"Yeah, the whiskey." I moved over to the stack of buckets, took off the stopper from the tiny hole in the lid of one of the buckets, then grabbed the thief — a tiny plastic spring-loaded tubule that allowed one to administer a tiny shot of booze from the inside of a carboy to the inside of one's belly. I clicked the top down and stuck it into the top of the bucket, retrieving a bit of the wines. "Here," I said, collecting the drips into a shot glass from the shelf.

He took the glass in his hand, gave it a swirl, then eyed me suspiciously. "This won't make me go blind, will it?"

"You'd be far less useful as an employee if you were blind, Joey," I said.

He laughed. "Not exactly reassuring."

"It's an old wive's tale," I answered. "It would take some *serious* oversight, or a really upset distiller, to brew something that had enough of the foreshots in it to cause permanent poisoning of the optic nerve."

He laughed again. "You know, for an idiot, you know a lot about distilling."

"Thank you, Joey." I gave him my best fake smile. "Bottom's up."

I watched as he brought the glass up to his nose. Just like I'd taught him, he nosed the glass for a few seconds, letting the aromas excite his salivation glands and get his mouth ready. Then he shot the liquor back into his mouth, swished a few times, and swallowed.

It was at that moment two things happened simultaneously. I began to laugh, even before I realized that the things were happening. What I noticed first were Joey's eyes, widened in an ill-contained horror. They bulged out with an intensity I hadn't seen since my last late-night accidental viewing of *Mars Attacks!*, an unfortunate "comedy" with bug-eyed Martian antagonists.

The second thing I saw was Joey's mouth opening once again, long before the entirety of the booze had had a chance to settle into his esophagus. Which meant that some of the liquor was coming back *out* of his mouth. He dribbled a bit, the liquid fighting with a weird groaning sound his vocal cords were attempting.

I lost it.

"Wh — what the — *hell* — what the *hell* was *that?*" The words finally erupted from his mouth, complete with a reenactment — in reverse — of the drinking process that had started the whole thing.

I couldn't stop laughing. "What do you mean?"

"What *is* this?" Joey asked. "It tastes… it tastes like shit."

"It's high-quality whiskey, Joey," I said. "It just hasn't been cut and aged yet."

He spat onto the kitchen floor, the shot glass in his hand still shaking. "It tastes like lawn clippings floating in diesel fuel."

"You're not far off, actually," I said, finally regaining some of my composure. "It's fresh because it's young. And it pretty much *is* fuel. High-octane stuff like this is typically around 180 to 190 proof before it goes into the barrel."

His eyes — somehow — got wider. "You — you made me drink this shit?"

"I *offered* it to you, friend. You're my partner, and I want you to be an *equal* partner. That means you should understand every step of the process."

"I don't think I need to understand *anything* if it means I have to poison myself for it." He paused, spat again, then swiped an empty glass near the kitchen sink and filled it with warm water from the tap. He guzzled the entire thing. "Shit, man, I think I'm actually *drunk* now. How much of this swill do we have?"

I roared in laughter again. "Relax. You're going to be fine. It won't hurt you." I did a quick calculation by counting all the buckets in the corner, then raised an eyebrow. "About thirty gallons."

"*Thirty* gallons? Christ — how much of it do we need? And you're wrong, old man," he said. "This stuff could *kill* someone."

"I'll keep that in mind."

I laughed some more as I cleaned up the splatter from Joey, all the while keeping an eye on the security monitor we kept in the back area that displayed the goings-on of the front bar and restaurant seating areas. We didn't often converse in the back, without a bartender or server up front, so I wanted to make sure no one was feeling lonely out there, or worse — taking it upon themselves to pour a drink or three.

Fellows was still seated in his spot at the bar, nursing the drink I'd poured him half an hour ago. I hadn't given much thought to his dilemma, but I knew from experience dilemmas like his didn't typically just go away on their own. I needed to ask Joey about it, and needed get his opinion.

I turned to find out where he'd gone. I saw him through the industrial metal shelves, hunched over the second security monitor.

The one that displayed the array of cameras we had on the lot outside, the alley in the back, and street in front of the building.

Joey suddenly appeared in front of me, the shotgun in his hand.

"We got company, boss," he said.

###

Continue reading *Mark My Words* by grabbing a copy!

AFTERWORD

If you liked this book (or even if you hated it…) write a review or rate it. You might not think it makes a difference, but it does.

Besides *actual* currency (money), the currency of today's writing world is *reviews*. Reviews, good or bad, tell other people that an author is worth reading.

As an "indie" author, I need all the help I can get. I'm hoping that since you made it this far into my book, you have some sort of opinion on it.

Would you mind sharing that opinion? It only takes a second.

Nick Thacker

ALSO BY NICK THACKER

Mason Dixon Thrillers

Mark for Blood (Book 1)

Death Mark (Book 2)

Mark My Words (Book 3)

Harvey Bennett Mysteries

The Enigma Strain (Book 1)

The Amazon Code (Book 2)

The Ice Chasm (Book 3)

The Jefferson Legacy (Book 4)

The Paradise Key (Book 5)

The Aryan Agenda (Book 6)

Harvey Bennett Mysteries - Books 1-3

Harvey Bennett Mysteries - Books 4-6

Jo Bennett Mysteries

Temple of the Snake (written with David Berens)

Tomb of the Queen (written with Kristi Belcamino)

Harvey Bennett Prequels

The Icarus Effect (written with MP MacDougall)

The Severed Pines (written with Jim Heskett)

~

Gareth Red Thrillers

Seeing Red

Chasing Red (written with Kevin Ikenberry)

~

The Lucid

The Lucid: Episode One (written with Kevin Tumlinson)

The Lucid: Episode Two (written with Kevin Tumlinson)

The Lucid: Episode Three (written with Kevin Tumlinson

~

Standalone Thrillers

The Atlantis Stone

The Depths

Relics: A Post-Apocalyptic Technothriller

Killer Thrillers (3-Book Box Set)

~

Short Stories

I, Sergeant

Instinct

The Gray Picture of Dorian

Uncanny Divide (written with Kevin Tumlinson and Will Flora)

ABOUT THE AUTHOR

Nick Thacker is a thriller author from Texas who lives in Colorado and Hawaii, because Colorado has mountains, microbreweries, and fantastic weather, and Hawaii also has mountains, microbreweries, and fantastic weather. In his free time, he enjoys reading in a hammock on the beach, skiing, drinking whiskey, and hanging out with his beautiful wife, tortoise, two dogs, and two daughters.

In addition to his fiction work, Nick is the founder and lead of Sonata & Scribe, the only music studio focused on producing "soundtracks" for books and series. Find out more at SonataAndScribe.com.

For more information, visit Nick online:
www.nickthacker.com
nick@nickthacker.com